Dear Reader,

Have you ever read a book wi... ...ck with you?

Well, imagine writing one and falling asleep dreaming about a character that you were allegedly done with.

James Goings cost me many hours of sleep, because he wanted you to get to know him better. James was first introduced in pages of *Let's Get It On*. He's the brother of Super Bowl hero Maurice Goings, but he's much more than that. He's been Maurice's cheerleader, business partner, and peacemaker.

Now it's time for James to take the ultimate gamble and fall in love. I hope you will enjoy this story as much as I enjoyed writing it.

As always, thank you for supporting me and happy reading.

Cheris Hodges

P.S. I'm only a click away. E-mail me at cheris87@
   bellsouth.net.
Join me on Facebook at www.facebook.com/
   cherishodges.
Or follow me on Twitter at www.twitter.com/
   cherishodges.

Also by Cheris Hodges

JUST CAN'T GET ENOUGH

LET'S GET IT ON

MORE THAN HE CAN HANDLE

Published by Kensington Publishing Corporation

BETTING ON LOVE

CHERIS HODGES

Dafina
Books

Kensington Publishing Corp.

http://www.kensingtonbooks.com

DAFINA BOOKS are published by

Kensington Publishing Corp.
119 West 40th Street
New York, NY 10018

All Kensington Titles, Imprints, and Distributed Lines are available at special quantity discounts for bulk purchases for sales promotions, premiums, fund-raising, and educational or institutional use. Special book excerpts or customized printings can also be created to fit specific needs. For details, write or phone the office of the Kensington special sales manager: Kensington Publishing Corp., 119 West 40th Street, New York, NY 10018, attn: Special Sales Department, Phone: 1-800-221-2647.

Dafina and the Dafina logo Reg. U.S. Pat. & TM Off.

ISBN-13: 978-0-7582-3147-5
ISBN-10: 0-7582-3147-4

First mass market printing: November 2009

10 9 8 7 6 5 4 3 2 1

Printed in the United States of America

ACKNOWLEDGMENTS

There are so many people that helped make my tenth novel possible. I'd like to say thank you to my parents, Doris and Freddie Hodges. Who knew that first typewriter would've led to this?

To Damon, thank you for being an inspiration.

I'd like to thank my agent, Sha-Shana Crichton for her tireless work.

To my sister, Adrienne Hodges-Dease, thank you for listening after all these years.

To the ladies of the Cheris F. Hodges Book Club, thank you for all of your support.

To my editor, Selena James, thank you for your hard work.

To all of the retailers who have welcomed me for signings in their stores, thank you.

CHAPTER 1

The only thing on James Goings's mind was getting away from the antics of his brother's over-paid football player friends and their constant need for high-stakes gambling and hounding every woman in a short skirt. For the last three hours, he'd been sitting in a private room in Harrah's casino in Las Vegas, losing his money to half of the Carolina Panthers' offensive line. And where had Maurice, his brother, been? In a corner, talking to his wife on the phone.

That fool should've just brought Kenya with him. Crossing the casino floor and ignoring the dings and bells of the slot machines, James decided that he'd had enough of Sin City and that he was going to go back to his hotel room, pack, and head back to North Carolina, where he'd have some peace and more money in his pocket.

When he passed the gold and glass baccarat room, a blur of black and silky hair slammed into him. The woman's purse hit the floor and seemed to explode. He reached down to help her pick up the contents of the purse: lipstick, a few coins and . . . Was that a *condom?*

Glancing at her as she stuffed her things in the overly full silver purse, he noticed how beautiful she was with her shiny black hair, sparkling brown eyes, and butter-rum skin. "I think this is yours," James said as he extended his hand to her.

"Oh my God," she said as she took the condom from him. A slight blush colored her cheeks as she attempted to close her hopelessly overstuffed purse.

James hid his amusement, but he had to wonder why she was bold enough to carry her own protection but embarrassed that he'd handed it to her. *She's definitely not a Vegas call girl if taking a condom from my hand makes her blush like that.*

Jade Christian had journeyed to Vegas with her girlfriends to have a wild weekend, à la Britney Spears, before returning to the shambles of her own life in Atlanta, Georgia. The condom was a stupid joke perpetuated by her good friend Serena Jacobs, who used sex as a weapon in her own life. She'd told Jade that the best way to get back at her boyfriend for cheating was to have an affair of her own. And what better place to do it than in Sin City?

Jade wasn't an angel, but she didn't subscribe to the notion that two wrongs made a right. At this moment, though, she could've stabbed Serena in the chest for slipping that condom in her purse. She could see how he was looking at her, and she didn't like it one bit.

"It's not what you think," she said.

"I'm not thinking a thing."

Jade rose to her feet, adjusted her purse on her shoulder, and smiled. "You're a terrible liar."

"I'd like to think that's one of my most redeeming qualities," he joked, then extended his hand to her again. "I'm James."

For a moment, Jade started to give him the pseudonym she'd been using all weekend when some lusty man approached her. But there was something about James. "Jade," she replied, with a smile.

"Beautiful name and it fits, because you're a beautiful woman."

The blush was back again, and for the first time, she regretted listening to Kandace and wearing a tight black lace dress that barely covered her thighs. He probably thought she was a Vegas call girl. She'd planned on wearing a nice pantsuit to the casino that night. But her girls had told her that part of her problem was that she'd allowed Stephen's rules of fashion to take over her life. What had that gotten her? The pleasure of seeing him with another woman, who had more plastic parts than a Barbie doll.

Stephen Carter, the owner of one of Atlanta's most upscale restaurants, had been her boyfriend, and she'd thought they would marry. They'd met when she applied for a job as his bookkeeper four years ago. She'd gotten the job and his heart, or so she'd thought.

Once they'd begun their relationship, he'd tried his best to change her. He'd had her dress as if she were a conservative forty-year-old woman instead of a vibrant twenty-nine-year-old with a lot of fun left in her.

He had hated her friends and had tried to introduce her to a set of women that he thought were more suitable for her to hang out with. Needless to say, she hadn't agreed with his assessment of her friends, and she'd refused to let him ruin those relationships. Especially after she'd discovered that before they'd met, he'd tried to sleep with Alicia Michaels, her best friend and party planner to the elite. But Alicia had shot him down, and he'd never gotten over it. Part of Jade had wondered, after the breakup, of course, if he'd dated her hoping to get closer to her friend.

Luckily, she had the kinds of friends that didn't sneak behind your back and try to steal your man. Alicia didn't want anything to do with Stephen, and she had been against Jade's relationship with him from the start. "I tried to warn you," she'd told Jade as they flew to Vegas.

"Are you enjoying yourself in Vegas?" James asked, breaking into her thoughts.

"Honestly, no. It certainly isn't what I expected."

"What did you expect?" His eyebrows rose, and a smirk spread across his lips.

"Not that, despite the dress and the contents of my purse. I was just looking for a chance to unwind and have some fun."

"And how were you going to do that?"

Jade was beginning to think that she'd been wrong about him as well, because she could've sworn that he was trying to proposition her. "Well, it certainly doesn't include doing anything I'd regret in the morning with some stranger. So if you think that a woman who carries condoms . . ."

"Slow down, sweetheart. I was asking because I want to go somewhere else myself and get away from my brother's cheating friends."

"Cheating men. What a surprise."

"They cheat at poker. The lone married man of the group is sitting on the phone, talking to his wife because he misses her so much."

Jade narrowed her eyes and then smiled. "Poker cheaters, huh? How much money did you lose?"

"More than I care to talk about. I know I'm not that lousy of a card player. There was some cheating going on."

"Want to win it back?" Jade rubbed her hands together. "I've been itching to release some tension and play a game of poker or something. My friends are in the baccarat room, because they're doing their thing."

James's face asked, "What's that?"

Jade laughed. "They like to stroke egos and win money. Not that they don't have plenty of their own, but when they come to Vegas, they like for someone else to take on the debt, if you know what I mean."

"I think I do. A bunch of beautiful women who charm old men into letting them play on their dime. No offense, but that sounds like a gang of gold diggers to me."

Jade rolled her eyes. "Typical. But what about these men who think all they need to do is flash some cash and a woman is all theirs? So my girls like to flip the script on them. There are worse things we could be doing."

"We?"

"They are my friends, and we're here together. And since it seems that you men lump us all together . . ."

"Whoa. Now, you're obviously angry at someone, and I'm going to assume that since I just met you, it isn't me," James said. "But on behalf of the asshole who pissed you off, I'm sorry."

Jade laughed heartily, realizing that she was projecting her anger on James and that he didn't deserve it. "No, let me apologize. About that money that you lost. Do you want it back?"

"Listen, as much as I do, those guys are some real cardsharps, and taking you up there would be like leading a bleeding baby seal into a tank full of hungry great whites."

She placed her hand on James's shoulder. "Never judge a book by its cover. Do you want your money back or not?"

CHAPTER 2

James didn't know why he listened to Jade and headed back up to the game room he'd dubbed "the players' suite." But they rode the elevator up to the fifteenth floor and walked into the room.

All the movement and talking stopped, and the men sitting at the different tables ogled Jade as she crossed the floor. Protectively, James wrapped his arm around her waist, and their stares became even more intense.

"Well, well, somebody called an escort service," one of the fatter men said before folding his poker hand. "James done got a woman."

"Shut up, Homer," James said. "Where's Mo?"

Homer, who really could use a low carb diet, rolled his eyes and said, "Where do you think? He's on the phone with his wife. I swear, that dude used to be fun. Want to get dealt in and give me some more of those long dollars?"

"I do," Jade said, then quickly took a seat at the table, across from Homer.

"Little girl, you're out of your league," Homer declared, and the other men laughed.

"Fat man, you don't know me. Let's do this," she said, then folded her hands underneath her chin. "How much?"

All the men looked at Jade as if she were an alien sitting at the table, demanding to be taken to their leader.

"Thousand," Homer spat.

Reaching into her purse, Jade pulled out a wad of cash. "Done."

James crossed over to her. Leaning over her shoulder, he asked, "Are you sure you can handle this?"

"There's not too much I can't handle," she said, brimming with confidence and bravado. Looking around the table, she imagined that every man sitting there was Stephen, and she was going to make sure that she stuck it to them.

"Little lady," Homer said, "would you like to deal?"

Taking the deck from his hand, Jade smiled, then shuffled the cards with the skill of the dealers on the floor of the casino. They'd underestimated Jade, and now she was going to make them pay for it.

"Five-card stud or Texas hold 'em?" she asked.

The men's mouths hung open like those of little hound dogs, and from the corner of the room where he was standing, James was enjoying the show. Jade looked as if she was about to beat the players at their own game.

When she dealt the first hand, Homer won and seemed to regain his swagger. But the next five hands went to Jade, and James loved every minute of it. Especially when she'd lean across the table to rake in the pot and the hem of her dress would inch up, exposing the sexiest thigh he'd ever seen. Her skin looked so smooth that he wanted to reach out and touch it. But there was no way he could do that. He didn't know a thing about her other than the fact that she was fine as hell.

After the sixth hand Jade won, she decided that she'd done enough damage. "Gentlemen, it's been real, but I think I've taken enough of your money." Pushing away from the table, Jade turned to James, who had the biggest grin on his face.

"Damn," he said. "Y'all got beat by a girl. Big, tough football players broken down by a beautiful lady."

"Shut up!" Homer snapped as he sulked.

Turning to Jade, James asked, "Are you ready to leave, or do you want to take the rest of their money?"

She looked at the angry faces of the men. "I think we'd better go."

James opened the door and held it for Jade to pass through. Once they made it to the elevator and got on, he turned to her and smiled again. "Fess up," he said. "You were a dealer at one of these casinos in a past life?"

"No," she said through her grin. "I grew up on a riverboat out in Mississippi with my parents. My father was a dealer, and when my mother was performing, I'd sit underneath the table while he took drunk people's money. The hand is truly quicker than the eye, and your friends made it real easy since they couldn't take their eyes off my chest."

Clearing his throat, James looked away because he couldn't take his eyes off her chest, legs, ass, or face. He didn't want Jade to think that he was just like everybody else.

"So, how much money did you lose? Because I think I won that back and some," she said as she started counting the stack of bills she had in her hand.

"If you let me take you to dinner, someplace off the Strip, we'll be able to call it even," he said. *Where did that come from? This woman has a lot going on with her, and you need to be going the other way.*

"I tell you what, I'll buy dinner and you pick the place," she said as she fanned the cash before stuffing it in her purse. "And hopefully, this will dispel your gold-digger notion."

"Something tells me that you're a woman full of surprises," he said as the doors to the elevator opened to the casino floor.

Jade stepped off. "I've heard that a time or two."

Walking about a step behind her, James suddenly wanted to see what surprises lay underneath her silk and lace. *It's just one weekend. We're adults, and she said she wanted to unwind. I know just how she can do that.*

Jade knew why James was behind her. Despite the fact that he had been a perfect gentleman so far, he was a man and he was staring. Turning around, she caught him with his eyes glued to her behind. Though part of her wanted to be irate at the fact that he was so blatant with his ogling, another part of her didn't mind his silent admiration, because it was so unlike that of many other men in the casino, who'd said some of the nastiest things to her and her friends. Still, she couldn't help but rib him a bit. "Maybe you should take a picture. It would last longer."

"Are you in the third grade?" he shot back. "Sorry, but I wouldn't be human if I didn't look. And what did you expect when you put that dress on, anyway?"

"Touché." She slowed her pace so that he could catch up with her.

James grabbed her hand and kissed it lightly. "Listen, there's a steak house downtown where we can go and talk. You're not a vegetarian, are you?"

"No, not at all," she said. "My grandmother was raised on meat. She's about a hundred now."

"That's what I'm talking about," he said, slipping his arm around her waist. "A woman who actually eats."

Jade didn't move his hand away, even though his touch seemed a little too familiar. But there was something about him that she liked, and he made her feel comfortable. Maybe the little packet in her purse would prove to be useful, after all. They were adults, and it was just one weekend. *I can't believe I'm even thinking about sleeping with this man,* she thought as they headed out the door.

CHAPTER 3

Don B's Steakhouse was the perfect romantic setting for a couple: the lights were low, and candles illuminated the dining room. In the golden glow, James thought Jade looked like an angel with a hint of something naughty below the surface. As the hostess led them to a table in the rear of the restaurant, the naughtiness about Jade piqued his interest.

Though he'd sworn off women, especially since his sister-in-law had tried to seduce him when she thought that his brother had cheated on her with the same woman who'd broken them up nine years prior, he was willing to spend his last few days in Vegas with Jade, since anything they had would be just a fling.

James hadn't had the best of luck when it came to the opposite sex, ofttimes finding out that the woman he'd been courting had her sights set on his famous brother or that she thought he was just too nice. Rather than deal with the fickle whims of women who wouldn't know how to handle a good man if he were standing in their face, James just focused on his career. But that didn't mean he couldn't have fun, and that was just what anything he did with Jade this weekend would be.

Reaching across the table, he stroked Jade's hand softly. "So, tell me something. Why are you here with your girls and not your man?"

She slid her hand from underneath his. "Who says I have a man?"

James leaned back in his chair, cupping his chin and peering at her. "Well, you're an incredibly beautiful woman, and some man would have to be a fool to let you stay single for too long."

"Smooth. If you want to know if I have a boyfriend, why don't you just ask? And for the record, I just got out of a situation. It was pretty ugly, hence the Vegas vacation."

James nodded. "Those things are always ugly."

"Spoken like a true heartbreaker."

Shaking his head, he smiled. "I don't break hearts, nor do I play games, so gambling isn't my idea of fun at all."

"Then why are you here?" She took the glass of water in her hand and brought it to her lips, but didn't sip. James couldn't look away from her plump lips, nor could he shake the thought of having those lips against his as she wrapped her legs around his waist.

"James," she breathed after lowering her glass.

Blinking, he said, "I'm sorry. You were saying?"

"If you're not a gambler, why did you come here?"

"I needed a break, or at least that's what my brother and his friends said."

"Break from what?"

"Work," he said. "According to them, that's all I do."

She nodded and smiled. "You're sure that's all you needed to get away from? There isn't some stalker ex-girlfriend that's going to jump out at us, is there?"

James laughed hollowly. His brother had the market cornered on stalking exes. Lauryn Michaels had been convicted of attempted murder and aggravated assault after she'd shot Kenya. The incident had shaken him, as well as his brother and his brother's wife, because for a while it didn't look as if Kenya would walk again.

Luckily, Lauryn had been sentenced to fifteen years in prison. James had never liked her, anyway, but he hadn't known she was as crazy as she turned out to be.

"No, there's no one lurking on my part. What about you?" he finally said.

She smiled. "I wish," she muttered. "I've been out west for three days, and my ex-boyfriend hasn't even noticed. Then again, that would require the grinch's heart to grow."

"Ouch. So that's where all the anger in the casino came from."

"Unfortunately, yes. I just don't understand why he felt as if he could treat me like I'm his servant and expect me to continue to take it. Now that he has his new eye candy, he thinks that I'm going to allow him to keep the money I invested in what I thought was going to be our future, as if it's okay that he left me for a plastic and collagen-injected Barbie doll." Closing her eyes, she took a deep breath, then opened her eyes and fixed her gaze on James. "That was more information than you wanted, wasn't it?"

"Yes. I tell you what, why don't we talk about something safer?"

"Like?"

"Religion and politics," he joked.

"Don't get me wrong," she said. "I can take rejection. It's the lies and backstabbing that I can't deal with. Why am I rambling on? You don't even know me."

"No, but I know this story," he said, reflecting on Kenya and Maurice's relationship. "But if you're meant to be with him, you'll get past this."

Jade folded her arms underneath her ample bosom and raised her eyebrows. "Hell will freeze over before I give him another chance."

"I've heard this before."

"Oh? Not from me."

"No, from my brother's wife. She walked in on him having sex with another woman, and nine years later they were back together."

"No offense, but your sister-in-law is a fool. If a dog bites you once, he'll do it again."

Before James could respond, the waitress walked over and took their orders. To his surprise, Jade ordered a hearty steak dinner with a loaded baked potato. Though she had drama and anger written all over her face, he wanted to take her into his bed and burn off every calorie of the meal.

"So, what are you going to do about him?" James asked after the waitress had walked away.

She shrugged her shoulders. "I don't know. The smart thing to do is to just walk away, and I would if I didn't have so much of my money tied up in his business. You know what, I don't want to waste another moment talking about him. I came here to have a good time."

"Are you having a good time?"

Her eyes sparkled as she sucked on her bottom lip, something James would've loved to do. "I think it's getting much better."

After dinner Jade and James headed out to explore downtown Las Vegas. The upper nineties had burned the desert earlier that day, but now it was much cooler. She shivered as they walked, taking in the lights and sounds, and James draped his arm around her since he didn't have a jacket to offer her.

"It sure does cool off quickly here," she remarked, falling into his embrace. "If I were at home, it would still be warm and the humidity would be unbearable."

"Where is home?" he asked.

"Hotlanta."

"Stop. I'm originally from Atlanta."

"Maybe that's why we connected," she said. "I knew there was something I liked about you."

James beamed and squeezed her a little tighter. She felt so good, soft and curvy like a woman should feel. Though he could tell she spent time in a gym, she didn't overdo it and try to become skin and bones. "Yeah, right. I bet if I lived in Atlanta, you'd pass me by on Peachtree Street without giving me a second glance."

Jade giggled. "Maybe, because you don't see too many straight men walking up and down Peachtree. Where do you live now?"

"Charlotte."

"Oh," she said, then looked pensive for a moment. "Bad memories in Charlotte?"

"We're supposed to be expanding the restaurant and opening up one in Charlotte because Johnson and Wales is there."

"We? As in you and Mr. Cheater?"

"Yes. But that's not going to happen. Not with my help, anyway."

"What's the name of this restaurant? When I go home, I want to make sure I don't patronize it."

"Chez Marcel."

"Stephen Carter's place?"

"Oh God, you know him? Please don't tell me you two are friends."

James shook his head furiously. "How did a woman like you hook up with a jackass like that?"

Jade chewed her bottom lip. "I wonder about that myself. How do you know him?"

James sighed and led her over to a bench. "My mother has a bakery on Auburn Avenue. She trained Stephen when he was a young pastry chef fresh out of culinary school. He couldn't cook worth a damn, but he charmed her. Then he stole her recipes. He tried to open a bakery and failed miserably. His next act was to reinvent himself as this hip restaurateur, offering overpriced food and fake ambiance. Buppies love it, but I think he's the biggest asshole in Atlanta."

Jade couldn't help but smile. Her gamble in Vegas was actually turning out to be a winning hand. "We should get him. Beat him at his own game and make him pay for what he's done."

"I'm not in the revenge or restaurant business," James said, pushing against his thighs.

"Think about it. What are the chances that we'd meet thousands of miles away from Atlanta and have one enemy in common?"

"Listen, Jade, I know he broke your heart, but what happens when you get the 'revenge' that you want? Where does that leave you?"

"With my own restaurant and, hopefully, Stephen busing my tables."

"I'm not going to get involved. Sorry."

She stroked his arm. "Do it for your mother."

"That was a low blow. My mom got over it and so did I. It might not hurt for you to try it."

Jade released his arm. "You're right, and I apologize for trying to drag—"

"Me into your mess. I know. Heard it all before." James rose to his feet, suddenly wanting to pack it up and head home. "I tell you what, why don't we head back to the casino and call it a night?"

"Wait," she said. "Now, I know I projected my anger on you, but what is this that you're giving me?"

James turned and cast a sideways glance at Jade. "We all have baggage. I always meet women who are probably really nice but always want to play games. I'm too old for that."

"What did she do?"

"I don't want to talk about it."

Jade placed her hand on his shoulder. "Come on. I spent the night talking about Stephen. You could at least tell me one story."

What the hell, he thought. *It's not like I'm going to see her again.* "My sister-in-law wanted to teach my brother a lesson when she thought that he'd cheated on her again. So, she tried to seduce me, caused a big riff between me and Mo. But everything is gravy now."

"Your sister-in-law sounds like a handful," Jade said, thinking that that sounded like a Serena trick.

"I love Kenya to death, but you women get emotional and start doing insane things. You're beautiful, and any man would be lucky to have you on his arm," James said. "Why waste your time on one who was stupid enough to let you go?"

"First of all, I'm not a piece of arm candy, which is what you men seem to want. You all take us to a dark place because you play with our hearts and minds," she snapped as she stood toe-to-toe with him.

"We don't take. You women give it as long as he has the money, the looks, and the power. Maybe you and Stephen deserve each other." He turned on his heels and stomped away.

Standing on the sidewalk, Jade shook her head as she watched James stalk away. She had been so wrong about him, and to think she'd even considered sleeping with him. Besides, she was going to stick it to Stephen, and she didn't need James Goings to help her do it. Who did he think he was, judging her because of what his sister-in-law had done? There were certainly worse things she could think of doing to Stephen, but all she wanted was to get her investment back.

I'm not going to do this. I'm not going to ruin my vacation by thinking of Stephen or James, she thought as she headed toward the bus stop.

CHAPTER 4

James didn't bother going into the room where his brother and his friends were; he wanted to be alone, so he headed to his hotel suite. Honestly, he wanted to find Jade and apologize for what he'd said to her downtown. He was judging her for what Kenya had done, and that wasn't fair. Still, what was it with women and wanting to get revenge for a broken heart? If he'd subscribed to that kind of thinking, then he would've spent his life trying to get back at women that had tried to use him to get closer to Maurice.

What was it about women and this need to hurt a man after a relationship ended? *They should just move on. I mean, it isn't as if there is a shortage of good men out there. Women just don't know a good man when he's looking them dead in the face,* he thought bitterly.

James had moved on after Annette Pemberton had played "Chopsticks" on his heart. They'd met right after Maurice had been drafted and James had moved to Charlotte with him. She'd seen him and Maurice talking at the draft party, which was held at the posh Westin Hotel in Uptown. Despite the fact that Lauryn had been draped on Maurice like a cheap suit, women had still thrown themselves at him. But Annette had had a better idea: to get to Maurice through his brother. She'd turned her attention to James, latching on to him while she tried her best to get into Maurice's bed and pocket. It hadn't taken long for James to see her game, but it also hadn't taken long for him to grow fond of her. He'd had thoughts of revenge, of humiliating her in front of Maurice and his famous friends, but instead, he'd ignored her calls and she'd gotten the message.

Annette hadn't been the only woman to try and use him to get a piece of Maurice. Several women in Charlotte had tried to get close to him with the hopes of getting next to Maurice. That was why he hadn't sought out anything serious, just a couple of encounters here and there. But casual sex left him feeling empty and like his father, the last person he wanted to be. Richard Goings had been an abusive womanizer who flaunted a string of affairs in his mother's face when he wasn't slapping her around.

James wasn't the kind of guy who believed in soul mates or love conquering all, because at some point, love caused pain. His father had hurt his mother, Maryann; Maurice had hurt Kenya; and he had countless friends who were paying alimony to women who they'd sworn to love forever. He wanted no part of that.

If Jade wanted to play games with her ex, that meant that she'd probably end up back in his arms before it was all over. He'd done the right thing by walking away. Still, for some unknown reason, he wanted to see her again. Well, he knew the reason, but after that scene downtown, he knew there would be no lovemaking in his suite tonight. Standing up, he headed for the door, deciding that it would be better to go into the noisy casino than lie in his suite, fantasizing about a woman he didn't even know. Heading to the casino floor, James figured he could lose a few bills at the slot machines. Picking a machine close to the baccarat room, he didn't pay attention to the bevy of beauties walking out of the gaming area, latched on to a few old men.

"Jade?" a woman said.

James's head snapped up, and he saw Jade heading in the direction of the women.

"I'm going to the room," Jade said. Then her eyes collided with his. The cold look that she gave him would've frozen the desert on a hundred-degree day.

The three women, who looked as if they could've been cover girls for any magazine, let go of their companions and turned to their girlfriend. Their eyes followed hers to James.

"Come on, girl," another one of the women said as they turned toward the elevator.

James knew he should just let her walk away, especially since she had the girlfriend network surrounding her. But he left his seat at the slot machine and crossed over to her.

"Excuse me, Jade. Can we talk?" he asked.

"Who are you?" the tallest woman asked, with her hand on her hip and attitude in her voice.

"I think I was talking to Jade," James replied, with a modest amount of respect in his voice.

"James, we don't have anything left to say to each other," Jade snapped.

"Then just listen," he insisted. "I want to apologize for earlier. I didn't mean to come off as a judgmental asshole."

Jade's face softened as her girlfriends looked confused and perplexed.

"Who is this guy?" one of them asked.

"Serena," Jade said, "let me handle this."

James held his hand out to Jade and pulled her away from her girls. "I shouldn't have left you downtown, and what I said to you was out of line. I didn't mean to judge you, but that's exactly what I did."

"Yes, it was."

He ran his hand over his face and tried to smile. "May I buy you a drink to make up for the error of my ways?"

She turned and glanced at her girlfriends, who had been watching the conversation intently. "I'd better not."

"Do I need to buy them drinks, too?" James asked.

"Yes," the tallest woman said, indicating that they'd been listening to the conversation intently.

James pointed them in the direction of the bar and let them pass.

Jade walked slowly, allowing James to catch up with her and her friends to get out of earshot.

"They are going to eat you alive, and I'm going to let them," she said, with a sarcastic smile.

"That's mean."

"So was leaving me at a bus stop downtown," she said.

"I know that was the wrong thing to do. Anything could've happened to you, and I would've never forgiven myself for that. I'm more of a gentleman than that."

"A man who admits when he's wrong? I can't believe it." Jade pushed her hair behind her ears and smiled at him. "Maybe I won't let them beat you up too badly."

James smirked and pulled a chair out for Jade at the table where her friends had taken up residency. "Ladies," he said, "what are we drinking?"

"Nothing until you tell us who the heck you are," the tallest woman said.

Jade cleared her throat. "How rude of me. Ladies, this is James Goings. James, these are my friends." She pointed to the tall, mouthy one. "Serena." Then she pointed to a leggy, caramel-colored sister with raven hair. "Kandace." And finally she pointed to the quietest woman of the trio. "Alicia."

James extended his hand to the women, who ignored his gesture, then sat down quickly. "Nice to meet you all," he said.

"So," Serena said, "I still don't know who you are."

Jade shot a warning look in her friend's direction. "We met earlier and had a little disagreement."

"Then why is he here?" Alicia asked, confusion clouding her comely face.

"Because he admitted that he was wrong, and how often have we seen a man do that?" Jade said, causing her friends to break into laughter.

James leaned back in the chair, feeling like the butt of their joke. But from his vantage point, he was able to admire Jade silently. She seemed like a different person with her friends; she was more relaxed, and she smiled a lot more. He imagined that the four of them together were a lot of trouble.

"Then I say Mr. James should order the best bottle of champagne on the menu," Serena said.

"That's fine," he replied, feeling as if he and Serena would never be friends. "I can do that." Waving for the waiter, James ordered a bottle of 1990 Veuve Clicquot Ponsardin and oysters on the half shell. The women looked at each other and smiled.

"You have great taste, James," Kandace said. "Where are you from?"

"Originally from Atlanta, but I live in Charlotte now," he replied.

"Atlanta? It's a small world," Alicia said. "We're from Atlanta."

"He already knows that, I'm sure," Serena said. "So, what do you do in Charlotte?"

Frowning, he said, "I work for a living."

Jade threw her hands up. "All right, enough of the third degree. James is all right."

Serena folded her arms across her chest and sighed. "Whatever."

"Goings," Alicia said. "Are you related to Maurice Goings?"

Rolling his eyes, he nodded. "That's my brother."

"Why does his name sound familiar?" Kandace asked.

Serena snickered. "Remember the guy whose fiancée left him at the altar for another woman? That's him. Oh, and he plays in the NFL."

"For the Panthers, right?" Alicia said. "I think I planned a few parties for him a couple of years ago."

Jade stroked her throat and then turned to James. "Once you get to know them, they are very nice."

"I'll take your word for it," he said in a tight whisper.

"We're not trying to give you a hard time on purpose," Alicia said. "It's just that we look out for each other, and we don't want anyone else taking advantage of our girl."

James knew they were talking about her ex, and he definitely didn't want to have this conversation again. "I totally understand," he said. "The last thing I want to do is to take advantage of your girl." His eyes never left Jade's face.

When is that champagne coming? Jade thought. The looks that James kept giving her did nothing but make her burn like a slow, smoldering fire. The fact that he had apologized to her had made her realize that she hadn't been wrong about him. He wasn't a total pig, and he was still sexy as all get out. The way he looked at her made her heart beat like a Congo drum.

"So, what are you doing in Las Vegas, James?" Alicia asked, causing Jade to stop thinking about tasting James's lips.

"Vacation with the guys," James said, looking away from Jade for the first time in what seemed like hours. "I guess it was luck that I ran into Jade when I did."

"Why's that?" Kandace asked, smiling, as if she knew something naughty had happened.

James turned to Jade and reached for her hand. "She's a hell of a poker player."

The women laughed. "Yes, she is," Alicia said.

The waiter walked over to the table and placed a bucket of ice with a bottle of champagne in it and the oysters in the middle of the table. Jade wanted to pour the contents of the bucket in her lap; maybe then she'd cool off.

After the group finished the champagne and the food, Jade allowed James to walk her over to the hotel where she and her friends were staying. "That was really nice of you to buy us that champagne, but it wasn't necessary," Jade said.

"I know, but I figured if they drank and ate, they'd stay off my back," he said, with a laugh. "But I was wrong. Serena's tough."

"She's a pussycat once you get to know her," Jade replied.

James extended his arm to her as they came to the intersection. "I wouldn't want you to get hit by a car," he said. "Your friends would hunt me down and kill me. You don't often find women as close as you all seem."

"Women have to stick together," she said, though the only thing she wanted to see together was the two of them. "Listen, about before and what I was saying about my ex . . ."

"We were having such a great evening, and now you're trying to mess it up," James said.

"What I'm trying to say is, I'm not some psycho ex-girlfriend with an ax to grind. I made a business deal with a man that I thought I was going to marry, and he took my money and cut me out of the business. That's not fair, and to allow him to get away with that would be wrong."

"I guess I can see why you're miffed. But still, why get revenge? Just get a lawyer."

She shrugged her shoulders. "That would be too easy, and there isn't anything in writing. It's going to be my word against his."

"I know a great attorney that can help you. My sister-in-law specializes in contract law."

Jade shook her head. "I'm not ready to go there yet. And I don't want to talk about it anymore."

Once they reached the door of the hotel, James was ready to tell her good night, but Jade didn't want him to walk away.

"You know," she said, "I never gave you your share of the poker money."

James smiled. "Keep it. Seeing the looks on those guys' faces was enough payment for me."

"So this is it, huh?"

"What do you mean?"

"Chances are we're probably never going to see each other again."

He nodded. "That's a shame."

Looping her arms around his waist, she looked up at him. "So, what are we going to do about it?"

"What do you want to do about it?" A hint of a smile spread across his full lips.

So many thoughts ran through her mind. She'd come to Las Vegas to do something she wouldn't normally do, to do something that would take her mind off Stephen and his antics. Boldly, she stood on her tiptoes and kissed James wantonly and brazenly, not caring who saw her.

He stepped back, savoring the taste of her kiss and smiling, as if he'd won a million dollars on a slot machine. "That was a helluva good-bye."

"I'd rather say good-bye after breakfast," she said. "Come upstairs with me."

"Are you sure?"

"What happens in Vegas stays in Vegas. I want to make something happen." She winked at him and headed through the door.

James wanted to rip Jade's dress off the moment

they stepped on the elevator, wrap her long legs around his waist, and bury himself inside her. He wanted to suckle her breasts until her nipples were swollen and full, but he showed restraint. It wasn't as if he was the type of man to have a string of one-night stands, but from the moment he saw her, sex was all that he'd thought about. Stepping closer to her, he stroked her cheek, then pulled her against his body. A soft moan escaped her throat as she felt his arousal.

He stroked her bare arms and sought out her lips again. "Where's your room?" he asked.

"Fifteenth floor."

Slipping his hand underneath her dress, he said, "Do you think we're going to make it?"

"Not if you kiss me again. This is wild," she moaned as his lips grazed her neck and he slid his finger inside the crotch of her silk thong. "As cliché as it sounds, I've never done anything like this before."

James lifted her leg and wrapped it around his waist as the elevator ascended to the tenth floor. "Neither have I," he said. He brought his lips down on top of hers, assaulting her mouth with a hot and demanding kiss. James felt her melt against him and nearly lose her balance. He backed her against the mirrored wall, casting a sidelong glance at their reflection. "You're beautiful, sexy, and you're making me so hot right now," he breathed against her ear.

The elevator's ding alerted the couple that they had reached their destination. Unfurling themselves from one another, they sprinted from the elevator, dashing down the hall to Jade's room. She fished her room key card out of the bottom of her purse while James stood behind her, stroking her back.

The moment they walked into the room, their clothes came off: she clawed at James's shirt as he unzipped her dress. Neither of them thought about anything but getting the other's clothes off. Her dress fluttered to the floor, his shirt was tossed across the room, and they stumbled backward onto the queen-size bed. They broke their kiss for a moment, as if they needed to take deep breaths.

"Are you sure you want to do this?" he asked.

"Yes," she breathed.

James continued his sensual assault of her body, taking her supple breasts into his mouth one at a time. She pulled at his hips, pressing him against the pulsating heat of her feminine core. Pulling back from her, he grinned. "Where's your purse?"

"Huh?"

"I need a condom."

Catching on to his joke, she laughed and reached down to retrieve her purse. Jade passed the condom to James and watched as he slid it over his thick erection. *What am I doing? I don't even know this man, but damn he's sexy as hell and I want this. There's no way I'm turning back now. . . .*

He drew her into his arms. "This is crazy, isn't it?"

Jade couldn't think of anything to say. Part of her wanted to tell him that she didn't do things like this, despite what she had in her purse. But the wanton sex goddess inside her said that the time for talk was over. She needed a release, and that was just what James was going to be tonight. She wrapped her arms around him and pulled him against her silently, telling him that she wanted him.

At her urging, James parted her thighs and found his way to her heat. It felt so good being inside her, feeling how hot and wet she was. He couldn't remember the last time he'd been with a woman who actually made him feel something other than obligation. Thrusting into her, he reveled in her body, the swell of her breasts against his chest, the curve of her bottom against his hands. What he didn't expect was for Jade to take control of his body the way she did, pressing him back against the bed and straddling his frame. She took the entire length of him inside her, moaning as she arched her back. James grabbed her breasts, teasing her hard nipples with his thumbs as they ground so hard that the bed rocked. He released a guttural groan as she clenched her body around him, seemingly milking his sexual energy. He didn't want to climax, not now, because he wanted to please her as she'd pleased him, but he couldn't help himself.

"Jade, Jade, Jade," he muttered, lifting her off him and laying her on her back. Using his tongue, he traversed her body as if she were the New World. When he reached the tops of her creamy thighs, he slipped his hand between them, using his finger to tease her throbbing bud.

It was her turn to call out his name as his lips and tongue replaced his finger. Jade's legs began to quake as she was about to come to her own climax. The pleasure that she was feeling was like nothing she'd ever experienced before. No man had ever taken the time to give her body the treatment it deserved, putting her pleasure above his own. She clutched his shoulders as his tongue danced in her G-spot until she couldn't take any more.

"Oh, James!" she exclaimed as she felt release.

Rolling over on his side, he pushed her hair back from her forehead. "You all right?" he asked.

"Um," she moaned.

"So what happens now?"

Jade shrugged. "I told you I've never done this before."

"Let's discuss it over breakfast, then," he suggested, with a smile. "Maybe I can have you for a midnight snack."

Jade threw her leg over his waist. "I think I like the sound of that."

CHAPTER 5

Waking up in James's arms didn't feel like the end of a one-night stand. Jade watched him as he slept, and smiled. Never had she been so satisfied and loved so expertly. Maybe it was Vegas, maybe it was the fact that she'd never see him again, that allowed her to be wild and wanton, but what was his excuse? He seemed to get more pleasure out of pleasing than anything else. She didn't know how to deal with the morning after, though, because she'd never had a one-night stand before. If this were a movie, she thought, she would have some jazzy line to say and would be able to go on with her Vegas vacation without a second thought about James Goings. But she knew that wasn't going to happen. This man was burned on her brain, etched in her soul, and flowing through her blood.

This is just lust, pure and simple, she thought, fighting the urge to stroke the side of his smooth face. Men like James weren't single, and she was sure that the only reason he'd slept with her was that he was as caught up in the "what happens in Vegas" adage as she was.

Just as she was about to drift off to sleep, there was a loud knock at the door, followed by, "Jade, open up!" The voice belonged to Serena. "Are you in there with that dude?"

Jade jumped out of bed, dashed to the bathroom, and grabbed a robe from the back of the door. She opened the door to the room a sliver and peered at her friend. "What do you want?"

"Why aren't you opening the door?"

"Because I don't want to."

"Ooh, you did it with that man. All right, score one for Jade."

"Can you go away?" Jade whispered, looking back to see if James had awakened.

"We have plans this morning, remember? Those investors that I told you about are waiting downstairs, at the breakfast buffet."

Jade slapped her hand against her forehead. "I totally forgot about that."

"I know where your mind was. But you need to get dressed and to get down there in five minutes," Serena said. "If you're going to stick it to Stephen Carter, you're going to need money. I didn't wine and dine these fools to let you blow it because you found a, um—how shall I say?—release."

"I'll be ready," Jade said. "But you have to go."

"Tell James hello." Serena sauntered away. Closing the door, Jade turned around to see James rising from the bed.

"Good morning," he said.

"Morning. I hate to rush you out of here, but I have a meeting in about three minutes."

"Wow. So that's how these things turn out?" he asked as he rubbed his eyes.

Shaking her head, Jade forced herself to smile. "What did you think was going to happen?"

"Possibly a replay from last night, but I get it," he said, keeping his tone light as he slipped on his pants. "Maybe I'll see you around."

"I hope so," she said, then dashed into the bathroom to shower.

As James walked out of Jade's room, he wondered how some people could do this type of thing on a regular basis. Honestly, he felt a little cheap. She had unceremoniously tossed him out of her room without much of a good-bye. He'd always figured that was the man's job. Needless to say, Jade had piqued his interest, but the feeling wasn't mutual. James knew when to walk away. As he headed back to his hotel, he replayed their night together in his mind. It was the best sex he'd ever had, and she was the most passionate woman he'd ever been with. Her taste was still on his lips. Once he got up to his suite, Maurice was there, waiting for him.

"You came to Vegas and lost your mind, huh?" Maurice said. "Who was the woman that you spent the night with?"

"Who said I spent the night with a woman?" James said as he plopped on the bed.

"I would hope that you didn't stay out all night with some man. Was it that chick you brought up there to the game room? Homer is still hot about losing all that money." Maurice laughed and reached for his cell phone. "What time is it back East?"

"Can you stop calling your wife for two seconds? Why didn't you just bring her with you?" James closed his eyes, and visions of Jade danced in his mind. Opening his eyes and sitting up, he found his brother staring down at him. "What?" he said.

"I'm trying to figure out why you have that goofy smile on your face," Maurice said.

"What are you talking about?" James touched his cheek, and he was smiling.

"All right, keep it to yourself, but if the sex was that good, then you might want to get her number so you two can hook up again."

"That's not going to happen. But why are you in my room?"

Maurice cocked his head to the side. "Because we were supposed to have breakfast with those brothers from the Las Vegas Chamber of Commerce."

"Oh, yeah," James said, sitting up and swinging his legs over the side of the bed. "What time is the meeting?"

"Ten minutes ago," Maurice said. "I'm always late, but you're supposed to be the responsible one."

Rising to his feet, James smirked at his brother. "So, go make the meeting and apologize for my tardiness. God knows I've done it for you more times than I can count. I'll be down in fifteen minutes."

Maurice laughed as he headed toward the door. Then he turned around and looked at his brother. "You know you're never going to live this down."

James nodded, noting the special glee Mo was taking in this temporary role reversal. "Whatever."

* * *

True to his word, James was dressed in a casual suit and sitting at the table with Maurice, Richard Harris, and Raymond Harris fifteen minutes later. Just as he was about to be briefed on what was going on, Jade walked by. She looked great naked, but in her heather and gray bandeau dress, which clung to her curves like a second skin, she looked more alluring. The chatter at the table stopped, and all eyes followed Jade as she and her friend walked by. Rising to his feet, James called out to her. When she whirled around and smiled at him, his heart tightened in his chest and he had to think to breathe.

"James, I didn't expect to see you here this morning," she said as she marched over to him and hugged him tightly.

"Stalker," Serena whispered loudly.

"Good morning to you, too," James replied as he and Jade separated.

Serena smiled smarmily and glanced at the other men sitting at the table. "Are we interrupting business?" she asked.

Richard stood and extended his hand to her. "Not at all. Would you ladies like to join us for coffee?"

Serena shook his hand weakly. "Actually, I've had my fill of coffee this morning. We're just leaving a meeting ourselves."

Jade smiled and turned to her friend. "I think I can stomach another cup of coffee."

"Have at it. I'm going to the business center to send a few e-mails," Serena said, then turned toward the exit.

James pulled an extra chair to the table and held it for Jade to sit down. "So," she said, "what big business deal did I walk in on?"

"Just a couple of guys bouncing ideas off each other," James said, unable to stop smiling. *Maybe I am wrong about her never wanting to see me again.*

"Well, if you have half the success that Serena and I did, then we're going to need to order champagne," Jade said, beaming.

"For your restaurant venture?" James asked.

Maurice cleared his throat. "I didn't realize that you were this rude, J."

"Sorry," James said, tearing his eyes away from Jade. "Maurice, this is Jade Christian. Jade, this is my brother, Maurice. The wonder twins over here are Richard Harris and Raymond Harris, a couple of Vegas's movers and shakers."

After everyone had exchanged hellos and handshakes, Jade and James returned to their conversation. "You're going to get back at Mr. Arrogance, after all, huh?" he asked.

"If that's how you see it. I think of it as getting my money back, and I deserve it," she told him.

"Still sounds like revenge to me," James declared.

Raymond and Richard finished their coffee and said good-bye to Maurice, James, and Jade. James hoped that his brother would leave the table as well, but Mo had other plans as he ordered another pot of coffee and a crumb cake.

"So, Ms. Christian," Maurice said as he waited for the server to return with his order, "are you the young lady who my friends say robbed them blind?"

Jade smiled as she poured the last bit of coffee from the carafe on the table. "Yes, and they deserved it because they underestimated me, and that's something that men ought to stop doing."

"Ouch," Maurice said. "Feisty. You remind me of my wife."

"Don't you need to call her?" James suggested.

Maurice nodded and winked at his brother. "Don't eat all the cake, and don't tell my trainer that I've gone off my diet."

Once Maurice had left the table, Jade smiled at James. "You're not slick. Why didn't you just tell your brother to beat it, kick rocks, or get lost?"

"That would've been rude." He smiled and fought the urge to kiss her as he'd done the night before. "Besides, I wanted to talk to you about last night and this morning."

"So did I. I know that things seemed crazy this morning, but I wasn't trying to ditch you, and if I had my way, we'd still be in bed right now," she said seductively.

"What happens next?" James asked.

"I don't know. I'm going to be working on this business deal and. . . ."

"And you live in Atlanta and my life is in Charlotte."

"Long-distance affairs never work."

James held back a sigh and said, "Then I guess we'll always have Las Vegas."

"I wish we could've met under different circumstances, maybe when you were still in Atlanta and before I knew that jerk," she said as she reached across the table and took his hand in hers. "When are you leaving?"

"In a few days."

"Then that gives us a couple days to spend together and make more memories." She smiled brightly.

James returned her smile and winked at her. "Let me take you to the Top of the World tonight."

"What is that?"

"A restaurant that's eight hundred feet away from business, nosy brothers, and girlfriends."

"And afterward?"

Licking his lips, he smiled. "Then we can do whatever you want to do, clothing optional."

A wicked grin spread across her face. "Mr. Goings, are you propositioning me?"

"If you have to ask, then I must not be doing something right."

Jade rose from her chair. "Then I say we have a date. Where would you like to meet?"

"In the lobby of the hotel, and if you have a dress similar to what you wore last night, please put it on."

"I will," she said, then walked away. James couldn't tear his eyes away from her tantalizing backside, which swayed like a palm in the breeze. He hadn't even noticed Maurice's return to the table.

"That must have been some great sex, because your nose is wide open," Maurice said when he sat down.

"Whatever."

"Could it be that my bitter brother has given up this notion that all women are the spawn of the devil?"

James shot his brother a cautioning look. "Listen, what happens in Vegas stays in Vegas. She lives in Atlanta and has some serious baggage. You'll never believe who she was dating back in Georgia."

"Who? Michael Vick?"

"No, and even worse. Stephen Carter."

"That asshole. The last time Kenya and I went to Atlanta, we almost went to his restaurant. But when

I found out he was the owner of the place, I told her I'd rather eat out of a Dumpster than drop a dime in the fool's place," Maurice spat. "I'll never forget what he did to Ma."

"Taking advantage of women seems to be a trait of his. He duped Jade into investing in his restaurant, and when he started seeing a profit, he dumped her."

"That's why you should never go into business with someone you're sleeping with."

"Or hire them as an attorney."

"Shut up. That was different."

James reached for the cake that the server had set in the middle of the table. "People do strange things in the name of love and then get upset when it blows up in their faces."

"That's the James I know and love. Mr. Cynical." Maurice reached for a hunk of cake and shook his head at his brother. "So, you two going out again?"

"Yep. We're going to say a proper good-bye."

"Don't mess around and fall in love," Maurice said in between bites of cake.

"That's the last thing that's going to happen," James declared.

Jade floated to her room. But her bubble was burst as soon as she saw Serena and Kandace waiting for her. "What?" she asked her friends.

"The question is, what are you doing?" Serena asked. "You don't know this guy from Adam's alley cat, and you're acting like a teenager in love."

"Lust," Kandace said. "Have you forgotten that you have bigger fish to fry?"

"Aren't you the same people that told me to come

here and have an adventure?" Jade asked as she slipped her electronic key card in the lock. "Matter of fact, had you not put that silly condom in my purse, James and I might have never hooked up, Serena."

Serena rolled her eyes. "Whatever. You need to focus. We have the funding that we need to purchase that restaurant in Charlotte right from underneath Stephen. You also have the means to tie his funds up in so much red tape that his little restaurant in Atlanta will be forced to shut down. We should be on a plane right now."

Jade opened her door, and her friends followed her into her room. "Another day and a half is not going to kill us. Besides, I have a date tonight."

Kandace and Serena groaned. "You know what?" Kandace said. "You're a glutton. What do you even know about this guy, besides how good the sex is?"

Jade smiled despite herself. "James is a special guy. I can feel it. But there's no need for you two to worry. Tonight is good-bye for James and me."

Kandace and Serena exchanged knowing looks. "Where does James live again?" Serena asked.

"Charlotte," Jade replied.

"Doesn't sound like good-bye to me, especially since we're trying to open a business there," Kandace said.

"Ladies, are we going to do some shopping this morning, or are you two going to stand here and critique my life?" Jade asked exasperatedly. "Where's Alicia?"

"I think she's playing baccarat again. You're not the only one having a Vegas fling," Serena said, with a snort.

CHAPTER 6

Once again, James was on the losing end of a poker game with the players. It didn't matter, though, because he knew he'd be a winner once he met up with Jade and they headed out for their date.

"You need to let that stripper play for you all the time," Homer said.

"She's not a stripper," James said as he pushed away from the table.

"She could be," Homer replied, licking his lips. "I'm still trying to figure out how you landed that."

"Don't be jealous, because your oversize gut and the milewide gap between your teeth run all the pretty ones away," James said as he patted Homer's ample stomach.

The other men at the table laughed and Homer scowled.

"Whatever, man," Homer snapped. "The only reason women want to get to know you is that your last name is Goings."

Any other day James would've reached over the table and attempted to strangle Homer for that comment. But at the moment, the only thing he wanted to do was get ready for his date with Jade, so he simply left the room.

James knew that Jade didn't want to get next to Maurice, like so many other women who'd tried to latch on to him in the past. After tonight he was sure that he'd never see her again. He still wasn't sure how he felt about that, because a part of him wanted to know everything about her, and the other part just wanted one more night with her in his arms. *I don't even know this woman to be going on like this. I need to take it for what it is, a vacation fling,* he thought as he entered his suite.

Jade paced the floor in her room as she searched for the perfect dress. She wanted James's jaw to drop to the floor when he saw her in the lobby, but if she didn't hurry, she'd be late. After another few moments of pondering what to wear, she decided on a slinky red dress with a V-shaped back and a neckline that was so low, she needed double-sided tape to keep from having a Janet Jackson-esque malfunction.

She reached down and strapped on her red sandals with the three-inch heels and prayed that James didn't have a lot of walking in mind for their date. Taking a glance at herself in the full-length mirror on the bathroom door, she smiled. Serena had a flair for picking out sexy clothing, and there was no way she would wear an outfit like that in Atlanta, where people expected her to be prim and proper or, as her friends called her, a doormat.

She'd allowed Stephen to walk all over her, but

she'd also thought he loved her and that they were building the restaurant for their future. Stephen's future just didn't include her, but some eye candy that he felt enhanced his image. His new woman made up for what she lacked in brains with silicone breasts. Snarling at the thought of Stephen and his new woman, Jade recalled how she'd found out that she'd been replaced.

Serena and Alicia had shown up at her doorstep early one Friday morning, armed with coffee and Krispy Kreme doughnuts.

"Hey, girls," Jade had said, blissfully unaware of the devastating news that they'd come to deliver.

Alicia had been the one to speak first. "Mocha latte with skim milk and no whipped cream. It's your favorite, right?"

"What's going on? You think coffee is the nectar of Satan," Jade had replied, ready to laugh at the thought of Alicia standing in line at Starbucks.

Serena, who had been uncharacteristically silent, spoke up. "There's an article in the paper about Stephen's restaurant and his plans to expand."

"Great. We did that interview weeks ago. It's about time the *Atlanta Journal-Constitution* ran this story." Jade reached out for the paper, but Serena didn't hand it over. "Serena, give me the paper."

Alicia had motioned for Jade to take a seat on the sofa. "This isn't going to be pretty or easy for you to take. Serena, give her the paper."

Jade had never been more confused than she was when she read the article about Stephen and his empire. She remembered talking to the reporter about their planned expansion into North Carolina, South Carolina, and Virginia, but who in the hell was the woman draped over him like a wet spandex bathing suit? She'd read the woman's name, but it was her title, "fiancée and business partner," that stood out the most.

"This can't be right," Jade had said as she stared at the picture. "Why is this woman in this picture, pretending to be me?"

"Because Stephen is a spineless punk, and he used you to get what he wanted, your investment in his sorry-ass restaurant," Serena had explained. "I say we roll up there and kick his ass."

Jade, feeling as if her entire world had just crumbled, had dropped the paper on the floor as she'd sobbed silently. It had taken her about twenty minutes to pull herself together, assure her girlfriends that she could handle this situation on her own. With red, puffy eyes and anger flowing threw her veins, she'd driven to Stephen's restaurant and stormed inside, ignoring the hostess as she bolted toward the office she and Stephen shared. When she'd opened the door, she found him and his new love on top of the desk, kissing like horny teenagers.

"Well, isn't this just cozy," Jade had said.

The two had pulled apart and looked at Jade.

"Who is this woman?" Stephen's lover had asked.

"A former employee," he'd replied coldly. "Jade, what is the meaning of this? Why are you storming into my office as if you have some right to be here?"

"You son of a bitch. I have fifty thousand reasons to be here. Employee? I thought I was supposed to be your fiancée!"

Rising to his feet, he'd stepped up to Jade. "You need to leave. You were my bookkeeper."

"Bookkeeper? That's all I was to you?"

"Yes, and I'd like it if you'd leave. My fiancée and I are busy."

Jade had slapped him as hard as she could. "Bastard! Give me my money back."

"We made a deal, and your money is tied up in—"

She'd slapped him again and then stormed out of the office. Her next trip had been to her lawyer, who told her there was nothing she could do to get her money back because they hadn't signed a contract.

A few days later, she and her girls had hopped on an overpriced flight to Vegas.

Jade shook her head, trying to clear away the ugly thoughts of her life. *I'm going to deal with Stephen when I return to Atlanta. But right now I'm going on my date.* She grabbed a sheer red wrap, draped it across her shoulders, and headed to the lobby.

When she found James standing near the front desk, dressed in a black tuxedo, carrying a dozen red roses, her breath caught in her chest. He looked as dashing as 007 himself, and the cocksure grin on his lips added to his appeal.

He strode over to her, smiling and holding the flowers and a pair of Toni Braxton show tickets out to her. "You look beautiful," he said.

Taking the roses in her arms, she willed her heart to slow down before saying, "You clean up well yourself."

"I have a car outside, and I'm ready to show you the world." James looped his arm around Jade's waist, and she knew that this was all a dream. Men didn't act like this, at least not the ones she knew or fell for.

"This is really nice," she said as they walked out to the limo that was waiting for them.

"Well, I figured that we should at least party like we're royalty this weekend," James said as the driver opened the door for the couple.

"James, this is too much." Jade eased onto the supple leather seat of the limo and closed her eyes. "We're just going to dinner, right?"

"Nope. Just relax and enjoy the ride, all right?" he said, with a wide smile. "Tonight, I'm your host, so be a good guest, okay?"

"If you say so," she replied, with a smile that matched his. "It's not often that I give up control."

"And that sounds like a problem to me," James said as he eased closer to Jade and wrapped his arm around her slender waist, pulling her closer to him as the driver peeled off from the curb.

The limo meandered slowly down the Strip, but neither of the passengers cared about the sights, the bright lights, or the people milling about. James locked eyes with Jade, drinking in her quiet beauty and trying to keep his hormones under control. That was hard to do because he knew what was underneath that dress. He knew that she had the softest breasts and the sweetest-tasting nipples that he'd ever put in his mouth. The passion and desire that were building in the backseat of the limo made him want to forget Toni Braxton and dinner, rip her clothes off, and make love to her until the sun rose.

"You're quiet," Jade said, breaking off their stare.

"So are you."

"This is weird," she said. "Because all I can think about right now is how much I want to hear Toni Braxton sing 'Breathe Again.'"

"Really?" James asked, not really buying it. He could feel the electric undercurrent that she was giving off and knew she wanted him as much as he wanted her.

I can't believe I just said that lame crap, Jade thought as she looked out of the window. Had she been honest, she would've told James that she'd always had a fantasy about having hot sex in the back of a limo. Of course, that fantasy wasn't going to happen, because she didn't want him to think that she was just a piece of sex. They were supposed to be taking the time to get to know each other, well, as well as they could over a few days. Sucking on her bottom lip, Jade turned to James and leaned against his shoulder. She knew this was a fantasy, a weekend affair.

Maybe we should skip the concert, he thought as he took her hand in his.

"What's the fragrance that you're wearing?" James asked.

"It's just some jasmine oil," she replied, her voice wavering as she closed her eyes and melted against him.

James took a deep breath, filling his nostrils with Jade's intoxicating scent. Damn, he wanted her. He wanted her more than he needed to take his next breath. Unable to control his desire any longer, he cupped her face in his hands and brought his lips on top of hers. Her lips were soft and tasty. A soft moan escaped her throat as his tongue danced into her mouth. With his hands firmly around her waist, Jade closed her eyes and lost herself in his kiss. She gripped his shoulders, sucking his tongue as if they would never have the chance to kiss again.

Pulling back, James looked at Jade with lust and desire in his eyes. "You know, I really don't give a damn about seeing Toni Braxton when you kiss me like that," he said.

"James," she moaned as he slipped his hand between her thighs. Her womanly core throbbed with anticipation as his fingers danced around the waistband of her lace panties. "We'd better stop before . . . ooh."

He dipped his finger in her wetness, touching the spot that he'd found the first time they'd made love. With his free hand, he raised the window between the driver and the backseat. "I want you so bad," he groaned. His erection pressed against his zipper, and the deeper he buried his finger inside Jade, the harder he became. "But I promised you a special night out."

Jade reached back and unzipped her dress. "I want you, too," she said as he pulled her onto his lap.

With hands faster than the eye, James reached underneath her dress and pulled her panties off. Jade was hot, and James felt the heat from her body immediately. In short order, he unzipped his pants, and Jade helped him push them down to his ankles. James's erection made a tent in his silk boxers, which brought a smile to Jade's face. She couldn't remember the last time that a man had wanted her as much as James did. Stephen had never made her feel desirable. Sex between them had been as bland as filling out income tax forms. How was it possible that she and this stranger had so much sizzle that they couldn't keep their hands off one another?

And speaking of hands, James knew just what to do with his, especially when he touched her back ever so gently, running his long fingers up and down her spine. He treated her body as if it was precious, worthy of adoration. Closing her eyes as James brushed his thick lips across her navel, Jade moaned in delight. James pulled her dress and strapless bra from her body in a quick motion, then laid her on the supple leather seat.

For a few moments, he just marveled at her body. To say she was perfect was an understatement. Her skin was softer and smoother than her silk dress. With his index finger, he traveled down her tantalizing frame. She placed her hand in the center of his chest as he covered her body with his lean, muscular one.

"This isn't really who I am," she breathed. "I don't just go around sleeping with men in the name of fun and games."

James gently kissed her cheek. "Jade," he said. "I'm not making any kinds of judgments. We're adults, and there isn't anything I want right now more than you. And I'm going to want you tomorrow and the next day, too."

She expelled a deep breath, happy with James's response. But in the back of her mind, she wondered if this was normal for him. Did he live his life having sex with no strings attached?

It's just Vegas. Let it happen and move on, the lust devil on her shoulder told her as James's tongue flicked across her hard nipple. Jade gave in to desire, allowing James to have control of her body. As he alternated between sucking and gently biting her breasts, she reached down and massaged his hardness with expert skill, nearly bringing him to the brink with her up and down strokes. He moaned with satisfaction as Jade moved her hand faster, then slowly again. Next, she decided to tease him with her wetness and pressed her body against the tip of his throbbing manhood.

"I need you now," she moaned breathlessly.

For two seconds, James wanted to dive into her hot body and just stay there until New Year's Eve rolled around. But with everything in him, he was able to pull back from Jade's awaiting valley. "Let me protect us," he said as he reached for his pants. Then he smiled at her. "Unless you have something in your purse."

She pinched him on the forearm. "Funny," she said. "Maybe you should be on stage tonight instead of the comedian George Wallace."

James pulled the circular condom packet from his wallet, then slid the sheath in place. Neither of them noticed that the limo had come to a complete stop. It didn't matter what was going on outside the limo as Jade pushed James onto the seat and climbed on top of him. She wrapped her legs around his waist and positioned herself on top of his erection. James pulled her against his chest as he felt the heat radiating from her womanly core. With her breasts pressed against his chest and his lips grazing her neck, James and Jade gyrated against each other, giving each other passion and pleasure that they'd never known. She moved her hips in a slow, circular motion, taking him deeper and deeper into her valley.

"James," she said, her lips pressed against his ear. "James."

His response was to take her chin in his hand

and capture her lips, as if they were the rarest candy that had ever been invented. As their tongues jockeyed for position, James shifted his hips and eased Jade onto her back. Breaking off the kiss, he used his lips and tongue to travel down to her cleavage. He stopped kissing her as she ground against him, nearly taking him to the point of no return. James knew that Jade had reached her climax a few times. Every time he felt her lips tighten around his manhood, he knew that she'd come. Three times.

But he wasn't done with her. He couldn't be, because there was no telling if he'd ever see her or feel her again. She shivered and sucked in her bottom lip as he slowly pumped in and out. Four times. She moaned with satisfaction, and James knew that he could release himself. He filled the condom with his pleasure, and then he and Jade lay in each other's arms, sweat making their bodies slip from the leather seats a bit.

"We're really going to have to stop this," Jade said, a wide smile plastered on her face.

"I totally agree," he replied and returned her smile. "We need more space."

Jade smacked his bare chest. "You know what I mean. It's like when we're together, we can't keep our clothes on."

"With or without your clothes, you're a beautiful woman."

"James," she said. "Seriously."

"Fine. If you want to spend these next few days just hanging out, we can do that. As a matter of fact, Homer and the boys are having another poker game tomorrow."

"I'm there," Jade replied.

"Great. But there is still the issue of you and me walking to your room after you take their money again. You're going to invite me in, and I'm going to have to say no."

"Who said I was going to invite you in?" she ribbed.

James clutched his chest. "And here I thought you liked me."

"I do." *And that could prove to be a problem, because this is just a Vegas fling.*

"Think the driver is back yet?" James asked.

"I hadn't even noticed that the limo wasn't moving," she said.

"Oh, it was moving, all right."

The couple dressed, and James tapped on the window between the front and the back of the limo.

"Yes, sir?" the driver asked.

"We're ready to go. Do we still have time to catch a nice restaurant for dinner?" James asked.

"Not on the Strip, but I know of a great place downtown," replied the driver.

James turned to Jade, who was straightening the hem of her dress. "Want to try it?" he asked.

"Sure. I seem to be doing a lot of new things with you tonight. What's one more?"

"That's fine," James said to the driver.

CHAPTER 7

By the time James and Jade finished eating dinner and hanging out in downtown Las Vegas, they were bone tired.

"I guess we should head back to the hotel. I'm sure my girls have been looking for me," Jade said as they slowly walked to the limo.

"They probably have. Your friends are a trip," he said. "You guys remind me of some of the guys my brother and I grew up with."

She smiled wistfully. Why did her mind have to dart back to that lying bastard Stephen? He'd never said anything nice about her friends, the women who had had her back since she was in college. *That's probably because Stephen had never had a friend he didn't betray.*

Despite the way they had treated him, James didn't degrade her buddies.

"What's wrong?" James asked when he noticed the perplexed look on Jade's face.

"Nothing. I was just thinking about something," she said quietly.

"Something or someone?"

"James, let's not bring reality into this," she said.

"So, you were thinking about Stephen. Let me just say this. Let it go. He's not worth it."

"He may not be worth it, but . . . Never mind. I don't want to talk about it. These few days are supposed to be about me and you having fun."

When they reached the hotel and took the elevator up to Jade's room, James pulled her against his chest and hugged her tightly. It was the kind of comforting hug that a man would give a woman he cared about. Jade pulled back from him and flashed a plastic smile. She was getting too comfortable with him. She was being drawn in by his gentle way and amazing bedroom prowess. But they were going back to their real lives in a few days.

"Good night, James," she said.

James glanced down at his watch. "It's more like good morning," he said, then leaned in and kissed her on the cheek. "Sleep well."

I'll be dreaming about you as soon as I close my eyes, she thought as he headed for the elevator. Jade slid her key card into the electronic lock and entered the room floating, with a big smile on her face.

"And just where in the hell have you been?" Serena snapped.

Startled, Jade nearly twisted her ankle as she walked over to the small sofa in her room. "Serena, what are you doing here?"

"Looking for you. I had a couple of bankers that wanted to meet with us this evening, and you were nowhere to be found."

"How was I supposed to know you were out setting up meetings? You didn't tell me, and I can't read your mind," Jade said, then fell back on the sofa.

"You were with that man, weren't you?"

"Sure was."

Serena shook her head. "I know you're having fun and that's what we came here to do, but don't forget that we have to take Stephen down also. To do that, we're going to need money."

Jade sat up and faced her friend. "I know what we have to do and that it is important."

Serena folded her arms across her chest. "Jade, I know how things are with you. You're a hopeless romantic. You thought things were going to work out with you and Stephen, despite the fact that all of us, even Miss 'I believe in love more than anything else' Kandace, tried to warn you about him."

Jade closed her eyes, tired of hearing about the biggest mistake of her life. "Serena, I know what I did, and I'm not following that same path with James."

"No one said that you were," Serena replied. "What do you know about James Goings?"

Jade could've answered that question in so many ways. She knew he was passionate, a lover that was all about pleasing her.

And he hated Stephen. What if James was a key part of the plan to make Stephen pay for being a total asshole? She opened her eyes.

"James knows Stephen," Jade said. "And he doesn't like him, either."

Serena shrugged her shoulders. "What does that have to do with anything?"

"Nothing, since he insists on staying out of this," Jade muttered in such a low voice that Serena didn't hear.

"The meeting has been rescheduled. Nine a.m., so you'd better go to sleep and be on time in the morning," Serena said as she stood up and headed for the door. "Make sure that you keep your business and your fun separate this time."

Jade gave Serena a mock salute as she walked out the door. Once she was alone in her room, Jade stripped out of her dress and crawled into bed. As she drifted off to sleep, the only thought on her mind was having James's arms around her.

James reached across his bed and was a bit startled to find the other side empty. Sitting up in the bed, he realized that he'd dreamed that Jade had spent the night with him. Swinging his legs over the side of the bed, James wondered if he was going to be able to push Jade out of his mind when he boarded the plane to Charlotte.

She's only in Atlanta, less than five hours away, he thought. *There is something special about this woman, and I want to get to know everything about her. This is insane. I came here to gamble and relax. Who knew I was going to meet this goddess?*

James headed for the bathroom to shower and start his day, even though he'd slept for only a few hours. He knew it was only going to be a matter of time before Maurice was knocking on his door, trying to find out what he had done the night before and with whom.

As he climbed in the shower, James thought about how his morning would be getting off to a better start if Jade was there with him. He'd love to see her with her hair wet and dripping. He'd love to see her face scrubbed free of make-up. Not that she wore a lot of it, but he wanted to see her completely naked and bare.

James knew that whatever he and Jade had wasn't going to last past this weekend and that he needed to stop letting her take up so much space in his mind, because when he returned to Charlotte and she went back to Atlanta, they were going to have only memories.

And then there was Jade's drama with her ex. Part of him wondered if the two would reunite when she returned to Atlanta. He'd seen it happen before. Kenya had sworn to him so many times when she was in college that she wouldn't pour water on Maurice if he was on fire. Now they were the happiest couple that he'd ever seen. Still, he knew Stephen, and he couldn't imagine him with a woman like Jade. Unless this wasn't who she really was.

She was fun, sexy, and smart. Everything that James envisioned his match to be. Not that he was willing to admit that he thought Jade was his match. The sex was good—no, phenomenal—but he wasn't going to pretend that in a few short days he'd met the love of his life. That stuff only happened in fairy tales, and they were in Las Vegas, not at Disneyland.

Shutting the water off, James climbed out of the shower and wrapped a towel around his waist. Just as he was about to start shaving, there was a knock at the door. He ignored it, figuring that it was his brother. But the knocking persisted. Grabbing the plush white robe that was hanging on the back of the bathroom door, James put it on and dashed to the door. Through the peephole, he saw Serena and Alicia standing at his door. Immediately, his mind turned to Jade. Was she in trouble? Did something happen after he left her last night? James snatched the door open.

"Ladies, is there something wrong with Jade?" he asked frantically.

Serena and Alicia looked at each other and then focused on James. "May we come in?" Serena asked.

"Yes, but what's the problem?" he asked as he ushered the women inside.

"You may be the problem," Alicia said.

James folded his arms across his chest, ready to toss these women out of his suite and find Jade himself. "What are you talking about?"

"Whatever you and Jade are doing has to stop. She just got out of a relationship, and you can't think that she's ready for something—"

James threw up his hand and cut Serena off. "First of all, does Jade know you two are here?"

"That's not important," Alicia said. "Look, you're probably a nice guy, and if you lived in Atlanta and could make Jade happy, we'd be cheering you two on."

"Ladies, I understand your concerns, but what goes on between Jade and me is our business," James said.

"Not really," Serena said. "Jade is our best friend, and we're not going to let her get used by another man. Who knows what your plans are or if you don't come to Las Vegas every weekend to sleep with different women?" Her neck rolled as she spoke. James thought it was cute that Jade's friends were looking out for her, but he didn't feel as if he had to explain himself to them.

"Ladies, I have a meeting I have to get to, and if you want to know what's going on between me and Jade, you're going to have to ask her," he said flatly.

"We're asking you," Serena snapped. "James, what are you trying to hide?"

James, struggling to keep his temper in check, walked over to the door and waited for Alicia and Serena to make their exit. When neither of them moved, he cleared his throat loudly. "Ladies, this was fun, but it's time for you all to leave," he said.

They walked toward the door. "James," Alicia said, "what can you offer Jade? You live in another state. She has a business that she needs to focus on. Just have your fun and move on."

"It's nice that you have your friend's back and you're looking out for her best interests. But she's a grown woman, and I think she can take care of herself," he replied.

Serena shook her head as she and Alicia headed out the door. James slammed the door behind them and muttered under his breath about nosy women. Part of him wanted to call Jade and let her know what her friends were up to. But, he understood their position and why they were looking out for their girl. Most men would say they were jealous, but James could tell that Jade and her friends were more like sisters. He and Mo had a similar relationship. James just wished that he had been there when Maurice first met Lauryn. Had Maurice stayed away from that freak, he and Kenya would've been happy a long time ago.

James headed for the phone to order breakfast, but before he could dial room service, there was a knock at the door again. Stalking to the door, thinking that it was Jade's friends again, James called, "Look, I'm not discussing this with you."

"Damn, bro," Maurice said. "I was just going to ask you if you wanted to go to breakfast with me and the fellas."

"Let me get dressed," James said as Maurice entered the suite.

"So where is she?" Maurice called out from the sitting room of the suite.

"What are you talking about?"

"Your date. I heard you had a limo and everything."

"Damn, you got spies?" James asked as he zipped up his jeans.

"Please, you're not that important, but Homer is still pissed that your little fling beat him out of all that money. He's on a mission to bring her down."

James walked into the sitting room, laughing. "Homer will get over it. Besides, Jade is coming to the game today."

Maurice shook his head. "This I have to see."

"You mean you're going to hang up the phone long enough to do something other than talk to your wife?" James asked, with a laugh.

"Shut up. Don't hate me because I love my wife. Who knew that I'd miss her this much?" Maurice said.

"Whipped."

"You're damned right, though I will deny it in public," Maurice said as he rose to his feet. "So, what did you and Jade do last night?"

"Things that grown people do, and you don't need to worry about it. Breakfast is on you, right?"

"Isn't it always?" Maurice said as they headed out the door.

"Well, you are the millionaire," James ribbed.

"Get it right. Multimillionaire," Maurice joked. "Seriously, though, what's up with you and this woman?"

James shrugged his shoulders. "She's fun, easy to talk to, and beautiful."

Maurice nodded but didn't say anything.

"What?" James asked. "I know that you, of all people, aren't judging me."

"No, I'm not, but this isn't you. You don't just

have flings with women," Maurice said. "But you've been acting a little like I used to, and nothing good is going to come from it. Trust me."

"Didn't you get Kenya out of the deal?"

"That's not the point," Maurice said. "You need to slow down. Maybe you will find the right one when you stop sleeping around with—"

"This is rich coming from you, the former king of groupie love," James said. "I don't sleep around as much as you think. But do you know how sickening it is for me to meet women who want to talk about you all the time?"

Maurice smiled and shrugged his shoulders. "Can you blame them? Make sure you tell them I'm completely off the market."

"Shut the hell up," James replied, with a smile. "I'm just saying, women in Charlotte are always trying to get next to me for a shot at you. It's crazy, and the beautiful thing about Jade is that she doesn't seem to care who you are."

"But you two are just hooking up here in Vegas. What happens when you get home?" Maurice asked as they headed for the elevator.

James shrugged again and fell silent. He knew that he'd never find a woman that could compare to Jade or that could turn him on with just a smile. Maurice was right, though. James had grown tired of meaningless sex and women who thought they were getting one step closer to landing a football player. "Who knows what the future holds," he finally said as they walked into the casino's restaurant.

"I know I can't wait to get on that plane and go home to my wife," Maurice said.

James lifted his arm and cracked a pretend whip. Maurice elbowed his brother in his side. "I am not *that* whipped!" he protested as they approached the table and joined the rest of their friends.

"Bullshit," Homer said. "All Kenya needs is a leash. That woman says, 'Jump,' and you ask her, 'How high?'"

"Well, gentlemen, one day you all will meet a woman who lights up your world," Maurice informed them. "But until you do, stop hating on me and my wife for having a good marriage."

Deion Richardson, an offensive lineman, nodded. "Mo is right. When you fall in love, you do what you have to do to keep that broad happy, because it's cheaper to keep her."

The men at the table burst out laughing, and Maurice shook his head in annoyance. "Whatever, fools," he said. "The love of a good woman has changed me for the better. If you all stop thinking with that small muscle in your pants, you might get a clue as to what the good life really is. Besides, Kenya didn't marry me for the money, and we won't be getting divorced for it, either."

James couldn't help but take his brother's words to heart. Could Jade be the light he'd been looking for? *What the hell? I just met this woman, and I'm not going to delude myself into thinking it's more than what it is.*

"What time do we get to take the rest of James's money?" Homer asked. "Matter of fact, I hope you bring your call girl with you."

"Jade isn't a call girl, and she's coming, so I hope you're ready to lose," James said.

"Whatever," Homer said. "She's fine as hell. But everybody is fine in Vegas."

"So what happened to you?" Maurice asked. "You look like the same ugly dude I see in Charlotte."

Homer tossed a packet of sugar at his friend.

"I'm not going to block for you the next time a pass is thrown across the middle and a DB is gunning for you."

"And you will never go on another trip with me," Maurice said.

James's cell phone vibrated in his pocket. He pulled the phone out and saw that there was a text message from the realty office in Charlotte.

James, we just got a call about brokering a deal for a restaurant in the Cherry neighborhood. It's an investment group, but the place is already being sought by a chef from Atlanta. Call me when you get a chance.

James dialed the office and excused himself from the table. The last thing he wanted to do was enter a bidding war for a property. No one ever seemed to win those.

Jade didn't want to get out of bed when her wake-up call rang. She was enjoying her dream about James. A dream that she was going to need to come true. She wanted his lips on hers again, wanted to feel his body on top of hers, just as it had been in her dream and in the back of the limo. Just as she was about to ignore the wake-up call, she heard banging on her door. She didn't even have to look to know it was Serena.

Pulling herself out of bed, Jade bounded to the door and opened it.

"So, this is how you do business? Our meeting is in an hour, and you're still in the bed," Serena said. "I have to ask if you're alone in there."

"Aren't we meeting those investors downstairs?" Jade asked, rolling her eyes at her friend.

"So what? You should be showered and dressed.

You do want your money back from that asshole, don't you?"

Jade sighed and picked up the phone to order some coffee. "You know I want to stop Stephen from opening that restaurant in Charlotte, which I would be paying for," she said while she waited for room service to come on the line. "And for the record, I slept alone last night."

Serena nodded. "Good. Kandace called a realty company in Charlotte to get a line on how much the property costs and to see if we can take it from Carter."

Jade ordered the coffee and told Serena to tip the delivery guy or girl, because she was going to take a shower. Once she was alone in the bathroom, she thought about what James had said to her the first night that they met. Was Stephen really worth her energy?

This is more than revenge because he cheated on you. This man robbed you of the majority of your savings. He deserves whatever he gets.

Jade hopped in the shower, ready to stick it to Stephen.

CHAPTER 8

After eating breakfast, James decided that he needed to be alone for a while. He was sick and tired of hearing Mo and his friends talk about football. He didn't give a damn about a three-four defensive scheme or if the new quarterback was going to work out and develop the same chemistry with Maurice that the one the team had traded had. James, who wasn't much of a football player, had run track in high school and college. Sometimes he worked out with Maurice and some of the other Panthers' players to stay in shape. But he was far from a gym rat.

James went to his suite to change into his swimming trunks and grab a copy of *USA Today* to read while he lounged. As he changed his clothes, he wondered if Jade wore a two-piece bathing suit or a sexy one-piece with a cutout mid section exposing her stomach. Shaking his head, he tried to push thoughts of Jade out of his mind. But he couldn't, and quite frankly, that startled him. He knew they were sharing a fling, but there was something about her that made him think there could be more going on.

But this is Vegas, and everything that's flashy and shiny isn't really what I need, he thought as he headed out the door.

James headed to the rooftop pool, picking a chaise lounge in the corner, away from the gathering crowd of morning swimmers. He leaned back and watched the people settling into their chairs and rubbing sunscreen on their skin. Most of the early morning swimmers were elderly people, who had probably been in bed, sleeping, while he and Jade were out in the limo. James began to read his paper, and his cell phone chimed again.

"This is James," he said into the phone.

"I know you're on vacation, but that group called again and they want to set up a meeting next week," said Amber Williams, the Brothers Realty office manager and James's assistant.

"All right. I'll meet with them, but let them know that we're not in the business of stealing property from underneath someone."

"Okay. So, how's Vegas?"

James looked up and saw Jade, Serena, and two men walking toward the bar on the other side of the pool. "It's fine," he said. "Something just came up. Let me give you a call back." Snapping the phone shut, James watched intently as the foursome ordered breakfast. Were these men the reason why Serena and Alicia had shown up at his suite? What kind of games were these women playing?

Be cool, he thought as he folded his paper and put it in his lap. Still, as he tried to calm himself, he wanted to go over there and find out who in the hell those men were. James knew he didn't have a claim on Jade and she was free to do whatever she wanted. That still didn't explain the intense jealousy building in the pit of his stomach.

"Well, Ms. Christian, your business plan is exceptional," said Christopher McAlster, president of Nevada State Bank.

"Is it exceptional enough for you to invest in my restaurant?" Jade asked, with a smile on her face.

"The market is so fickle right now. But from what you've shown me about Charlotte, North Carolina, this might be a good investment," Christopher replied.

Serena looked from Christopher to his second in command, Richard Habersham. It seemed as if they were going to be shot down by the bank. Richard's face was emotionless and stoic.

"*Might* be a good investment?" Jade repeated. "Mr. McAlster, this is the best investment opportunity that will come your way this year."

Christopher looked at Richard, who gave him a slight nod.

"We're willing to take a chance on your restaurant," Richard said. "But here are the terms of our investment." He reached into his briefcase and pulled out a contract.

"Let me see this," Serena said as she took the contract from Richard's hands. Silently, she read over it. "This reads more like a loan document. We're not looking for a loan. Charlotte is the number two banking center in the country. I'm sure we can get loans there with lower interest rates."

Christopher cleared his throat, then said, "Well, the restaurant business is risky, and I can't in good conscience allow the bank to just hand over money and not know when we're going to see a profit. It would be different if the restaurant was going to be here in Las Vegas."

Jade squared her jaw. "Serena, let me see those papers."

"I tell you what," Serena said as she handed the contract to Jade. "This interest rate is way too high. The monthly payments are a little more than we are willing to pay and . . ."

Jade flipped through the papers and then asked, "Where do I sign?"

Serena flashed her friend a look that said, "Have you lost your damned mind?"

Christopher smiled and pulled a pen from his slacks' pocket. Jade took the pen from his hand and then turned to Serena. "We need this, and we're going to pay this loan back. This restaurant is important to us, and it will be a success."

"I tell you what," Christopher said. "Let's order breakfast, and I'll see what I can do about this interest rate. Ms. Christian, I like your spunk, and I do believe your business is going to be a smashing success."

Jade smiled and shook hands with him. Richard cleared his throat, then said, "I'm going back to the office, Mr. McAlster, unless you need me for something else."

"No, Richard, that's all," Christopher said.

Serena and Richard rose to their feet at the same time. Serena turned to Jade and whispered, "Make sure you get a lower interest rate. This loan is one step below highway robbery."

Jade nodded and pinched her friend on the arm

as she took her leave. Once Christopher and Jade were alone, his true colors began to shine through.

"You know you're a beautiful woman," he said after ordering two mimosas and eggs Benedict and bacon for both of them.

"Thank you, but what does that have to do with you lowering my interest on this loan?" Jade asked, smiling at him again.

Christopher placed his hand on top of her knee and stroked it. "That's all up to you."

She pushed his hand away. No matter how much she needed the money, she wasn't going to let this sleazy old man try to get her into bed. "I don't think I like the way you do business, Mr. McAlster."

"Please, call me Christopher. You know, I keep a suite in this casino hotel. Penthouse suite, actually. It's private, even the balcony. Have you ever made love on a balcony with the sun's rays caressing you like a lover's kiss?"

The bartender set their drinks in front of them, and Jade picked hers up, holding it tightly in her hand. "No, I haven't, and if you were the last man on earth, I wouldn't touch you with a ten-foot pole and a vibrating sex toy."

Christopher smiled. "I don't have to approve this loan."

"Then don't. Because if you think I'm going to hop into bed with you for money, you're a damned fool. That's not how I do business."

He ran his index finger down her arm. "You'd love it. I know how to make a woman scream."

Without giving it a second thought, Jade tossed her drink in his lecherous face. "You bastard! You can take this loan and stick it up your flabby ass."

"Is there a problem over here?" a voice asked from behind Jade. She turned around and was happy to see James standing there.

"No," Christopher said, rising to his feet. Though he tried to stand toe-to-toe with James, he was about three inches shorter than James.

"Well, it looks as if the lady doesn't want to be bothered," James said gruffly.

"What business is it of yours?" Christopher demanded hotly as he wiped his dripping face with his hand.

"Leave her alone, or you're going to give the word *swimsuit* a new meaning," James said.

Jade smiled as she watched the scene unfold. She hadn't even known James was at the pool, but she was happy that he was there.

"Are you threatening me? Do you know who I am?" Christopher said, his voice rising with indignation.

"Do I look like I give a damn who you are?" James snapped as he took a step closer to the man. Jade grabbed James's arm.

"He's not even worth it," she said.

Christopher grabbed the loan papers and ripped them in half. "Good luck finding the funding you need now, you bitch."

Without hesitation or a second thought, James balled his fist and punched Christopher, knocking him to the ground. "Didn't your mother teach you that it's not polite to call a woman out of her name?" Turning to Jade, James asked her if she was all right.

Sighing, thinking that she'd been so close to having the money that she needed to finally give

Stephen what he deserved, she said, "Can we get out of here?"

The few people who were at the bar, munching on breakfast and sipping mimosas, were watching intently. James nodded. "Let's go." He wrapped his arm around her waist and didn't even look back to see if Christopher had gotten up. Once they were inside the hotel and on the elevator, James asked, "Who was that guy?"

"A banker," she replied. "Serena found him, and we should've left when his assistant pulled out loan papers instead of an investment agreement."

"I hope I didn't overstep my boundaries, but when I saw you toss your drink in his face, I had no idea how he would react, and I didn't want to see him put his hands on you."

Jade hugged James tightly. "You know, I'm really glad you were there. He was a total sleaze. Sometimes I have to wonder where Serena finds these people."

James held his tongue. He hadn't told Jade about the visit her friends had paid him. At least he knew that Jade wouldn't do *anything* for money. That made him smile.

Jade was silent as she and James entered his suite. Her hopes of getting her money back from Stephen were dwindling like a campfire in a typhoon. The only thing she could do now was pray that the realty company Kandace had contacted would start a bidding war for the property that Stephen wanted. One way or another, Jade wanted him to pay for what he had done to her. But was it worth it?

She was tired of meeting with shady investors and

of sleepless nights because her mind was filled with schemes to bring Stephen down. But being with James for the past few days had really set her mind at ease. She had no problem sleeping because she looked forward to dreaming about him. And he made her feel safe. That was important to her because she had always had to take care of herself. Her mother and father had spent the majority of their time working on riverboats, and Jade had had to fend for herself from an early age. Sometimes she'd been dropped off at her mother's parents. But living with them had been like being in boot camp. She'd been expected to cook, clean, and still pull down As and Bs in school. Her grandfather had been a borderline alcoholic, and no one had known what to expect whenever he walked into the house. Jade had always envied people who had normal parents and a family life that offered safety and security. All she remembered of her childhood was constantly waiting for the other shoe to drop.

College had been a time of change for Jade. She had had her first real taste of freedom, and she'd loved it. Kandace had been her roommate at Spelman College in Atlanta. By chance, they'd met and clicked with their neighbors, Serena and Alicia. Their friendship had been the best thing that had ever happened to her. Around the Atlanta University Center, they'd been known as the Four Musketeers. They had had each other's backs when they were college students and still did as adults.

Still, Jade wondered if this was something they should let go. Maybe she should just sue Stephen and forget trying to ruin him. Karma would get him in the end, wouldn't it?

"Are you all right?" James asked.

"What? Oh, yes, I'm fine."

"Uh-huh, I'm really convinced," James said as he led Jade to the sofa. "What was that guy talking about? What do you need funding for?"

"There's a property that we want to buy. It's no big deal. I know my business plan is well written," Jade said. "We'll find legitimate investors."

"I hope things work out for you guys. Your friends seem very protective of you," he said.

"It's just because of the Stephen thing. I'm not fragile," Jade said as she sat on the sofa. "But we do look out for each other."

"Oh, I believe that, but there's nothing wrong with that," he said.

"They have a name for men like you," Jade said, with a smile on her lips.

James released a low chuckle. "Do I want to know what it is?"

"Amazing," she said. James took a seat beside her.

"I can say the same about you," he said as he took her hand in his.

Jade chewed her bottom lip, wanting to ask James if this was more than a weekend thing and if there was a chance that something more would develop between them. But she didn't say anything; she just smiled at him.

"Are you hungry? I can have room service bring you some breakfast," James said.

"No, I'm fine. Hey, is the poker game still on for today?"

"Yes, but if you want to skip it . . ."

"No, no, I need to get rid of some stress. Taking those dudes' money will help," she said.

James stood up. "All right. What do you say we go get a massage? It's way too early to be stressed out."

Jade rose to her feet and kissed James on the cheek. "I really like the way you think."

James and Jade headed to the spa, and for the next three hours, they indulged in facials, full-body massages, manicures, and pedicures. Jade watched as the masseuse worked on James. As he lay on the table, she marveled at the shape of his shoulders. They looked strong enough for her to lean on, cry on, and cuddle up to every night.

What in the hell is wrong with you? she thought as she forced herself to look away. *James has a life in another state. You can't get caught up in wanting something with him that has no chance. Besides, it's a weekend fling, and there's no need to read anything more into it.*

She turned back to him, this time focusing her gaze on his back as the masseuse moved her hands down his lean yet muscular torso. Jade already knew that his skin was smoother than silk, and touching him turned her on in every way. Part of her wanted to push the masseuse aside and finish the job herself.

"All done, sir," the woman said.

"Umm, that was great," James said as he sat up on the table.

The masseuse handed him a robe, then walked past Jade, with a smile on her face. "Do you want me to give you two some time alone in here?" she whispered, as if she felt the desire between them.

Jade nodded. "Thank you," she replied.

As the masseuse headed out of the room, Jade followed her and locked the door.

"What are you doing?" James asked, with a sly smile on his face.

"The massage and everything was great, but I know the ultimate stress reliever," she said as she crossed over to him.

"Do tell," James said, wrapping his arms around her waist.

Jade shrugged her shoulders, causing the over-size terry cloth robe she was wearing to fall down, exposing her bare flesh. James stepped back from her and watched as she did a slow striptease for him. Jade untied the terry belt and twirled it as if it were a feather boa. James couldn't help but laugh.

"I'm guessing you don't have an exotic dancer's background," he said as he walked over to her and slipped his hands underneath her robe.

"Are you saying you don't like my dancing?" she asked as she seductively rubbed her body against his. Jade rocked her hips back and forth until James's manhood sprang forward.

"Um," he said. "I didn't say I didn't like it." He thrust his pelvis into hers. "I think you can feel that."

"Oh yes," she said, then dropped her robe. James lifted her and sat her on the edge of one of the massage tables. He spread her legs apart and ran his index finger down her inner thigh. Next, he lifted Jade's legs onto his shoulders and buried his face in her wetness, kissing her most sensitive parts until her legs quaked. James treated her like a Georgia peach, slowly nibbling and sucking, all the while enjoying the sweet nectar that flowed from her. She closed her eyes and pressed her hips deeper into James's kiss.

Jade couldn't count the number of times that he

made her climax as he tasted her. But her throat was sore from calling out his name. Shivering, she grabbed James's shoulders. "I want you inside of me," she moaned.

He pulled back from her, looked into her eyes, and smiled. "You got me."

James picked Jade up and wrapped her around his waist, using the edge of the table to keep them balanced. In one swift motion, he was inside her, swimming in her wetness. Jade screamed out in pleasure as he found her spot. Her fingernails bit into his shoulders as he pumped in and out, turning her on as no other man had ever done.

He repeated her name as if it were a mantra or a prayer, because she felt so good against him, so raw. Before he could stop his explosion, James had climaxed. It was at just that moment when they both realized that this time they weren't protected.

"I can't believe we just did that," she said as she reached for a robe.

"We got carried away, and I know it's no excuse but . . ."

"When's the last time you were tested for any sexually transmitted diseases, and what is your HIV status?" she asked in one breath.

"I had a complete physical about two months ago, and everything was fine."

"But that was two months ago."

"What about you?" he asked. "You know, it works both ways."

"Well, about two weeks ago I thought I was going on a honeymoon overseas, and I had a battery of tests run and was given a clean bill of health."

James ran his hand across his face. "Are you on any birth control?"

"Yes, I take the pill." Jade sucked in her bottom lip nervously. She hadn't been taking it regularly, because she'd figured that once she and Stephen got married, the next step would be having a child or two.

"Okay, so we should be all right," James said as he put his robe on. "Let's get out of here and get ready for the game. I'll buy you lunch."

"Not really hungry, but I do hope that your cocky friends are ready to be eaten alive," she said. But all the while, Jade wondered what the consequences of their irresponsible actions would be.

CHAPTER 9

Later that afternoon James and Jade headed to the players' suite, where Maurice and the rest of the crew had set up the poker game. They didn't say much to each other. Jade was worried that she'd done the one thing she'd always promised herself she wouldn't do. She was afraid that she had gotten pregnant without having a husband, a house with a white picket fence, and everything she needed to give a little one the stable family life she hadn't had as a child.

Though her parents had been married, she didn't have a traditional childhood. At an early age, Jade had seen how women and men used each other as pawns. Even in her parents' marriage, she'd seen how her mom would use her feminine wiles to get her father to do things that she wanted. And as she'd sat at her dad's feet underneath the poker table, she'd seen how he used his charm and good looks to get lonely women to bet more than they should in games that the house would win.

Jade wanted to give her child, if she ever had one,

a normal life. If James had gotten her pregnant, there would be nothing normal about this child's life. They barely knew each other, and who was to say he wouldn't question the child's paternity?

"Baby girl," Homer said, "are you in or out?"

"I'm in and the name is Jade. I'm not a baby, nor am I a girl." Jade placed her bet and then glanced at James. *Will he just chalk this all up to a Vegas fling? He's probably never going to call me so . . .*

"Is your mind someplace else?" Maurice asked Jade.

"What?" she asked.

James walked over to her with a drink. "Leave the lady alone, fellas. Remember what happened last time."

Maurice folded, and Homer was about to rake in the pot. "Not so fast, fat boy," Jade said as she spread her cards across the table, revealing a royal flush. "You lose again."

Homer's mouth fell open like a trap door. "How in the . . ."

Jade reached over the table and raked the money up. "I'm just better than you, and the sooner you realize that, the more money you will have in your pocket."

James and the others laughed and hooted as Homer rose from the table like a child who'd just been told that Santa Claus wasn't coming to his house.

"This is some straight-up bull," he said and headed for the door.

"Dang, man, you're a sore loser," Maurice called after his friend.

Jade took the deck of cards in her hands and

began shuffling it. "Who's next?" she asked, with a sly smile on her face.

The other men in the room backed away from Jade as if she were the grim reaper.

"I think you've taken enough of our money," Maurice said. "I'm going to order some food."

When the room was cleared, James took a seat across from Jade. "If you weren't such a cardsharp, I'd take you on," he said.

"Maybe I'd let you win a few hands," she said as she shuffled the deck again. "Then again, if you've been getting beat by these guys, you must really suck at cards."

"I don't really like to gamble. There aren't many sure things in life, so why willingly go into something with so much risk?"

We took a big risk earlier today, she thought but didn't say anything.

"Are you hungry?" James asked. "Maurice is buying, so we may as well take advantage."

"You and your brother are close, huh?"

"Yeah."

"He seems like a nice guy for a professional athlete," she said. "But I'm glad you're the one who found me in the casino a couple of days ago."

James smiled tensely. "I have a question. What happens after we get on our planes and go home? I'm feeling a connection with you that I'd like to explore, but . . ."

"I don't know how these things work. You read about people who skip off to Las Vegas and marry a stranger, or people who have weekend flings and move on. But you're a man that a woman would be a fool to let get away," she said. "Still, you know what

I'm dealing with, and I'm pretty sure your opinion of me trying to bury Stephen hasn't changed."

James nodded. "You're right about that. Is it really worth it?"

"Can we not do this again?" she asked. "The last time we had this discussion, it turned into an argument, you left me standing at a bus stop, and then you had to buy a bottle of champagne and oysters. Do you really want to go there again?"

James reached across the table and grabbed her hands. "You are one feisty woman, and Stephen Carter is going to be in for the fight of his life. Just make sure this is about the money and that you don't want him back in your life."

"I'm not your sister-in-law," Jade said. "If a man cheats on me, it's a wrap. I'm not the forgiving type."

"That's harsh."

"And what do you call someone deliberately betraying you? If you love someone, why do you need to be with other people? What's the lure of other women, and why lie?"

James threw his hands up. "You're preaching to the choir over here."

Jade smiled. "And that's why I like you. You're so different. An honest man. Who would've thought that you all still existed?"

"Come on. Let's get something to eat, and then we can figure out what to do with the rest of the afternoon, since I know the guys aren't going to play with you anymore."

Jade chuckled softly. She was going to miss him when this Vegas excursion was over. *Well, Charlotte is only four hours away,* she thought as they headed into the sitting area of the suite, where a couple of hotel workers were setting up lunch.

After Maurice and the other Panthers' players filed into the sitting area, James watched Jade as she fixed her plate and wondered why they couldn't continue to see each other after they left Vegas. She liked him and he liked her. But there was the whole Stephen thing and her nosy-ass girlfriends. Still, Atlanta wasn't that far away from Charlotte, and it was home. He turned away from her. These weren't the kinds of thoughts he was used to having about a woman. James was strictly about his business and not relationships—especially a long-distance one with a woman who had baggage like Jade. It was one thing to have great sex with her for a few days while they were in Vegas, but what would happen when they returned to the real world?

"James," Maurice said, breaking into his thoughts.

"Yeah," James said, looking up at his brother.

"So, you and Ms. Jade are still kicking it, I see."

"Don't start this," James said.

Maurice shrugged his shoulders. "I'm just saying."

"Saying what?" James asked.

"Nothing, because here she comes," Maurice said as he stepped aside to let Jade join them. "Hello, Jade."

"Hi," she said as she took a seat beside James. "I hope you didn't lose too much money in the card game."

Maurice smirked at her. "Right. Where did you learn to play poker like that, and can you teach me?"

"I'm the daughter of a riverboat dealer, so my card

skills came naturally," Jade said as she picked up a barbecue rib.

"All right," Maurice said. Before he could continue, his cell phone rang.

"I bet that's your wife," James said as Maurice opened the flip phone. His brother didn't have to respond, because the next words that came out of his mouth confirmed who was on the phone.

"Hey, sweetheart. I can't wait to come home, too. I miss you. Next time I go on a trip with these guys, we're going to have to make sure that you're not in court," Maurice said as he walked away from Jade and James.

"He really loves his wife?" Jade asked.

"Yes," James said. "Kenya and Maurice were made for each other."

"Is their relationship the reason you think that I'm going to take Stephen back?" she asked, then bit into her rib.

"Maybe," James said, then rose to his feet. "But I'd rather not think about you being with Stephen, because for the next twenty-four hours, you're still mine."

Before Jade could respond, her cell phone rang. She placed her rib on the plate, wiped her hands, and answered the phone, knowing full well who it was.

"Hello, Serena," she said without looking at the caller ID.

"You've really done it this time," her friend hissed. "What the hell was James Goings doing with you when you were talking to Christopher?"

Jade stood up and walked away from James and out of earshot of everyone else in the room. "Serena, as soon as you and his little flunky left, Christopher was all hands."

"What? Are you serious? That slimy old . . . I'm sorry, Jade. I had no idea he would try something like that. His bank came highly recommended."

The men behind Jade erupted in laughter, causing Serena to inquire where she was.

"I just finished playing poker with some of James's friends, and his brother had a buffet set up."

"What is it with you and this James guy? And he obviously doesn't—"

"Doesn't what?"

"Promise not to get mad," Serena said.

"No."

"Come on, Jade. We were just looking out for you."

"We? What the hell did you and Alicia do?"

"And why couldn't it have been Kandace and Alicia?" Serena asked, with a nervous laugh.

"Because I know you and Alicia don't mind your business. So what did you do?"

Serena sighed. "We told James that maybe he should leave you alone because you have a lot going on and you don't need another man who doesn't have a future to offer you."

"Oh my God! I can't believe you two would do that. Have I ever gotten involved in your relationships?" Jade said in a near whisper.

"So, you're in a relationship with a man you meet a couple of days ago? This is why we went over there," Serena said.

"You know what I mean," Jade said. "James and I aren't in a relationship, but whatever we're doing is none of your business."

"The last time I heard you say something like this, you ended up losing fifty thousand dollars."

"Good-bye, Serena," Jade said, then snapped her phone shut. She turned around and saw James walking toward her.

"Is everything all right?" he asked.

"Not really. Why didn't you tell me that my friends gave you an order?"

James shook his head and snickered. "Obviously, I didn't listen to them, now did I? Besides, I can understand where they are coming from. Just didn't appreciate their tactics."

"Tactics?"

"The double-team. When I saw Alicia and Serena at my door, my first thought was that you were in trouble. Something flowed through me that made me nervous. Then, when they got to the point of why they were there, it pissed me off."

"You could've told me," Jade said. "Then I could've told those heifers about themselves."

James wrapped his arms around her. "It's all right," he said. "Your friends love you, and they have your best interests at heart."

"What about you?"

"What do you mean?"

"Do you have my best interests at heart?"

"Of course I do."

"So, I guess asking you to get me another rib wouldn't be too much, huh?" she asked, with a smile on her face.

"Come on. We'll eat ribs together."

* * *

After Jade and James had eaten and laughed long enough with the Panthers' players, they headed up to the pool on the roof to spend some time alone. Jade didn't want to deal with her girlfriends, and James was tired of hanging around Maurice's offensive line. James got them a bottle of chardonnay, and they settled into two lounge chairs near the pool.

"This is really nice," Jade said. "There must be a special going on downstairs, since there aren't a lot of people up here."

"Or the buffet is on sale," James said as he filled their glasses. Jade picked up her glass and took a sip.

"I think your brother cleaned out the restaurant," she said. "Those ribs were awesome."

James laughed. "I still can't get over the fact that you actually eat more than a salad. Most women don't want to show a brother that they can eat."

"I cook, too. Well, occasionally."

"You're from Atlanta, so that doesn't shock me," he said as he set his glass beside his chair. James reached for Jade's foot and removed her shoe. Then he began to massage her foot.

"Ooh, you're spoiling me," she said as she closed her eyes and threw her head back. "That feels so good."

"I'm glad you're enjoying it," James said. "I'm thinking about going to Atlanta in a couple of weeks. What are the chances that you and I will run into each other?"

"If you're going to give me another foot massage, then we will definitely be seeing each other," she said as he began to work on the other foot.

"Sounds good to me," he said as he worked his way up to her calf. "You know what they say about good things. I'm going to have to head back to Charlotte in the morning. But I don't want today to be the last time I see you."

Jade sat up and looked directly into his eyes. "Neither do I. The last thing I thought I was going to find in Las Vegas was a guy like you."

"See what happens when you open your mind?" he said. "You were ready to write me off when we first met."

"Thank goodness you didn't let me," she said.

James pulled Jade into his arms and kissed her on the cheek. Part of him wanted to tell her to forget about Stephen and getting revenge on him and to move on. He had something she could focus on, a future with him. But he didn't say anything, and they watched the sunset in silence.

Jade felt so comfortable in James's arms that she didn't want him to let her go. And she didn't want him going back to Charlotte. She turned her eyes upward and smiled at him.

"What's calling you back to Charlotte?" she asked.

"Business. Maurice and I run a realty company. Well, I run it, and Maurice lends his name and face to it. There's some buyer that's being really aggressive about getting some property, and it seems kind of fishy. I need to be there to handle it."

"Is there anything that you don't do?"

"We'll discuss that later. But right now I want to talk about you spending the night with me."

"Well, I have been neglecting my friends since we hooked up," she joked. "Of course I'll stay with you tonight. Especially since you haven't told me when you're coming to Atlanta."

James kissed her on the forehead. "Keep playing with me and I'll be waiting at Hartsfield-Jackson when you fly back."

"That wouldn't be so bad," she said. "But you have work to do. Besides, when I get back to Atlanta, it's back to the grind."

"The grind or the plot?"

"The plot?" Jade asked, playing coy.

James shook his head. "I know you're going to try and get Stephen. I just hope I don't read about your wedding announcement when I do come to Atlanta."

"If this wine wasn't so good, I'd toss it in your face. Everyone doesn't end up like your brother and sister-in-law. I'm pretty sure Maurice never took her money and then . . . Never mind. It's your last night here, so why don't we spend our time doing something else other than arguing?"

"And just what do you suggest?" James asked, with a slick smile on his face.

Jade rose to her feet and held her hand out to him. "Come with me," she said. "And I promise that you're not going to forget this night."

"All right. You don't have to tell me twice," he said as he took her hand and they headed downstairs.

CHAPTER 10

James looked at Jade and shook his head. Was this what she meant by an unforgettable night?

"You're serious about this?" he asked.

"You know my friends were not trying to come here with me. But I've always wanted to come to Circus Circus."

James chuckled. "So where to first?"

Jade pointed in the direction of the Adventuredome, the hotel and casino's indoor amusement park. James liked seeing this side of Jade. She was fun and adventurous and had a childlike quality that was endearing. But James could only image how she would act if someone crossed her. In a way, he almost felt sorry for Stephen, but the guy deserved a lot more grief than what Jade and her friends were trying to do. A man like Stephen Carter was a damned fool to let a woman like Jade go and to steal from her. Then again, Stephen was known to take things that didn't belong to him. He had stolen those recipes from James's mother. Stephen couldn't cook, and his bakery had failed without Maryann having to sue him. James had wanted to pound Stephen into the ground when he found out what he'd done to his mother. It had taken everything in Maryann to stop James and Maurice from going after Stephen. She had known that he couldn't cook.

Jade grabbed James's hand. "Come on. Let's get on the roller coaster." She practically dragged him to the line for the massive coaster. "This is going to be so much fun," she said.

"I'm guessing you like putting your life at risk on these things," James said.

"When I was a lot younger, my parents and I would go to amusement parks, and I always wanted to get on the roller coasters. At first I was too short. But when I met the height requirement, I rode them all. Sometimes, I go to Six Flags just to unwind."

"Six Flags, huh?"

"Yes. And I've actually thought about riding the Drop Tower at Carowinds."

"That's a ride I won't be taking with you. But I'll be sure to be waiting for you on the ground," James said.

She laughed, and moments later they were being locked into the coaster's car. As the car zoomed up and down, round and round, and upside down, Jade screamed and threw her hands in the air. James held on to the metal bar for dear life. When the ride was over, Jade was ready to go again and James was searching for a drink.

"You don't want to go again?" Jade asked.

"No, I have a better idea. Why don't we go see the clown show?"

"James Goings, I can't believe you're a chicken." She flapped her arms as if she were a chicken.

"Call it what you want, but I have no reason to get on that ride again."

"Boo!" She stuck her tongue out at him as if she were three years old.

James pulled her against his chest and brushed his lips against hers. "You're a big, sexy kid," he whispered.

"And there are kids watching us right now," she said as he cupped her behind.

"Good for them." In one quick motion, James covered Jade's lips with his, gently sucking her bottom lip. Kissing her was like an addiction, and he knew there was no rehab he could enter into to cure himself.

Pressing her hand against his chest, Jade broke off the kiss and stared into his eyes. "The clown show? Are we going to go or . . ."

"Yes, we are," he said, taking her hand in his.

"You know," she said, her lips close to his ear so that no one else could hear her, "we really don't have to watch the clowns, because I can think of a more amusing way to spend your last night here."

James turned around and faced her with a slick smirk on his face. "What's that?"

"Trust me, it's going to be magical," she said.

"It always is."

Jade led James out of the amusement park. They walked out into the lobby of the casino hotel and headed for the tram.

"Where are we going now?" he asked as he glanced at his watch. It was still early by Vegas standards, but James knew he was going to have a serious case of jet lag when he returned to Charlotte. But he was going to have to deal with it, because there was no way he was going to walk away from Jade right now without knowing when he'd see her again.

"There's something at the Luxor that you have to see," she said. Her eyes sparkled with excitement, and James liked this side of her. She wasn't like any woman that he'd ever met. But part of him wondered if this was something that was just too good to be true. Was that Jade?

Once they were on the tram, James pulled Jade into his lap. "You know, this has been the best trip to Vegas I've ever taken," he said.

"Me too," she said. "You just better make sure I have just as much fun when you come to visit me in Atlanta."

"Oh, you'll have fun, but we will not be taking a trip to Six Flags."

"Well, it sounds like someone is chicken," Jade joked.

"No, but if you want a thrill ride, I have one for you." He pulled Jade against his chest and kissed her on the cheek.

"You're a bad man, Mr. Goings." She wrapped her arms around his neck and brushed her lips against his.

"What? I can launch the ride for you any time you want."

"Not until after the show," she said. "Then I'm going to take you up on your offer. Let's see how thrilling you can be."

Moments later James and Jade arrived at the Luxor and headed for the Atrium Showroom to catch a magic show.

In the darkness of the theater before the magic

show started, James held Jade's hand and she never wanted him to let it go.

This is crazy, she thought. *Everything ends as soon as he steps on the plane. Maybe he will come to Atlanta, maybe, not. I'm not going to wait for him. That would be crazy, or would it?*

The stage lights came on and the show began. As the emcee spoke of the magic of Las Vegas, Jade glanced at James and smiled. It did seem as if magic had a hand in their meeting.

After the magic show, James and Jade headed back to his hotel.

"What time is your flight in the morning?" she asked as they got on the elevator.

"Nine."

"Then I guess you need to go to sleep, huh?"

James wrapped his arms around her waist. "You know, I'd sleep a lot better with you in my arms tonight."

A slow smile spread across her lips. "You know you're not going to sleep tonight," she said.

"You're going to keep me up?"

"And you're going to love every minute of it," she said as he unlocked the door to his suite.

It was 6:00 a.m. and James didn't want to get out of bed. Jade slumbered in his arms, naked. He ran his finger down the length of her arm. What were they really doing? Was this going anywhere once he left Vegas? James knew all too well how women made choices in the heat of the moment that they regretted later. He had seen Kenya do it. What if Jade did the same thing? When she arrived in Atlanta, would she run back into Stephen's arms if he said the right things?

James didn't like the thoughts he was having. Jade had stirred something inside of him, and he was looking forward to exploring it. Still, he had a nagging feeling that once the fantasy became reality, things were going to change. He eased from the bed in an effort not to wake Jade. But his efforts were in vain.

"Where are you going?" Jade asked.

"To shower. I didn't mean to wake you up," he said.

"It's all right." Jade got out of the bed and walked over to James. "I'm just glad you're not trying to sneak out of here without saying good-bye."

"You know I wouldn't do that," he said. "Want to join me in the shower?"

"Did you really have to ask?" she said as they raced to the bathroom.

After taking a long shower that was more erotic than cleansing, James dressed and sent his luggage downstairs. Jade rushed back to her hotel to change so that she could ride to the airport with James.

When she arrived at her room, she wasn't surprised to see Serena waiting outside her door.

"I bet I know where you're coming from," Serena said as Jade slipped her key card in the lock.

"I'm sure you do," Jade said as she opened the door. "What do you want?"

"I guess I owe you an apology. Who am I to question your judgment? But know that I was just trying to look out for you and—"

"Serena, I'm fully capable of looking out for myself. But if the shoe was on the other foot, maybe I would've done something similar. Still, James seems to be a good guy."

"And so did Stephen. All right. I'm going to stop going there, because you know what they say. What happens in Vegas stays in Vegas, right?"

"Actually, no. James and I are going to see each other again. Remember, his mother still lives in Atlanta."

"Oh, yeah, that's right. So you and this man who you have slept with for four days are going to have a long-distance relationship. Just how do you think that is going to work out?"

"It doesn't matter what you think, because this is my business, my life."

"Fine, but I hope you don't end up hurt again, Jade."

"You know what, Serena?" Jade began. "All men aren't all bad. I feel that something about James is different."

"Whatever."

"I don't have time for this. I'm riding to the airport with him," Jade said. "I need to change my clothes."

"Don't let me stop your fun," Serena replied sarcastically, then walked out of the room.

Jade shook her head. Serena might not admit it, but she had some issues with men. Jade wondered who had hurt her friend so badly. But she wasn't going to spend too much time thinking about Serena's issues. She needed to get ready so that she could head to the airport with James.

In the back of her mind, she had to wonder if this thing with James would end today, when she waved good-bye to him at the airport terminal. What if James had another life in Charlotte and he was going back to it?

This man could be married with three children and . . . Stop it! You're beginning to think like Serena, she thought as she slipped into a pair of jeans and a tank top. Jade grabbed her sunglasses and headed for the lobby. When she arrived downstairs, she found James leaning on the counter, with a pair of black shades covering his eyes. He was dressed in a pair of khaki shorts, a white linen shirt, and a pair of brown sandals.

His look was very casual, yet sexy at the same time. Jade walked over to him and encircled his waist with her arms. "Are you sure you have to leave?" she asked.

"Unfortunately, duty calls. We'll see each other soon," he said. "I'll be in Atlanta in two weeks, and you and I have a date."

Jade smiled. "I'm looking forward to it. This is crazy, isn't it?"

"What do you mean?"

"No one comes to Vegas and has this happen to them," she said. "This is one for a movie or fairy tale."

"I guess this was a good gamble to take," he said as they headed outside to an awaiting cab.

As they rode to the airport, Jade watched the scenery of the desert as it flew past them. She knew that since James was going to be gone, she'd be able to focus on getting that property in North Carolina that Stephen thought was his. All Stephen had had to do was be honest with her, but he had lied and stolen her money. He wasn't going to get that property in Charlotte. *I'm just going to have to keep my*

*plan under wraps. I don't want James to know that I'm
still seeking revenge.*

James was beyond tired when he arrived in Charlotte. But instead of going home and getting into
bed, he headed into the office to take a look at the
file on the restaurant property that someone was so
determined to purchase. Walking into the dark
office, James couldn't help but think about Jade and
the things that they could do on his solid oak desk.
He placed his hand flat on the desk and smiled.
Soon his attention turned to the file that he'd asked
his assistant to leave on his desk for his perusal.

The restaurant was located in a neighborhood
that was in the process of being revitalized. The
realty company that made the initial offer had given
the owners a lowball figure, which had risen considerably since there was currently more interest in the
property. Now the owners wanted at least seventy-
five thousand dollars more for the building. James
thought that was too much. But the commission
on the sale of that building for that price wasn't
something to sneeze at. The money would give
James a chance to go take a real break from the
business and would really give Maurice a chance to
see what it was like to sell property without his help.

That would give him a chance to spend more
time with Jade, he thought, with a smile, as he took
a seat behind his desk and dove deeper into the file.
The people who had contacted Brothers Realty had
claimed to be an investment group. Maybe they
were a part of the redevelopment of the Cherry
community. James knew he'd never heard of the

group before, but that didn't mean anything when it came to Charlotte real estate. People were coming into town like carpetbaggers these days, trying to buy any and everything that was for sale. Most of the properties were sold for a higher profit to developers who wanted to build something. Everyone profited from it, and that was why James didn't mind doing the bulk of the work at the realty company.

James closed the file and leaned back in his chair. Despite the fact that he was trying to get some work done, he drifted off to sleep and dreamed of Jade.

CHAPTER 11

Jade sat in Kandace's downtown Atlanta office, reading the latest issue of *Black Enterprise* magazine, as she waited for her friend to set up a meeting with the Realtor in Charlotte. She'd only been back in town for three days, barely enough time to recover from jet lag. But time was of the essence when it came to getting this property out from underneath Stephen.

"Yes, we can be in Charlotte tomorrow," Kandace said in an ultraprofessional tone. "I look forward to putting a face with the voice as well."

She hung up the phone and turned to Jade with a wide smile on her face. "It sounds very promising. We're soon going to be the owners of a restaurant in Charlotte."

Jade dropped her magazine. "Great. But why do we have to go meet with the Realtor?"

Kandace shook her head. "No one does a million-dollar deal over the phone. You know what? While you and Serena were trying to line up funding with those bankers in Vegas, you should've hit up your new friend's brother."

"No," Jade said. "James doesn't have anything to do with this, and I didn't want him to think I was trying to get next to him to gain access to his brother."

"Oh my God," Kandace said. "Serena was right. You really do think you and James have something more than a fling."

"Don't go there. And just so you know, whatever James and I have is our business. You, Serena, and Alicia don't have to approve."

Kandace held her hand out like a cat's paw and hissed at Jade. "You don't have to be so mean. Isn't that guy from Charlotte? At least you will get to see him in his natural habitat, and you'll see if this thing you're trying to build is real. I'm all for love, unlike Ms. Serena. But do you think it's wise to start something so soon after what went down with Stephen? You could be on the rebound and end up with—"

"I can handle this," Jade said firmly. "But it's good to know that I have one friend in my corner."

Kandace leaned back in her chair. "Jade, you know I have your back, through thick and thin."

Jade smiled. "Well, hopefully, there's going to be more thick than thin these days. Even if we don't get this property, I hope the price goes up so high that Stephen can't afford it."

"How are you going to get your money back?"

Jade shrugged her shoulders. "I probably won't get it back. But I'll be damned if I'm going to sit by and watch him become a success when he knows that he wouldn't have been able to do this without my dumb ass."

"You were in love. He made it seem as if you two were going to get married and run this culinary empire together," Kandace said. "He's a damned fool, because you have an amazing business mind."

Jade folded her arms across her chest. She didn't feel as if she had a great business mind. Right now she was unemployed, because her last job had been as Stephen's bookkeeper. "Maybe I should open my own accounting firm, since I don't have anything going on right now."

"That's a good idea," Kandace said. "And I'll be your first client. You know I need you to do my business and personal taxes."

"Normally, I would say I don't need charity, but business is business," Jade said.

"Alicia and Serena are supposed to be meeting us for lunch so that we can go over our plan for the meeting in Charlotte," Kandace said. "I'm feeling some Chinese. What about you?"

Jade, who was staring out of the window, nodded absentmindedly.

"Jade, are you all right?" Kandace asked, noticing her friend's silence.

"What if this isn't worth it?" Jade said. "If I focused my energy on me, then I'd accomplish a lot more."

"And Stephen will get away scot-free. Jade, he can't get away with what he did. This is more than just revenge. He needs to learn a lesson."

"Let me use your phone for a second," Jade said as she reached for Kandace's desk phone. Then she dialed the number of the Fulton County Department of Health. "Yes," she said when someone answered. "I'd like to report some health violations at Chez Marcel. When I ate there two days ago, I found a live roach in my house salad." After giving a few more bogus details about her dining experience, Jade hung up the phone with a promise that a health inspector would visit the restaurant in a few days.

Kandace nearly fell out of her chair laughing. "My goodness, girl. Remind me not to get on your bad side. Stephen is going to flip."

"I hope he didn't get his cooling system fixed," Jade said, with a snicker. "At least there will be some sort of violation."

Kandace shut her computer down. "Come on. Let's get to P.F. Chang's before we have to wait two hours for a seat."

As they headed out the door, Jade couldn't help but feel reenergized about giving Stephen just what he deserved. She could do that and start her firm at the same time. Kandace was right; he needed to learn a lesson and she had fifty thousand reasons to teach him.

Kandace and Jade arrived at P.F. Chang's at the same time as Alicia and Serena.

"I can't believe everyone is on time," Jade said as they walked into the restaurant.

"Some of us have jobs and only an hour for lunch," Alicia teased.

"Whatever," Jade replied.

Serena, who was sending a text message on her BlackBerry, looked over at Jade and shook her head. "I can't believe you're not somewhere talking to James. Have you heard from him since you've been back from Vegas?"

"Wow! Are you still in my business?" Jade snapped.

"Ladies," Kandace said, "we're here to talk about our meeting with the realty company in Charlotte. Can we keep the personal barbs to a minimum?"

"Always the voice of reason," Alicia said as the hostess led them to a table in the rear of the restaurant. "But for real, Jade, has Mr. Wonderful called you?"

Jade rolled her eyes. "No. But I didn't expect him to." Jade wasn't about to tell her friends that she was worried that James hadn't reached out to her. She knew that he was busy with work, and she'd only been back in town for three days. Still, part of her had to wonder if James had even given her a second thought since he'd returned to his real life.

James hung up the phone with the owners of the restaurant that the Atlanta-based investment group wanted to purchase. The price had risen considerably because the first buyer had matched the second offer that James had countered with.

"Amber," he called to his assistant. "What time is that meeting tomorrow?"

Amber walked into his office with an electronic calendar. "Ten a.m."

"All right. Thanks for all your research on this project," he said. "I can't believe that the owners want to inflate this price even more."

Amber leaned against the door and shook her head. "Sounds like the beginnings of a bidding war to me. Aren't there other restaurants these women could purchase?"

"According to all the e-mails that I've gotten from them, they want this property. I know Cherry is undergoing a change, but it's not happening as fast as people think it's happening."

"At least the commission is going to be great," she said, with a smile.

"And ten percent of it is yours," James said, then rose to his feet. "I'm going to head out for lunch. Maurice is allegedly coming by. If he gets here before I do, tell him to wait."

Amber smiled and nodded. "Do you think he'll sign a football for my sorority's charity auction?"

"Ask him. I'm sure he'll do it," James said, then headed out the door. When he got to the parking lot, he pulled out his cell phone and scrolled down to Jade's number. He wanted to call her, but what if she was busy? What if she'd moved on from their Vegas fantasy and back into Stephen's arms?

There's only one way to find out, he thought as he pressed the talk button.

"Hello," Jade said, with a singsong quality to her voice.

"Good afternoon, beautiful."

"Hi, James," she said.

"I didn't catch you at a bad time, did I?"

"Kind of. I'm having a lunch meeting with my alleged business partners. Can I give you a call back?"

"Sure," he said. "I'll talk to you later."

James couldn't help but wonder if those business partners included Stephen Carter. *She can't be stupid enough to go back to a man who robbed her of fifty thousand dollars.*

As James got in the car, his phone rang. "This is James," he said.

"Hey, brother-in-law," Kenya said. "I just called the office, and Amber said you were going to lunch."

"Yeah, what's going on?" Even though Kenya and Maurice had a solid marriage, James still felt a little protective of his brother and sister-in-law.

"Where are you eating? I want to join you because I need your help on something," she said.

"On what?"

"A surprise for your brother."

"That man doesn't need any surprises. He has everything."

"Almost everything. James, promise me that you will keep this to yourself, okay?"

"I promise," he said.

"I'm pregnant."

"What?"

"Yes, while you guys were in Vegas, I had my annual checkup and found out. But I don't just want to tell Mo over dinner, especially since his birthday is coming up."

"Kenya, Mo is going to be so happy. He really wants to be a father, and thank God, you're going to be this child's mother."

"So, you're going to help me?"

"Yeah. Why don't I pick up something and come by your office? Have you started having those crazy cravings yet?"

"No. But I would like something cheesy."

"I'll hit Fuel Pizza and get us a few slices."

"Don't forget the hot wings," she said before saying good-bye.

About forty-five minutes later, James arrived at Kenya's office with five slices of pizza and a large order of hot wings.

He placed the pizza box on her desk and opened

it. "I got cheese, barbecue chicken, Buffalo chicken, pepperoni, and the works," he said.

"Which one do you want?" Kenya asked as she reached for the cheese slice.

"Thankfully not the cheese," he said as he grabbed the works slice. "Any preference as to what you want to have?"

"Are we talking about the baby?" she asked in between bites.

"Yes."

"I'd love a little girl, but it doesn't matter as long as the child is healthy."

James shook his head as he took a big bite of his pizza slice with the works. "I can't have a niece that looks like you. Mo and I would never have any peace."

Kenya set her slice on a napkin and looked at James. "Excuse me?"

"We'd be chasing the little boys away with a shotgun. Besides, the first child is always a boy. Little James."

She laughed and reached for the hot wings. "If I have a son, I pray he won't want to follow in his father's footsteps and play football. It's hard for me to watch Maurice get hit, and if it's my son on the field, I might be tempted to deck a kid."

"Come on. If you have a boy, he has to play some sport."

"There's basketball, baseball, and track. Anyway, I want your mom to come to Mo's party so that she can be there for the announcement. I was thinking about having two cakes. A birthday cake and a future daddy cake. What do you think?"

"That's a lot of sugar, and you know Mo is going

to already be overstimulated," James said, with a laugh. "But his birthday is next week. Are you sure he won't find out about the baby before then?"

"Find out what?" Maurice said from the doorway.

"I guess he did," Kenya said. "We were planning a surprise party for you."

Maurice walked into the office and kissed his wife on the cheek. "I don't want a party."

"Why not?" James asked.

"Because it's just a reminder that I'm getting old," Maurice said, then took a wing from the box.

"Thirty-one isn't old," Kenya said. "And don't go there about NFL age. You're having a party, and you're going to like it."

Maurice bit into his wing and shook his head. "I guess the boss has spoken," he said after swallowing. "Can we at least keep it small?"

Kenya wiped her hand on a napkin. "All right. But you're really going to love this party."

James bit the inside of his cheek to keep from saying anything. He couldn't wait until his brother found out the real reason behind the party. "Are you still coming by the office?" he asked.

"Damn, I forgot all about that," Maurice said. "I wanted to take my wife to lunch, but it looks like she couldn't wait for me today."

Kenya rolled her eyes. "Whatever. Neither of you told me how Vegas was."

Maurice chuckled. "I know one of us had more fun than the other. Isn't that right, James?"

As if on cue, James's cell phone rang. He looked down at the caller ID and saw that it was Jade. "Hello," he said as he stepped out of the office.

"Hi, James," Jade said. "Sorry about earlier."

"You were on my mind, and I decided to call," he said.

"I'm glad you did. I was beginning to think that you'd forgotten all about me."

"How could I ever do that?" he said. "What did Nat King Cole say? 'You're unforgettable.'"

"James," she said, and he could imagine her blushing on the other end of the line.

"Did you have a good meeting?"

"Yes, and I'm going to be in Charlotte tomorrow. Do you think we can see each other?"

"Sure. Well, I have a meeting in the morning, but I can clear my schedule in the afternoon."

"Good."

"Just good? I was hoping for great or you telling me that you're jumping for joy," James quipped.

"I love how humble you are," she shot back.

"That's just my way. How long are you going to be in Charlotte?"

"Just for the day. I don't want to spoil your trip to Atlanta. You know what they say about too much of a good thing," she said.

"That it's never enough."

"You're so funny. It's really good to hear your voice," she said in a serious tone. "Part of me wondered if Las Vegas was just a beautiful dream that I'd woken up from three days ago."

"It was no dream, because if it were, I'd still be asleep. We had fun in Vegas, but I'm looking forward to getting to know the real you and showing you the real me," he said.

"James," Maurice called from the hallway outside of Kenya's office. "We need to talk."

"Duty calls. I'll see you tomorrow," James said into his phone.

"I'm looking forward to it," Jade replied before hanging up.

James turned to his brother. "What's so damned important?"

"Try and talk her out of this party thing," Maurice whispered.

"How about no?"

"Come on, James," Maurice pleaded. "I don't feel like standing in front of a room of people celebrating my road to retirement."

"Where is all this coming from? You haven't lost a step. You guys made it to the NFC championship game last season, and if it wasn't for the quarterback getting hurt, y'all probably would've won a second Super Bowl."

Maurice leaned against the wall and looked at his brother. "We got a new coaching staff coming in, and from what I hear, Coach Lukeman runs the ball more than he passes it."

"All right, but everyone knows that you're the star of this team," James said. "There's no way the new coach is going to bench or trade you."

Maurice shrugged his shoulders. "There's no way to know that. That's the nature of the NFL. Kenya really loves it in Charlotte. What happens if I get traded?"

"Did you see something on ESPN this morning that put you in this funk?" James asked.

"Yeah. I saw who Carolina named as the head coach."

"You don't know what that man is going to do.

Don't ruin this for Kenya. She really wants to give you this party."

"Why? You know what? It doesn't matter. If she wants to give me this party, then I'm going to party. You bringing your Vegas babe to the shindig?"

"Maybe," James said. "And thanks for interrupting my phone call with your melodrama."

"Oh, you two have been talking since all that sex in Vegas?" Maurice grinned. "You know what they say. You can't turn a—"

"Don't go there. Jade and I are getting to know each other, and I think I'm going to like her. Therefore, you're going to have to respect her."

Maurice threw his hands up in surrender. "My bad, player. But let me speak from experience. Don't let a big butt and a smile get you into something you can't get out of."

"This isn't Lauryn Michaels we're talking about," James said. "Jade doesn't have a golden shovel in her hand."

Kenya walked out into the hallway. "Is this a meeting of the all-boys club?"

"No," Maurice said as he wrapped his arms around Kenya's waist. "My brother fell in love with vacation booty."

"You married vacation booty," James shot back. "No offense, Kenya."

"Totally different circumstances," Maurice said. "We have history."

"Leave James alone," Kenya said. "People find love in unexpected places. I have a meeting in Matthews. Will you guys lock up?"

Maurice kissed his wife on the cheek. "You know I will."

"I'm going to get out of here, too," James said. Then he pointed at Maurice. "You need to come by the office. There are some things you need to sign, and Amber wants you to sign a football for a sorority auction."

"All right. I'll stop by after my workout," Maurice said.

James watched as Kenya and Maurice walked to the elevator, hand in hand. His brother didn't know how lucky he was. James couldn't help but wonder if he'd ever settle down and have a family.

CHAPTER 12

The next morning Jade met her friends at Kandace's office. She was excited about going to Charlotte, but it had nothing to do with their meeting with the realty company. She couldn't wait to see James. Then again, what if he was totally different in his real life? Would they have the same passion that they'd had in Vegas?

What if Serena and Alicia are right? No, James and I are starting something special, and despite what my friends say, we're going to be fine, she thought as she parked her car and got out.

"It's about time you got here," Serena said. "Are we ready to go now?"

"I'm going to drive myself," Jade said.

"Somebody must have made other plans," Alicia said.

Kandace smiled and nodded at Jade. "You know what? You and Serena need to stop being haters and let Jade enjoy whatever she and this guy are doing. She deserves to be happy."

"Blah, blah, blah," Serena said. "Can we just get

going? Some of us don't want to spend all day in Charlotte."

Jade rolled her eyes and shook her head as she got back into her car. To her surprise, Serena climbed into the passenger seat.

"Just so you know," Jade said as she started the car, "I will leave you on the side of the road if you start talking crap about me and James."

"Oh, shut up. I hope this will be your wake-up call," Serena said. "I have nothing else to say about this thing you're doing with a man you know nothing about."

"I knew a lot about Stephen, and where did that get me?"

"Touché."

As they drove to Charlotte, Serena kept her word and didn't say anything about James. "I heard the price of the restaurant went up to a million dollars. Do you think Stephen can afford that?" Serena asked after they'd driven for about an hour.

"Not according to the books that I saw last. He could've gotten a loan, but Stephen doesn't have the best record of paying people, if you know what I mean."

"Oh, I know," Serena said. "For every one person who thinks Stephen is the cat's meow, there are four people he owes money to. I had no idea when you first started dating him that he was such a louse."

"Well, I should've known that he was a piece of crap when Alicia told me that he'd hit on her. I really thought Stephen and I were building something," Jade said as she gently chewed on her bottom lip.

"I know I'm not supposed to say anything, but don't you think you're making the same mistake again? You and this guy had a wonderful weekend in Las Vegas, but you live in Atlanta, and he lives in Charlotte. If he casually slept with you the way he did, then there's a chance he may have a stable of women in Charlotte as well."

Jade rolled her eyes. "If that's the case, why does he want to see me? If he has all these women, don't you think he'd get all the sex he wanted from them?"

"You can't think this is more than sex," Serena said in a matter-of-fact manner.

"Don't worry about what I think. This is my business and my love life. Maybe if you had one of your own, then—"

"Please don't go there," Serena snapped. "Unlike you, I don't need a man for validation or safety. Maybe you should go see a therapist about your issues."

Jade slammed on the brakes, despite the fact that they were driving up Interstate 85. The car behind them darted into the next lane, and the driver flipped Jade off after leaning on the horn.

"Have you lost your damned mind?" Serena demanded.

"You have nerve saying I have issues when you treat men like disposable diapers. So, I didn't have the best parents in the world, but that has nothing to do with . . . Just shut up," Jade said as she pressed down on the gas pedal.

"Look, I'm sorry," Serena said. "I didn't mean to sound as if I was judging you."

"I'm driving." Jade reached for the volume button on the radio and turned it up.

Serena turned and looked out the window.

* * *

James walked into his office at about 7:30 a.m. Shortly after he arrived, Amber walked in with muffins and a box of coffee cups from Starbucks.

"Good morning," she said. "I thought we'd feed the people who are going to make us millionaires."

"We haven't made any deals yet," James said. "What kind of muffins are those?"

"Blueberry and banana-nut," she said. "The coffee is hazelnut."

James smiled and nodded with approval. "What would I do without you?"

She shrugged and headed for the conference room to arrange the coffee and muffins. Glancing down at his watch, James saw that he had time to call the owners of the restaurant and try to negotiate a better price for the property before the investors from Atlanta arrived. He wanted to get this meeting over with as soon as possible because he couldn't wait to see Jade when she came to town.

"Amber," James called out. "Can you get me a lunch reservation at Ruth's Chris?"

"Yes, sir. Are you taking these people to lunch?"

"No, this is personal," he said, with a sly smile.

She walked into his office and eyed him, as if he'd been replaced by an alien. "Personal? As in you have a date? What's really going on?"

"Wait a minute," James said as he rose to his feet. "Why are you having such a hard time believing that I have a date?"

Amber shrugged her shoulders. "Well, I've been here for two years, and I have yet to see you with a date."

"Unlike my brother, my love life isn't often plastered across the newspapers," James said. But the truth was, he didn't take women out. The few women he had dated in Charlotte hadn't moved him to set up lunch dates or anything that didn't involve a bedroom. But there was something different about Jade, something special. He just hoped that she had given up her quest to bring Stephen Carter down. Karma would take care of that slick bastard. However, James would introduce her to Kenya, who was a lawyer. Maybe she could help Jade recover her money.

Why didn't I think of this before? he thought. James picked up his desk phone and dialed Kenya's office.

"Kenya Goings," a woman said in an ultraprofessional voice.

"Good morning, Mrs. Goings," James said.

"James, what's going on?" Kenya asked.

"I have a friend that I think you can help," James said. Then he began to tell her Jade's story.

"Wow! Women still do that stuff?" Kenya said when James was finished. "It doesn't matter how in love people think they are, there is a reason for contracts. I wouldn't even go into business with Maurice, and I'm about to have his baby."

"Well, I don't know how Stephen conned her into doing that, but that man is the same fool that tried to make my mother's desserts his own."

"I remember that. So, Stephen Carter is still at it," she said. "Tell your friend to call me. And I'll even make sure the *AJC* covers it."

"I'm sure she will be happy to hear that," James said. "How are you doing?"

"I had to battle morning sickness this morning,

but your brother was working out in the basement, so he doesn't have a clue."

"Are you sure you want to wait until his birthday party to tell him you're pregnant?"

Kenya sighed. "Yes. It's only a few days away, and hopefully, it will get him out of this funk he's in."

"Yeah, he was telling me about that. He's worried about this off-season and what the new coach is going to do."

"I just hope he doesn't get traded, because I don't want to leave Charlotte right now. Well, I have to go. My first client is here and on time."

"All right," he said, then hung up the phone. He glanced at his watch and saw that it was 9:45. He wondered if his meeting was going to start on time.

It did. At exactly 10:00 a.m., Amber walked into his office to let him know that the investors from Atlanta had arrived.

"And they really are all women," she said in a whisper.

James stood, straightened his tie, and nodded toward Amber. "Well, let's go. I hope they brought a cashier's check. I talked to Roderick, and he said he's ready to get rid of this property."

Amber smiled, secretly hoping that this deal would go down and she'd be able to purchase a loft in NoDa, Charlotte's arts district.

They walked down the narrow hall and into the conference room. When James looked around the room and saw the familiar faces, he shook his head. "Is this a joke?" he asked. Then his eyes locked with Jade's. Trepidation flickered in her brown eyes as she stood up.

"What are you doing here, James?" she asked in a shaky voice.

"This is my company. The bigger question is, what are you all doing here?" said James.

Kandace dropped her head in her hands. "This is so not happening. I had no idea that you were the owner of this realty company."

"Seems like someone should've done a little more research," Serena said cattily.

"Oh, shut up," Kandace shot back.

James held his hand up. "Ladies," he said, "we can still make this purchase happen. I spoke to Roderick Harrison, one of the owners of the property, and he and the others are ready to sell. The price is one and a half million."

Kandace pulled out a financial statement. "That's a lot more than this building is worth."

"But it's a lot more than Stephen can afford," Alicia said.

Jade shook her head, trying to quiet her friend.

James turned to Amber. "Can you excuse us for one moment?"

Amber nodded, but her face was a ball of confusion. James knew he was going to have to explain everything to Amber later. Once she was out of the room, James slammed the door shut and cast a contemptuous glance at Jade and her friends.

"Just what in the hell is going on? Did you all have me waste my time trying to secure this property for you all in order for you to get it out of Stephen Carter's price range?" James slammed his hand against the table. "Do you realize how much time I wasted because you all want to play high school games?"

"Who said we don't have the money to buy this restaurant?" Serena asked, rising to her feet.

"Sit down," Jade said. "James, I had no—"

"What? You had no what?" James bellowed. "I told you that I didn't want anything to do with your little scheme, and what did you do? You put me right in the middle of this shit. Roderick lists a lot of his properties with us."

"And what's your point?" Serena snapped.

"Get the hell out of my office!" James exclaimed.

"Wait," Jade said. "We can purchase this restaurant." She looked to Kandace. "We have the capital for it, right?"

"So you're going to buy this restaurant and do what with it?" James asked heatedly. "It's in the center of a revitalization project that needs a restaurant, even if it is Stephen Carter's."

"You know what?" Alicia said. "We never said that we weren't going to keep a restaurant there. Your concern shouldn't be what we're going to do with the property, but if we can pay for it."

"My concern is for this project and this city," James said. "The revitalization of Cherry is important in more ways than one to this city."

"Whatever," Serena said. "I'm sure you're going to get a profit from this sale, so don't act like you're being Mr. Community Nonprofit."

"Serena, I really don't give a damn what you think. All of you get the hell out of my office," James stormed.

Kandace, Alicia, and Serena headed for the door. Jade lingered behind, hoping to appeal to James on a different level. She reached out and touched

James's arm. He jerked away from her as if her hand were a flame.

"I thought I asked you to get out of my office," he said.

"James, let me explain. . . ."

"Explain what, Jade? That you're a child and you had to go ahead with this scheme against Stephen? I told you there were other ways to get your money back from Stephen. My sister-in-law is willing to help you get your money back. But this, this is too much."

"Too much?" she asked.

"Just go. Obviously, you're not the woman I thought you were."

"What are you saying?" Jade asked, anger flickering in her eyes.

"I don't think I can be any clearer," James said, then stormed out of the conference room.

Jade started to follow him, but she stopped herself in the conference room, with a queasy feeling in her stomach. Slowly, she walked down the hall and met up with her friends.

"Were you able to get through to him?" Kandace asked.

Jade shook her head somberly. "He's very upset," she said. "He thinks we're playing a game."

Serena rolled her eyes. "We can find someone else to broker the deal."

"And I know a chef that will come here and work in this restaurant," Alicia said. "We can get it renovated and everything."

"Then we should just go to the owners ourselves," Kandace said.

Jade pressed the elevator button. "Let's just get out of here."

As the doors to the elevator opened and the women stepped on, Jade saw James slam into his office. The cold glare he gave her made her shiver as the elevator doors closed.

Amber rushed into James's office, not bothering to knock on the door. "What happened?" she asked.

"The deal fell through."

"What?" she said, not attempting to mask her disappointment. "But they seemed so ready to . . ."

"Amber, it's done. Sorry that I got your hopes up," he said.

"Wow," she said sadly. "Do you still need that lunch reservation?"

"Nah. Wait a minute. Why don't I take you to lunch? I know it doesn't make up for the commission that you lost, but it's the least I can do."

"Thanks," she said, then walked out of the office.

James picked up the file he'd been reading, but his mind wasn't on work. It was on Jade and her friends. Just what in the hell were they thinking? Granted, he didn't want to see Stephen bring his pompous ass to Charlotte, but Roderick didn't deserve to be screwed by these women and this game of cat and mouse they were playing. And why did Jade feel as if she had to do this? He'd thought that he'd changed her mind about getting her pound of flesh from Stephen. What did this mean about her feelings for the man? He'd seen this too many times. Too many women claimed to hate a man and then ended up in his arms when the smoke cleared. Even if she didn't end up with Stephen, why would he want to be with a woman who was so vindictive?

Stephen did steal from her. I guess I'd be pissed off, too, but there are other ways to do things, he thought as he picked up the phone to call Roderick. As he was dialing the number, his cell phone rang.

"Yeah," he said, without looking at the caller ID screen.

"James, it's Kandace. Can we talk?"

"About what?"

"My friends and I want to purchase the restaurant, and Alicia knows a chef who can come in and make a go of the restaurant."

"Knowing what I know about why you all want to buy this restaurant, I find it hard to believe that you're being honest with me."

"If we're willing to invest more than a million dollars in this, why do you feel as if you have any right to question me?" Kandace snapped.

"I'll call Roderick and the bank. We can get this rolling," he said. Part of him wanted to ask about Jade, but he didn't.

"Jade's going to meet you in your office at two p.m. with the check and everything," Kandace said.

Before James could protest, Kandace hung up the phone. Part of him wanted to see Jade, but he still had too many questions about her character and where her heart was.

Jade grabbed Kandace's shoulder as she heard the tail end of her conversation with James. "Why did you do that?" she demanded. "I don't want to go to his office for anything."

"Whatever. You didn't drive to Charlotte to let a

misunderstanding come between you and this man that you can't stop talking about," Kandace said.

Serena rolled her eyes. "I think he showed you who he really is. He didn't even give you a chance to explain—"

"Serena, shut up," Kandace said. "This is Jade's business, and she likes this man."

Alicia folded her arms across her chest. "Are we really buying this property? Because if we are, then there are some things I need to start getting in order."

All eyes were focused on Jade, who didn't say a word.

"This is our chance to put all our investment money to use," Kandace said. "Remember when we were in college and we started this account? We said that we were going to start our own business one day. Thank God we got out of the dot-coms before they went bust. That money is just sitting there. Now we have a chance to teach Stephen a lesson and make a profit."

"Fine," Jade said. "I'll take the check to James, but I really think this is the last time that I will see him."

"Hallelujah," Serena said. "And can we make a promise that none of us will ever mix business and pleasure again?"

"Yes," the other three women said.

"Can we go get something to eat?" Alicia said. "We should check out what our competition is going to be."

"I heard Ruth's Chris is pretty good," Serena said as they got into their cars.

"Then that's where we're going," Jade said as she slid into the driver's side of her car.

CHAPTER 13

James and Amber sat near the wide window in the front of the restaurant. "So you're serious?" Amber asked, with a wide smile on her face.

"Yes, the sale is back on, and you're going to get your commission," James said as he reached for his glass of water.

Amber clapped her hands, trying to keep her composure. "This is great," she said. "That money is going to come in real handy. But I have to ask you. What's the deal with you and those women? It's like you all know each other or something."

James took a sip of water, then set the glass beside his napkin. "We do. Actually I met them in Las Vegas and . . . It's a long story," he said.

"Oh," Amber said, understanding that she needed to leave it alone.

James turned and looked out the window and saw Alicia, Serena, Jade, and Kandace walking up the sidewalk. *I'll be damned,* he thought.

Amber noticed his glance and turned to take a peek out of the window. "So, which one of them do you like?" she asked. "I'm thinking the one in the middle."

James looked and saw that she had pointed out Jade, who was tossing her hair back. He couldn't help but think how soft Jade's hair had felt against his cheek when they'd lain together in bed. Jade had a lot of soft places on her, starting with her hair, then her lips, and every inch of skin on her body felt like silk. But he had to wonder about her heart. Was she just as cold as Serena and Alicia? Had she let the situation with Stephen change who she was?

"Am I right?" Amber asked her silent boss.

James nodded, despite himself. "Her name is Jade Christian," he said.

"And I'm guessing she is the one you were supposed to have lunch with."

"Yeah, but I'm beginning to have second thoughts about her," he said in a whisper.

"What?" Amber asked as she leaned into James so that she could hear him more clearly.

Serena tapped Jade on the shoulder repeatedly. "Would you look at that?" she said, nodding toward the front window of the restaurant. "It's James and his assistant about to kiss."

Jade looked at the window and her jaw dropped. *That son of a . . . I guess I was wrong about you, James.*

"We don't have to eat here," Alicia said as she noticed the pained look on Jade's face.

"No, we're going to eat here, and I'm going to give him a piece of my mind," Jade snapped. "You know he had the nerve to try and call me out, and all the while he's been sleeping with his assistant."

"I hate to say I told you so," Serena said. "But I told you that he was going to be a different man in Charlotte than who you met in Vegas. That's just how men are. On vacation they are one way but—"

"Please shut up!" Kandace said. "They were just talking. Damn! Jade, don't let Serena and her bitterness make you jump to conclusions. That's his assistant. They are probably having a business meeting. And if you're going to go up in this restaurant and act a fool, let me know and I will go someplace else for lunch."

"Me too," Alicia said.

Jade looked back in the window and saw James looking at her. Did she see a longing in his eyes? How could that be when she'd seen him kissing that girl? Or had they kissed?

"Can we go in?" Serena said. "Standing on this sidewalk isn't going to—"

"All right," Jade said, turning her back to James. "Let's eat and get the hell out of here."

Kandace tapped Jade on the shoulder. "Don't forget, you have a meeting with James at two. So, get yourself together and head to his office and get our property."

"And when do we get to tell Stephen that his dream of owning a restaurant in Charlotte is over?" Alicia asked as they waited for the host to seat them.

"Let me handle that," Jade said. "That's the least I can do to that bastard."

"Can you record it?" Serena asked. "I want to see his face when he finds out that he's been played."

Jade glanced over at James's table. *Why is he looking over here?*

"Jade," Serena said.

"What?" Jade mumbled.

Serena noticed her friend's stare and shook her head. "Get over it, girl. You have bigger fish to fry."

The host led the women to a table that gave Jade a perfect view of James and his "date." She should've known something was going on with him and his comely assistant. But how cliché was that for the boss to be sleeping with the secretary?

"Should I go over there and say something to him?" Jade said, more to herself than to her friends.

"Yes," Alicia and Kandace said in unison.

"No," Serena replied. "He's not your man. You two had a fling in Vegas. Let it go."

What if I don't want to? Jade thought as she looked at him. James locked eyes with her, and Jade knew she was going to have to go over and say something to him. Rising to her feet, she headed to his table without saying a word to her friends.

James watched Jade as she walked over to his table. He hoped there wasn't going to be a scene, and he willed himself to keep his attitude in check. Amber looked up and saw Jade coming their way.

"I'm going to powder my nose," she said seconds before Jade arrived at the table.

"You didn't have to drive your girlfriend away," Jade said once she reached the table.

"Amber is my employee," James said.

"So you kiss all your employees?"

"What the hell are you talking about?" he asked through clenched teeth.

Jade leaned into his ear. "I saw you and Amber."

James raised his right eyebrow. "What are you talking about?"

She pointed to the window. "Right there."

James shook his head. "You must be having hallucinations, because Amber and I did not kiss. We were simply talking."

"Sure you were," she said. "You know what? You had the nerve to talk about me and what I was doing, but you're just as—"

"Jade, really," he interrupted. "You're going to do this in the middle of this restaurant? Aren't you coming by my office later? Can't we just talk then about what you think you saw?"

Placing her hands on her hips, she backed away from James. "Fine. I'll see you at two."

As Amber returned to the table, she noticed that James didn't look too happy. "Is everything all right?" she asked.

"Fine."

Before they could say anything else, a blond waitress came over to take their orders. James smiled as Amber ordered a grilled chicken Caesar salad.

"You have something against steaks?" he asked after he ordered the rib eye steak lunch special.

"I don't eat red meat," she said. "But everyone talks about this place, so I figured I might as well try it out. And since lunch is on you, how could I say no?"

James laughed, but he couldn't help thinking about how he and Jade had shared steak dinners that night in Vegas. The dinner had been great, but dessert had been even better.

"James," Amber said, breaking into his thoughts. "Yes?"

"Have you called Roderick and told him that the deal is back on? Where is your mind?" Amber asked.

James stole a quick glance at Jade and her friends. There was no question as to where his mind was.

* * *

"Well?" Serena said when Jade sat down. "What did he have to say for himself?"

Kandace shook her head. "Serena, can we please get through lunch without you telling us about the evils of men?"

Serena rolled her eyes and folded her arms across her chest. "You know, you all can say what you want about love and falling for this man or that man. But in the last twelve months, all of you have been crying over some dude."

"And you haven't, because super Serena doesn't allow anyone to get close to her," Jade said.

"Ladies," Alicia said, "this is not the place to have this kind of discussion. People are looking at us as if we're the stars of *Sex and the City.*"

Jade and Serena looked around the restaurant and saw that a few patrons were staring at them and soaking up every word they were saying. One of the older women sitting closest to their table shot Jade and her friends a condescending look and shook her head.

"You're right," Jade said. "We're making asses of ourselves right now, and that old lady over there looks as if she's going to have the manager kick us out of here."

Serena cut into her grilled chicken. "All I'm saying is the next time any of you come crying to me about some guy, I'm going to remind you all of this."

Kandace and Jade looked at each other and laughed. "You know," Kandace said, "this reminds me of college."

"Please," Alicia said.

"It does not," Serena said. "At least in college, you were expected to make mistakes. We're adults and—"

"Excuse me, ladies," the waiter said as he walked over to their table. "Does anyone need a refill?"

"We're fine," Alicia said, with a smile. The waiter nodded and walked away.

The women finished their meal in silence, until Jade noticed James and Amber leaving. She could've sworn she saw him put his hand on the small of Amber's back. "Just look at that," she mumbled.

"You're just getting on my nerves now," Alicia said. "Obviously, you like this guy. Stop acting like Serena and go talk to him."

"I'm going to talk to him at two and give him the check for the restaurant," Jade said, with a bit of an attitude.

"We're not talking about talking business with the man," Kandace said.

Serena snorted. "If you were smart, you'd limit it to just business."

Jade ran her fingers through her hair and looked down at her steak. The last time she'd had a steak was the first time she and James met. How had everything just blown up like this? When they left Vegas, they were supposed to be on their way to starting something special, something real. He had to realize that this thing with Stephen was strictly business and that it had nothing to do with them. But what was the deal with him and the assistant?

After lunch Alicia, Serena, and Kandace headed back to Atlanta, leaving Jade to handle James alone. Paying for the property wasn't the problem; Jade just didn't know if she was going to be able to get through to him. She had to explain to him that she wasn't in love with Stephen and she just wanted her money back. And maybe a pound of flesh for her heart being broken for all of Atlanta to see.

Jade slid into her car, glanced down at her watch, and saw that it was 1:30. Just what was she going to do for the next half an hour? She decided to drive by the restaurant she and her girls were about to purchase. She was looking forward to owning something, even if she didn't have a clue about running a restaurant.

As she pulled up to the building, she was surprised to see Stephen and a woman standing in front of it. They looked as if they were arguing, and Jade couldn't help but smile. She brought her car to a stop and exited it. She approached the duo without being seen.

Stephen was visibly livid. "What do you mean someone outbid me on this property?"

Jade looked at him and drank in the features that used to drive her crazy. His skin was still the color of creamy caramel, and his sparkling gray eyes still looked as if they could see through her soul.

As he waved his hands in the air, she thought about how those big hands used to massage her shoulders as she sat at the desk in his office, balancing the books. At the time his touch had been something that she craved. But sex between the two of them had been as exciting as watching paint dry. Stephen had had to be on top. And despite the size and warmth of his hands, foreplay had been a foreign concept to him. Stephen always did what made him happy and satisfied his needs.

Jade approached the duo, but neither of them noticed her walking toward them.

"This was the perfect location," Stephen raged at the woman, who, Jade assumed, was his Realtor. "I don't understand how you didn't know that someone else was interested in it."

"The new buyer came out of nowhere," the woman said. "They purchased the land and the restaurant for a price higher than you could afford."

Stephen glared at her and shook his head. "You should've been on the job."

Jade cleared her throat, alerting Stephen that she was there. He turned around and locked eyes with her.

"What are you doing here?" he asked.

"Just came to check out my investment," Jade said, with a sly smile on her face.

"Investment?" he quizzed.

"Yes, this will be my restaurant and land. If I were a nastier person, I'd have you arrested for trespassing," Jade snarled.

Stephen narrowed his eyes into little slits that reminded Jade of a snake. "How could you do this to me? You know how much time and money I have invested in this Charlotte expansion."

"I only know and care about the fifty thousand dollars you stole from me," Jade snapped.

Stephen waved his hand dismissively. "Are you still on that? You invested in my restaurant on your own. You weren't under duress when you gave me that money."

"No," Jade said, stepping closer to Stephen and pointing her finger in his face. "I invested in your restaurant because I thought we were going to be married. I was trying to support you and be there for you."

"Did I ever give you a ring?" he returned.

Jade glared at him. "You bastard."

"So, I'm going to have to scout some new locations, but I will open up a Chez Marcel in Charlotte, and whatever little restaurant you plan to open here will fail. You don't know the first thing about running a restaurant."

"And neither do you!" Jade exclaimed. She fought the urge to slap him. "Get off my future property."

Stephen shook his head. "Your mistake, babe. When it all blows up in your face, call me and I may bail you out."

Jade clenched her jaw. "Hell will freeze over first. No one needs you, Stephen. Well, maybe your over-inflated fiancée, but I don't."

Stephen and the Realtor headed to his car, and Jade stood in front of the restaurant. She closed her eyes and envisioned a crowd of people waiting to get in.

I'd better go give James this check, she thought as she turned and headed for her car.

CHAPTER 14

James tried to focus on his work. But every five minutes he was looking at the clock to see if it was two o'clock yet. He wanted to hear what Jade had to say, but more importantly, he couldn't wait to see her again. Even though he was pissed with her, he couldn't deny that he still had it bad for Jade. He couldn't deny how sexy she had looked in her business suit or how the gray pencil skirt had held her curvy hips the way he wanted to hold her against him.

Shaking his head, he turned back to his computer and the e-mail he'd been writing for the last fifteen minutes. He looked at his watch; it was about two seconds closer to two o'clock than it had been when he looked the last time.

Amber tapped on his cracked door. "James, Jade is here to see you," she said.

"Send her in," James said, then wiped his sweaty palms on his slacks. Seconds later Jade walked in the door, and his breathing went shallow.

"Here's the payment for the property," she declared without saying hello.

James took the check from her hand and nodded for her to sit down. "We need to talk," he said.

"I thought you had your say already, James," Jade said as she sat in the chair across from his desk.

"Maybe I came across too harsh. That wasn't my intent. It's just I was surprised to see you and your crew in my conference room this morning. Then, when I found out that Stephen was trying to purchase the same property, it . . ."

"Caused you to act like an asshole instead of a businessman," Jade pointed out, finishing his sentence for him.

"If that's what you think. But what I realized is that what you and your friends do with your money is your business."

Jade nodded. "And I guess whatever you do with your assistant is your business," she said.

James smirked. "Are you seriously on that again? First of all, Amber is fresh out of college and way too young for me. Secondly, she's my employee, and I have too much respect for my company to try and do something with her, and finally, there's too much work to be done here for me to be distracting my assistant." He rose to his feet.

"I saw you kiss her," Jade said, standing up and facing him.

"That was just your imagination," James said, stepping closer to her. "Or maybe you wanted a reason to be pissed off at me."

Jade wanted to step away from him, and at the same time she wanted him to wrap his arms around her and kiss her as if the world was going to come to an end. For what seemed like an eternity, neither of them moved; it didn't even seem as if they took a breath. But in one swift movement, James lifted Jade into his arms and brought his lips down on top of hers. She hungrily sought out his tongue and wrapped her legs around his waist.

James brushed some of the papers on his desk to the floor, then laid Jade across the wooden desktop. She reached for the waistband of his slacks as he unbuttoned his shirt. The demi bra she wore barely contained her perky breasts, and when James slipped his hands underneath the lacy garment, she moaned with anticipation. His fingers brushed across her erect nipples as she stroked his erection.

"Is the door locked?" she asked.

James shrugged. He didn't care if the door was open or not, but he pulled away from her and locked it. "Happy?" he asked as he kicked out of his slacks.

Jade dropped her silky panties, along with her skirt, on the floor. "Why don't you come over here and make me happy?" she said, with a smirk on her face.

James crossed over to her and smiled as he took her into his arms. "Even though I was pissed with you, I wanted to do this the moment you walked into the building."

He sat her on the edge of the desk and spread her legs apart. Then he planted his face between her thighs. With his tongue, he sought out her throbbing bud of sexuality. Jade struggled to keep her voice down as James lapped her womanly juices, which sprang from her like a summer's rain.

"Oh," she moaned as his tongue danced across her most sensitive area.

Jade clamped her thighs together around James's

ears as he deepened his kiss, sucking on her throbbing bud as if it were a piece of magical candy. She held on to his shoulders as her legs began to quake. Seconds passed like hours as James continued tasting her. When his tongue danced against her inner thigh and his finger probed her valley of desire, Jade melted into a pool of heated lust on his desk. James inched up her body, taking his time and tasting every bit of exposed flesh. Each kiss made her shiver with a wanton need to feel him inside her. Then, when she felt his manhood growing against her thighs, her juices began to flow like a river.

"I need you," he breathed against her ear after covering his erection with a condom. "I need you, Jade."

She lifted her leg, giving him all the clearance he needed to dive in. As their bodies melted together, they gave in to the passion and pleasure they felt. Jade was hot and wet, and James could barely contain himself as she pressed her hips into his and ground slowly against him. With her head thrown back, she tightened her thighs around him and called out his name as he reached her G-spot. James thrust into her, making Jade scream with delight. She tightened her muscles around his manhood, bringing him to climax just as she reached her own orgasm. Jade fell backward onto the desk, and James collapsed on top of her. Sweat covered their naked bodies, and for the moment it didn't matter that James's phone was ringing and Jade had papers stuck to her backside. In their minds, they were in the most perfect place on earth.

"Don't you think you should answer that?" Jade asked as the phone kept ringing.

"Why do you think voice mail was invented?"

She gently stroked his back and brushed her lips across his. "This is dangerous," she said.

"What do you mean?"

"I could get used to this, and since we're going to be doing business in Charlotte, you will be seeing a lot more of me."

"And the dangerous part is what?"

Jade dropped her arms from around him and turned her head to the side. "You don't see this as being a problem? Have you ever known a long-distance 'thing' to work out?"

James ran his forefinger down the center of her breasts. "Let's call it what it really is. A relationship. I hope that's the direction we're moving in. Otherwise, you're wasting my time. I don't want a bed partner, although we haven't done much in a bed, have we?"

She swatted him on the shoulder and smiled. "But—" she began, and James placed his finger to her lips to silence her.

"There are no buts. If you're ready to try something new, then here I am. But if you're still hung up on your ex and you have to go out of your way to get revenge, then this can be our good-bye."

Jade pushed his hand away. "It's not about revenge, and I'm not hung up on Stephen," she said.

"Really?"

Squirming underneath him, she wiggled out of his embrace and swung her legs over the side of the desk.

James, now standing, planted himself in front of her. "Tell me the truth," he said. "You wanted this property because Stephen was going to buy it. I understand that you're angry, and you have every right to be. But, at what point does that anger become unhealthy?"

"He humiliated me. And I know you might think I should get over it and let it go, but I poured a lot of sweat and tears into his restaurant. While he was out front socializing with the best Atlanta had to offer, I was trying to make sure he had money to pay the staff, the decorators, and I was the one who got all the publicity for that restaurant. I used my contacts from college to get people to give a damn. And to open the newspaper and see I'd been replaced! Not just in the relationship, but in the business, too. Well, James, that was the straw, and the camel's back was already cracking."

"I told you that my sister-in-law is a contract attorney and she can help you," he said. "But that has nothing to do with you and me. I want you, Jade, want you for more than just sex. There's something about you that's intriguing, that's special, and I want to uncover every bit of it. I want to know what makes you happy so I can stop you from ever being sad. I want to know what makes you who you are." He stopped when he saw tears welling up in her eyes. "What's wrong?"

"This feels so right, but I haven't had the best of luck with relationships, and sometimes the men . . ."

"You've never been with me. I can't promise that every day is going to be sunshine and roses, but most days will be. I don't want a bunch of women. I know all I need is one woman, who can be everything that I need, want, and desire."

Jade sucked her bottom lip in and tried to quell the emotional storm brewing inside. When James spoke, she believed him. And she wanted to believe that he was the man for her, but she'd had these thoughts before. "James," she whispered as he took her into his arms, "this is crazy."

"Once you pay for that restaurant, we're no longer in business together. And we are never going into business together. Just let go and get what's coming to you, woman," he said as he cupped her bottom.

"And just what would that be?" She felt his arousal against her legs and smiled because she was just as ready for round two.

Then there was a pounding knock on the door. "James, what in the hell are you doing in there?" Maurice yelled.

"Damn it. He would pick today to show up when he's actually supposed to," James whispered.

"Your brother?" asked Jade.

James nodded as he and Jade began dressing. Once they were clothed and his office had some semblance of order, James opened the door.

Jade smiled weakly at Maurice as she headed out. "I'll see you later," she said to James.

Maurice smirked and took a seat across from James's desk. "Well, well," he said.

"Don't start, Mo," James warned.

"I'm not starting anything. It looks like you just finished something up in here, though," Maurice said.

"Why are you here?" James asked, clearly annoyed with his brother.

"Didn't you say we needed to discuss some business?" Maurice asked. "I came to work, but it looks as if you were putting in work." He laughed at his own joke; then he noticed the serious look on his brother's face and stopped laughing. "Look, you're single. Kenya and I have used her desk a time or two. Never in the middle of the day, though. Poor Amber was in the lobby, watering flowers, and those plants in the lobby are plastic."

"Shut up." James laughed despite himself. "Are you serious, though?"

Maurice nodded. "I always thought you and Amber would get together, since she is the only woman that you allow to be around you on a consistent basis."

"I don't play where I work, all right?" James said. "And don't let Jade hear you make those quips about Amber."

"So this thing is serious? Come on, James. I know you're not that damned . . ."

"Think about what you're getting ready to say, because you have no room to talk," James said.

Maurice threw his hands up. "All right, but hear me out. You and this chick met in Vegas, right? She hopped into bed with you and didn't know you from Adam's alley cat. Do you really think that's the kind of woman that you need to be getting serious with?"

"Sort of like the kind of woman you were about to walk down the aisle with a couple of years ago?"

"That's why I can recognize a gold digger when I see one," Maurice said. "There's something about that chick that isn't right."

"Whatever, Mo," James said.

"Come on. Why is she in Charlotte?"

"Because she just bought a restaurant," James snapped. "It was a million-dollar investment, so she's not trying to get my money."

"Women like that . . ."

"Like what? Beautiful and sexy? What? They don't usually want me? They're just using me to get to your ass, right?"

Maurice rose to his feet and shook his head. "That's not what I'm saying, and you know that."

"Did you listen to me when I told you about Lauryn?" James asked.

"No, but don't you think you should learn from my mistake?"

"I think you should mind your damned business," James replied. "Jade isn't anything like Lauryn."

"You don't know that," Maurice said. "And you're not going to be sure until it's too late."

James folded his arms across his chest and leaned back in his seat. "If you have some legitimate business here, then let's get to it."

"Man, I forgot what I came here for. Just make sure that she's really worth it." Maurice turned and headed out the door.

James chewed his bottom lip and tried not to let what Maurice had said perplex him. But was he right? Did Jade have an ulterior motive as to why she wanted to be with him?

I'm not going to let Maurice get to me, he thought as he began to pick up the papers he and Jade had brushed aside.

Jade sat in the parking lot, wondering what she was going to do until she and James linked up again. She realized that she had no idea where he lived, and even if she had his address, she wasn't that familiar with Charlotte. The look on Maurice's face had told her that he knew what had happened in the office. Jade's cheeks burned as she thought about what Maurice was thinking when she walked out of the office as if her skirt was on fire.

Just as she was about to start her car, there was a knock on her window. Frazzled, she looked up and was surprised to see Maurice standing there. Jade rolled her window down and offered him a shy smile.

"What's going on?" she asked.

"That's a good question. Got an answer?"

"I don't understand." Jade furrowed her eyebrows and shrugged her shoulders.

"What's going on with you and my brother? The real deal?" he asked.

"That's between me and James," Jade said. "And if you have any questions, maybe you should ask him."

"But I'm asking you. Here's the thing. I love my brother, and I don't want to see him hurt by some gold digger who realizes that the last name Goings will open a lot of doors for her in Charlotte and Atlanta."

"Hold up," Jade said. "You don't know me. You don't know a thing about me."

"I know the type. I hope you are aboveboard, because if you hurt my brother, let's just say I'll go out of my way to make your life hell."

Jade opened the car door and got out. She stood in Maurice's face, even though she was several inches shorter than he was. "So you're making assumptions about me and threatening me? Just who in the hell do you think you are?"

Maurice shook his head, his face contorted with a deep scowl. "This isn't even about me—"

"You're right. It's about me and James. He may be your brother, but last time I checked, he was a grown-ass man who didn't need you playing his savior."

"Women like you are common," he said. "You

know that James can do a lot for you in Charlotte and Atlanta. I believe you're using him."

Jade dropped her head and laughed sarcastically. "Yeah, I am using him. I started by giving him a million dollars for some property that my investment group bought here. And I'm using him for some of the best sex of my life. Yes, Maurice, you've figured me out."

He stepped back from her, still scowling. "Whatever you're doing, you'd better make sure that you—"

"Maurice," James called out. "What the hell is going on?"

Jade and Maurice turned around and watched James stalk in their direction.

"One of y'all need to answer me," James snapped. "What's this all about?"

Jade looked at Maurice. "I think you and your brother need to talk."

James glared at his brother. "If this is what I think it is, my brother needs to leave."

"Fine," Maurice said. "If I'm overstepping, then whatever. I'm out."

James turned to Jade. "I'm sorry about that," he said.

"I guess I shouldn't be upset, since my friends did the same thing to you. But your brother seems to think I'm some kind of gold digger."

"That's because he has issues," James said. "Come on. Let's get out of here."

As Jade got in her car to follow James, she couldn't help but wonder if Maurice's words were going to have an effect on him.

CHAPTER 15

James led Jade to his ranch-style house in a new subdivision on the outskirts of town. His house sat at the rear of the cul-de-sac and gave him more privacy than he had a need for. But as he looked in his rearview mirror and saw Jade's car behind him, he suddenly thought about what he could use all that privacy for.

They pulled into his driveway and got out of their cars. "Hungry?" James asked.

"I'm still kind of full from lunch. Ruth's Chris was nice," she said, with a smile.

"Well, I was going to show you my culinary skills," he said.

"Umm, sounds intriguing. I guess I could eat something."

Jade followed James to the front door. When she walked in, she was surprised by the decor in the house. It wasn't the typical bachelor pad; the place was cleaner than her Atlanta penthouse and was decorated in earth tones. Part of her had expected to see a leather sectional and a sixty-inch flat-screen TV.

But she should've known better. James had class and his home reflected that.

"Nice place," she said.

"Thanks," he said, then nodded toward the over-size sofa. "You can have a seat if you like."

Jade sat on the sofa and melted into the cushions. "This is heaven," she whispered.

James eased beside her and took her into his arms. "My brother was out of line, and I hope you don't hold his ranting and raving against me."

"Your brother was trying to look out for you. He just went about it in the wrong way." Jade turned and faced James. Their lips brushed against each other, and Jade smiled. "Maurice isn't going to be a problem, is he?" she asked.

"Hell no. If my brother had better judgment when it came to women, he would be celebrating ten years of marriage and probably would have a couple of kids running around here."

"You guys are big on family, huh?"

James shrugged. "We just want to make sure that our kids will have it better than we did. Our father wasn't a very good role model."

Jade nodded. "I can understand that. Growing up on a gambling boat leaves little room for a normal childhood. My friends say that I'm always looking for a sure thing to make up for all the craziness that surrounded me when I was growing up."

"Everybody wants to have something in their life they can depend on," James said as he stroked her cheek. "I hope that when the time comes for me to have kids, I will be that father that they can always depend on."

"You want children?"

"One day. It's not like I'm getting any younger. I'm thirty-five, you know. And here's a secret. Mo is about to be a father. Kenya's going to make a big announcement at his birthday party next weekend."

"Really?" she said, not that interested in knowing about Maurice's happy news.

"I'm going to need a date for that party," he said.

"Are you sure Maurice is going to allow me to attend his party?"

"You're going to be with me. There won't be a problem at the door. What time are you leaving tomorrow?"

"Trying to get rid of me already?" she jokingly asked.

"No, because if I had my way, I wouldn't let you leave. But I wanted to call Kenya and see if we could get an appointment with her."

"Oh," Jade said as she cupped James's face in her hands. "I'm flexible."

"Don't I know it."

Jade gently squeezed his cheek. "Funny."

James held her tighter. "You know you're very flexible," he said, then kissed her on the forehead. "What do you want for dinner?"

"Umm, surprise me," she said as she dropped her hands. "As a matter of fact, I just want to watch you cook. Please tell me you wear an apron."

"How about no?" James rose to his feet and headed to the kitchen, with Jade in tow.

As they entered the kitchen, she marveled at the size and style of it. The stainless-steel appliances looked as if they had been taken from Rachael Ray's kitchen. A set of gourmet pots hung above the stove. When James opened the refrigerator, Jade wasn't surprised to find it fully stocked.

"Are you sure you live alone?" Jade asked. "This place is so not what I expected."

"Don't you think I'm a little too old to live like a frat boy? You know you'd be talking a lot of junk about me with your girlfriends if you came in here and it looked like a tornado had been through here. Besides, I have a cleaning crew that comes in once a week."

"And I was about to be impressed because I thought you cooked and cleaned," she said as she took a seat on a stool near the marble kitchen island.

"It's hard to believe that I'm not perfect, I know," he quipped. "But somehow you will have to carry on."

Jade tossed a dish towel in his direction. "Whatever."

James ducked out of the way of the towel, then turned back to the refrigerator. He pulled out the ingredients for a grilled chicken dinner.

She looked at the food and wrinkled her nose. "Chicken?" she asked.

"Yes, and your heart will thank me," he replied.

Jade smiled. "You're looking out for my heart now?"

He winked at her before saying, "Among other things."

About forty-five minutes later, they were sitting down to a dinner of teriyaki grilled chicken breasts, brown rice with pineapple, and steamed green beans. The flickering glow of two tapered candles lit the dining room. Jade glanced over her wineglass at

James as he cut into his chicken. She couldn't remember the last time that a man took the time to cook for her and make her feel this special.

"Something wrong?" James asked when they locked eyes.

"No," she said. "Nothing's wrong."

A smile spread across James's lips. "You really wanted another steak, didn't you? You don't like the chicken, huh?"

She set her wineglass down. "I like the chicken, and everything is wonderful. The food, the company, everything."

James scooted his chair closer to hers. "So what's with the long face?"

Jade placed her hand on his thigh. "You make me feel things that I never thought I'd feel. It's like you provide what I've been longing for, and I keep looking around the corner, waiting for the other shoe to drop."

"You're borrowing trouble," he said. "I think you should stop that."

She wanted to say that she would and that she would let things come as they may, but that was not the kind of woman Jade was. She did borrow trouble, even if being with James seemed like the most natural thing to do. But was it too good to be true?

Jade squeezed his thigh and returned to her meal. "You're right," she said. "I should stop."

Later that night Jade lay in James's arms, unable to sleep. Her mind just kept wondering if she was really going to find happiness with James Goings. She didn't tell him that this evening was one that she'd dreamed of. James made her feel safe. He gave her everything that she had missed growing up. Everything that she had missed in her relationship with Stephen. James made her feel as if she was a priority, and that was something that she'd never felt before. With Stephen, she had felt like an obligation that he didn't really want to deal with. Jade had known long before the story showed up in the paper that things with Stephen had been changing, but she hadn't wanted to be alone. Looking over at James, Jade wanted him to be her everything. But how were they going to make this relationship work when everyone seemed to be against them being together?

One thing is certain, she thought as she turned and faced James. *At least he's not hiding a wife, girlfriend, or baby mama, like Serena alleged.*

The next morning James woke up before Jade did. Her warmth in his arms made him not want to move. Were he given a choice, he'd lie with her like this all day. He brushed his lips against her forehead, then slipped his arms from around her and got out of the bed, hoping not to wake her up. James had noticed that Jade had tossed and turned for hours before she'd drifted off to sleep last night. If she was resting now, the last thing he wanted to do was disturb her. James headed into the kitchen and dialed Kenya's office. He knew his sister-in-law was in, despite the fact that it was just a little after seven.

"Kenya Goings," said a female voice.

"Aren't you up bright and early this morning?"

"Well, had I stayed at home a minute longer, I would've killed your brother," Kenya said in an exasperated voice.

"What's wrong?" James asked.

"Actually, he kept talking about how you're making a huge mistake with this woman from Vegas. I told him he needs to mind his business, but that fool wasn't hearing me. Then I had morning sickness, and Mo was standing outside the bathroom, trying to be helpful but getting on my nerves," she said. "So, what's the deal with you and the Vegas showgirl?"

"Did he tell you she was a showgirl?" he asked incredulously. "That dude is tripping."

Kenya sucked in a breath. "Honestly, I'm not even going to repeat some of the stuff Maurice said about your friend. Trust me, you don't want to know."

James slapped his hand against his forehead in frustration. "Your husband has issues. Jade is a woman who runs her own business. She makes me happy, and I hope I make her happy, too. She is the reason why I'm calling."

"Really? What's going on?"

"She needs some legal advice. Do you think you can fit us in today?"

"Umm," she said. James heard her typing on her computer. "I have an opening around ten."

"Cool. We'll see you then," he said.

"James," Kenya said, "you deserve to be happy, and don't let anyone—especially your brother—tell you otherwise."

"Thanks," he said. "That means a lot coming from you."

"Well, I hate to cut this lovefest short, but I have some briefs to get ready and file with the clerk of the court before nine," she said. "I'll see you guys at ten."

When James hung up with Kenya, he had a smile on his lips. His sister-in-law was a good friend to him, despite the incident that had happened between them when she thought that Maurice had cheated on her. He turned to head back to the bedroom, but Jade met him in the hallway, with nothing but the bedsheet draped seductively over her naked body.

"You know, when I woke up and you weren't there, I thought last night was a wonderful dream," she said.

James closed the space between them and pulled her against his body. "Is that so?"

She nodded and smiled. "But luckily, I was wrong. I did sleep in your arms all night."

He brushed his lips against hers, then said, "You know, we can have breakfast in bed, because Kenya can't see us until ten."

"What I want to do in bed right now has nothing to do with breakfast," she said, then dropped the sheet.

In one quick motion, James scooped Jade up in his arms and dashed into the bedroom.

After spending half of the morning making love, Jade and James pulled themselves out of bed in order to make it to Kenya's office for their ten o'clock meeting.

When they arrived at her office, James spotted Maurice in the lobby. "Jade"—who was getting on the elevator—"you go ahead and go up. I need to talk with my brother," he said as they approached the elevators. James grabbed Maurice by the elbow. "What's up?"

Maurice looked from James to Jade and shook his head. "You tell me," Maurice said. "I came to surprise my wife and make sure she was all right, and lo and behold, my brother and his woman are here." Sarcasm flowed through Maurice's words like a river.

"I spoke to your wife this morning. It seems like you can't stop talking about me and my woman," James retorted.

"James, what do you really know about Jade Christian and her crew?"

James furrowed his eyebrows and shook his head. "We're not going through this again."

"I hired a private detective," Maurice said. "And in twenty-four hours, he found out that those women are known for bilking the rich and famous out of their money. Especially that Serena Jacobs, and you know what they say about birds of a feather. How did you and Jade meet? Do you think that you running into her was an accident?"

Running his hand over his face, James wanted to write his brother off, but the things he said made more sense than he wanted to admit.

"And Jade was involved with who before you two started sleeping together?" Maurice said pointedly.

"Mo," James said, holding his hand up, "why are you so invested in what I do and who I do it with?"

"Because we've been down this road once, and I don't want to see another crazy bi . . . James, if I'm wrong about her . . ."

"You are, so why don't you take all this energy that you're putting into nosing around my life and put it into making sure the Panthers don't trade your ass," James said as he pressed the elevator up button.

The doors opened, and the brothers stepped

onto the elevator. Maurice glared at James. "That was a low blow."

"And calling Jade a showgirl wasn't?"

"I forgot, you and Kenya tell each other everything," Maurice said, with a laugh.

"That's not funny," James said, fighting back his own laughter.

"Whatever, man. I know you and this girl are having a good time right now, but what are you going to do when this thing runs out of steam?"

James cast a sidelong glance at his brother. "When did you get a crystal ball, and why haven't you used it in your own damned life?"

"Stop comparing this situation to what happened with Lauryn," Maurice said.

"As soon as you stop doing it, I will," James snapped. "This isn't even about you. Or is that the problem?"

"Not this shit again," Maurice grumbled.

"Yes, this again. You have to be the center of damned attention, don't you? Or is it that you're the only one who can have a stable relationship and a family? The rest of us are just supposed to be envious of what Maurice has, because we mere mortals will never have that."

"That's bull and you know it," Maurice snapped. "But if I see you walking into fire, am I just supposed to let you get burned?"

"If that's what I want, then yes," James said. "And you're going to show Jade some damned respect."

Before Maurice could reply, the doors to the elevator opened.

"We'll finish this later," Maurice said as he bounded toward Kenya's office.

James shook his head and followed his brother to Kenya's door. "You know Jade's in there with her, right?" James asked as he grabbed his brother's elbow.

"And?"

"Mo, Jade is a potential client. What are you going to do? Just burst in there?" James asked.

"Why are you so insistent on involving that woman in our lives?"

James shook his head. "I'm sick of trying to explain myself to you." He sat down in one of the chairs outside of Kenya's office. Maurice sat beside him.

"All right. Fine," Maurice said. "You do what you want to do with that chick, but mark my words. This relationship is a mistake."

James wanted to punch his brother, choke him, or just push him down a flight of stairs. Then he thought about it. It was as if their roles had been reversed. James had said far worse to Maurice when he and Lauryn were together. But the difference was he'd been right.

What if Maurice is right now? the skeptic in James asked. He rubbed his neck and turned away from his brother. Jade wasn't running game, she wasn't trying to use him, and Maurice needed to mind his own damned business.

CHAPTER 16

Jade watched Kenya as she typed information into her computer, and she felt hopeful. Hopeful that there was a law somewhere that would allow her to atone for her stupidity and get her money back.

"A lot of courts do look seriously at verbal contracts," Kenya said as she printed a document. "I'll bet he's going to use the gift defense."

"The what?" Jade asked.

"In a lot of these cases that I've seen, when a woman sues a man that she used to date, he claims that she gave him money as a gift."

"Trust me, that fifty thousand dollars was no gift. I thought it was an investment in my future."

Kenya pulled her reading glasses off and stared at Jade. "Just one question," she began. "Why didn't you get something in writing?"

Jade sighed. She'd been asking herself that same question since she'd seen the picture of Stephen in the *AJC*. Shrugging, she said, "A serious lapse in judgment? I thought we were in love with each other. The last thing I expected was to be replaced by a bootleg Barbie doll."

"This is a costly mistake," Kenya said. "But he still took your money, and that's wrong. We can get this lawsuit filed and maybe get a court date for next month some time."

"How much is this going to cost me?" Jade asked, a little surprised that Kenya had taken her case when several other attorneys had turned her down.

"Don't worry about that," Kenya replied. "This man needs to learn a lesson, and I'm more than willing to help teach it." She extended her hand to Jade. "Besides, he tried to take advantage of my mother-in-law as well, so I'm guessing this is a pattern with him."

Jade enthusiastically shook Kenya's hand. "Thank you so much."

"Don't thank me until I win," Kenya said. She handed Jade her business card. "If you have anything that shows you were his employee and you two had more than a personal relationship, I'm going to need that."

"I have some old pay stubs and W-two forms from the restaurant," Jade said. She wished she had listened to Alicia when she'd told her to find another job once she and Stephen began sleeping together. Hell, she wished that she had walked away from Stephen when Alicia had told her that he'd tried to pick her up.

"All right," Kenya said. "And I play to win, so Stephen is going down."

Jade smiled brightly. "I like how that sounds." In the back of her mind, Jade wondered how in the world Kenya dealt with being Maurice Goings's wife.

Kenya and Jade walked out of the office, talking as if they were old friends. But their chatter stopped when they saw James and Maurice standing toe-to-toe, arguing.

"You're acting like a damned fool!" Maurice boomed.

"Learned from the best, because you are a damned fool," James shot back.

Kenya rushed toward the battling brothers and grabbed her husband's arm. "Do I need to remind you two that this is a place of business? Why are you two out here acting like Neanderthals?" she demanded.

Maurice cast a sidelong glance at Jade but held his tongue.

"Let's go," James said as Jade walked over to him.

Jade looked from him to Maurice and shook her head. "Maybe we all need to sit down and talk," she said. "Kenya just took me on as a client, James and I are going to be seeing each other a lot more, and I don't want you two to keep fighting."

"Sounds logical to me," Kenya said.

Maurice and James remained silent.

"Guys," Kenya said, "stop acting like children and come into my office."

They headed into Kenya's office, and Kenya perched on the edge of her desk, looking at the frown on her husband's face and shaking her head. "What's the problem?" she asked.

Maurice looked in Jade's direction. "Tell me something," he began. "How much money do you and your friends make from all these men you take advantage of?"

"What?" Jade snapped. "You're mistaken."

"Serena Jacobs is your friend, right?" Maurice continued.

"So? Since when am I responsible for what someone else does?" Jade retorted.

"Yeah, Mo," James said. "I mean, do you want to be judged by the company you keep? Remember when the city thought you were the second coming of Rae Carruth?"

Kenya waved her hand. "Don't go there. Look, guys, we're going to be a part of each other's lives for the immediate future. I'm not going to mediate arguments every time the four of us get together."

Maurice looked from Jade to James. "All right. I hope I'm wrong about you, Jade. My mother raised me better than this, so if you make my brother happy, then I guess I should mind my business."

"Thank you," James said.

"But," Maurice said, "don't let me be right."

Kenya reached out and smacked Maurice on the shoulder. "Be nice."

"I am being nice," Maurice said, sounding like a child that had been scolded by his mother.

James and Jade chuckled quietly. It was now obvious to Jade how Kenya dealt with being Mrs. Maurice Goings. She held her own with him and stood her ground when she needed to.

"All right," Kenya said. "Now all of you can get out of my office, and I can get to work."

James rose from his chair and crossed over to his sister-in-law, then gave her a quick peck on the cheek. "Thanks," he said.

Maurice stood and opened the door for the couple as they left. Jade glanced at him, wanting to tell him that he was wrong about her and her friends. Instead, she kept her thoughts to herself as she and James said good-bye.

"How did things go with Kenya?" James asked once they were in the parking lot.

"A lot better than they seemed to go with your brother."

James fanned his hand as if he were swatting away an annoying gnat. "Maurice is just being Maurice. You know, he had the nerve to hire a private investigator to check up on you and your friends."

"What?" Jade asked incredulously. "How could he invade my privacy like that?"

"I know," James said. "But you don't have anything to hide, do you?"

Jade stopped walking, placed her hands on her hips, and glared at him. "I know you better be joking. Or . . ."

James crossed over to Jade, wrapped his arms around her, and kissed her on the neck. "Of course I was joking. Why is this bothering you so much?"

"Because I don't want to have your brother looking at me as if I'm some leech on your neck, and I don't want you caught in the middle, having to choose."

"That's not going to happen," James said. "Maurice will get over it, and you and I are going to be fine."

"The stuff he said about Serena . . ."

"I don't care. You're not Serena, and whatever she has done or is doing has nothing to do with you."

She wrapped her arms around his neck. "I'm glad you feel that way."

James pulled Jade against him and thrust his pelvis into her. "I'm feeling a lot of things right now."

"You are so bad," she whispered as she felt the thickness of his erection.

"Let's get out of here and have lunch in my bed," he breathed against her ear.

James didn't have to say another word as Jade grabbed his hand and pulled him toward the parking lot.

CHAPTER 17

James and Jade entered his house, locked in each other's arms. She craved his touch as he opened the front door, and didn't want to wait until they were in the bedroom to feel the heat from his hands and the passion of his kisses. As soon as they stepped into the foyer, she slipped her hand inside his slacks. The move excited James even more than he already was. She gently stroked his shaft up and down. A soft moan escaped his throat as he backed against the wall. She unbuckled his slacks and slid them down his hips. His erection sprang forward from his boxers. Jade continued to stroke him as she dropped to her knees. Softly, she breathed against his pulsating manhood; then she took the length of him into her mouth.

James threw his head back in ecstasy as Jade sucked softly and slowly, then faster and harder. He buried his hands in her silky hair as her tongue glided across the tip of his penis. Then she took him inside her mouth again, deeper than before, and James groaned in delight as the wetness of her mouth enveloped his swollen member.

As she took him to the edge of a climax, James pulled back. "Damn," he murmured, then lifted her into his arms. James carried her to the sofa and gently laid her down. Then he pulled her skirt up to her waist. "It's my turn to taste you," he said, then planted his face between her quivering thighs. Hungrily, he lapped at her sweet juices, wrapping his tongue around the trembling bud that held her pleasure.

Shivering, she cried out in pleasure as James sucked, licked, and kissed the hidden areas between her wet folds of flesh. Just as she was about to reach her own climax, she grabbed his neck, wanting him to stop, but James kept licking, kept kissing, and Jade let nature take its course. The waves of pleasure that flowed through her body were beyond description. Every fiber of her being was touched by passion, desire, and longing. James had awakened her body in ways that she'd never known.

Pulling back, he looked up at her and licked his lips. "Delicious."

Jade wrapped her legs around his waist and let him know that she was ready to have him deep inside.

"Not here," he said. "I need more room than this sofa."

James scooped Jade into his arms and headed for the bedroom. She pressed her lips against his neck, gently kissing and licking him. James was so aroused and so ready to take her to bed that it took everything in him not to drop her before getting her between the sheets.

"You're driving me wild, baby," he said as he placed her against his soft cotton sheets. He ran his hand between her breasts, relishing the softness of her skin. He dipped his hand between her thighs and felt the wetness awaiting him.

Before he dipped inside her, James reached into his nightstand drawer and grabbed a condom. Jade watched with eager anticipation as he slid the sheath in place. He took her into his arms and kissed her with a fiery passion that made her teeth chatter. She was already hot, but his lips and tongue made her hotter. Jade grasped his shoulders, forcing him onto his back. Then she mounted his erection, taking the length of him inside her love. He held her hips, getting into a slow and steady rhythm. They rocked back and forth, enjoying the heat from one another.

She felt as if this was the first time she'd made love. James wanted to please her as much as she pleased him. They had a mutual need and desire, which weren't complete until they'd both had their fill.

James moaned as Jade moved faster. He dropped his hands, allowing her to take total control. With her head thrown back and her eyes closed, she rode him like he was a champion stallion. Over and over she called his name. His reply was an incoherent cry, alerting her to the orgasm building inside him. As he exploded, she fell against his chest, holding him tightly as she shivered from her own climax.

He kissed her gently on the collarbone. "You're amazing," he whispered.

"So are you," she replied quietly.

"Are you sure you have to go back to Atlanta tonight?" he asked.

Jade nodded. "I'm sure Serena, Alicia, and Kandace

are waiting on me so that we can figure out what our next move is with the restaurant."

James cleared his throat. "Yeah, I almost forgot about your business here."

She groaned, as if she felt an argument coming on. "James, do we have to do this?"

"We're not doing anything. I know why you all wanted that restaurant and—"

"Shh. You're about two words away from ruining the afterglow." She leaned in and kissed him on the tip of his nose.

"I hope you all can make this restaurant work," he said. "And that's all I'm going to say about it."

"Thanks. Now, can you just hold me until I have to leave?"

James tightened his embrace. "You don't have to ask me twice."

It was nearly 9 p.m. before Jade hit the road for home. Despite his best attempts at coaxing her to stay, Jade told him that she had some things she needed to take care of in Atlanta. Honestly, she didn't want to go. She wished that she could stay wrapped up in James's arms forever. But she had to face Stephen, especially since he knew that she was the reason that he couldn't purchase the restaurant that he'd been coveting for years. Of course, she wasn't going to tell James any of this, because she knew how he felt about her battle with Stephen.

Jade glanced at him as she opened her car door, waved, and smiled at him. *He'd understand if the shoe was on the other foot. I can't just let Stephen get away with what he did to me. This is business. Nothing personal,* she thought.

Still, Jade wondered if Stephen was worth all the

effort that she was putting into him. He'd made it clear that he wanted nothing to do with her, other than keeping the money he'd bilked her out of. What if James really walked out of her life because she wouldn't let this thing go?

She was about to cross the state line into South Carolina when her cell phone rang. Jade had no doubt as to who was on the other end.

"Hello, Serena," she said when she answered.

"Where are you?"

"On my way back to Atlanta. What's wrong?"

"Guess who I ran into today," Serena said.

"Who?" Jade asked, not really wanting to play a guessing game.

"Stephen. He came by my office, demanding to know how you got enough money to buy his North Carolina restaurant," Serena said smugly. "He nearly had a coronary when I told him how we're opening a restaurant there, and master chef Devon Harris is thinking of running the place."

"Is that true? How in the world did you get Devon Harris to—"

"It's not a done deal, but we're working on it," Serena admitted.

"Serena, why would you tell him that if we don't have Devon? And when did *we* decide that we were really going to do this restaurant?"

Serena sighed into the phone. "Let me get the girls on a conference call. If you'd have come back earlier, we could've talked about this. I guess you were busy with that dude."

"His name is James, and I'm getting pretty tired of your smart-ass comments about him."

"Some things are more important than your

precious boyfriend, okay? We've got to make our money back from this restaurant purchase, and it would be helpful if you were in town, since we got into this because of you."

"Don't act like you didn't have a choice," Jade snapped. "I was willing to let this go in the beginning, but you were the one who said Stephen needed to learn a lesson."

"And he does, but this is our fight and you're phoning it in."

"Whatever. Maybe we should forget about this."

"Hell no! We got a million reasons to make this thing work. You know how long we've been investing and saving money so that we could do something special with it. Now we've put it into this restaurant, and you want to quit."

"I didn't say I wanted to quit, but let's make this about more than getting revenge on Stephen."

"Sounds like James talking and not you. Hold on."

Jade waited for Serena to come on the line with Alicia and Kandace. She knew this was a conversation she didn't want to have.

"What's the deal, people?" Kandace said. "I was in the middle of something important."

"I'm sure your Twinkies will wait for you," Alicia said.

"For your information, I have a project that I'm working on, and it's cupcake night, so there," Kandace replied.

"Ladies," Serena interrupted. "We have a more pressing matter at hand. Ms. Jade is having second thoughts about things."

"That's not what I said," Jade snapped. "Look, we've been so focused on getting revenge on

Stephen, but what if we just forget about him and focus on making this restaurant work?"

"Uh-oh," Alicia said. "Sounds like somebody is going soft. Have you forgotten what Stephen did and the money he—"

"No, I haven't. That's why I'm suing him," Jade said. "But this can't be a collective thing. We're not vindictive bitches who have to prove anything to Stephen."

"But you're suing him? Why?" Serena asked. "Isn't it going to cost more to do that than to open this restaurant? Hell, we could sell the place to another developer if we can't get Devon on board."

"I'm suing him because it was my money and it's the mature thing to do," Jade replied.

"According to who? James?" Serena asked.

"All right," Kandace said. "We're not going to solve anything over the phone, and I really have some work to complete. Can we meet for breakfast in the morning?"

"Sure," Jade said. "I'm hanging up because it's dark out here and I need to focus on the road." She clicked her cell phone off before anyone could reply.

Seconds later her phone began to ring again. "Damn it," she muttered as she answered. "What now?"

"Is that how you answer the phone when you're driving?" James asked.

"I thought you were someone else," she replied, with a smile spreading across her face.

"Where are you now?" he asked.

"In the backwoods of South Carolina. I should be home in another hour."

"I really don't like you driving late like this," he said. "And I'm sorry if that sounds paternalistic."

"Are you worried about me?"

"What do you think?"

Jade continued smiling. She couldn't remember the last time she'd been treated this way or had a man in her life that was genuinely concerned about her and not just about what she could do for him. "Well, I'm a big girl, and I follow all traffic laws," she said jokingly.

"I'll bet. You don't strike me as a girl who follows the rules, and I mean that in a good way."

"Sure you do," she said, with a laugh. "And I guess you're Mr. Straitlaced."

"I used to be. You must be rubbing off on me," he quipped.

"You're confusing that with me rubbing you," she said.

"Funny. I don't want to distract you, so do me a favor and give me a shout when you arrive home so that I know you're safe."

"All right," she said. "I'll talk to you soon."

After hanging up with James, Jade pressed the gas pedal to the floor. She couldn't wait to get home so that she could crawl under the covers and call her man back.

James hung up the phone with a satisfied look on his face. But when his phone rang and he saw Maurice's number on the caller ID, his mood changed. Despite the fact that Mo had claimed that everything was squashed with Jade, he knew his brother probably had more to say. Part of him didn't want to answer the phone, but he picked it up, anyway.

"What's up?" James said.

"Is your chick still there?"

James sighed and said, "Are you talking about Jade? If you are, no."

"Sorry. Meet me at the Blake Hotel's bar. I got to tell you something."

"Do you realize that one of us has to go to work in the morning?"

"Negro, it's only eleven o'clock."

James exhaled, then agreed to meet his brother. *This man always has some damn drama going on with him.*

Fifteen minutes later, James was walking into the hotel's bar. Maurice was sitting on a stool, with a smile on his face and a bourbon in his hand.

"What's so important?" James asked.

"I'm not getting cut or traded. My agent called, and the Panthers have offered me a contract extension. Drinks are on me," Maurice announced.

"Okay, so you couldn't tell me this over the phone?" James asked as he waved for the bartender. He ordered a Crown Royal on the rocks and turned to his brother, who was still smiling like the cat who ate the canary. "What?"

"Something's going on with Kenya," Maurice said.

"What do you mean?"

"This morning she was sick. Lately, she's been eating some weird shit, and she hasn't been complaining about cramps. I think my wife is pregnant."

"Uh, don't you think she would've told you if she was?" James asked, trying not to ruin Kenya's birthday surprise.

"Maybe she doesn't know for sure. Man, if I'm

going to be a father, that is the best thing that could ever happen to me."

"Better you than me," James said.

"There you go. You know you want some kids."

"Yeah, when I get married. I refuse to be another one of those men who make babies but don't take responsibility for them. You know, like our sperm donor."

Maurice shook his head. "Don't remind me of that bastard. That's why I want a son, so I can teach him what I never learned. I just hope Kenya's ready for a family. She works so much, and then she took on that case with your lady friend. She's going to be going back and forth to Atlanta. If she's pregnant, she's going to have to quit this job."

James laughed and slapped his brother on the shoulder. "Let me know when you're going to tell her that, because that's going to be better than any TV drama. Kenya isn't quitting her job because you said so."

"Why does she need to work? I have more than enough money to . . ."

"Mo, Kenya doesn't give a damn about your money. She works hard because that's who she is. Let that woman work. I don't get you. One second you're talking about all the gold diggers in the world, and the next you want your wife to sit at home and live off you."

"That's because she's a woman that deserves to be taken care of," Maurice said. "Just like our mother, who still works at that bakery despite the fact that she doesn't have to."

"Mo, where do you come up with this caveman bullshit of yours?" James asked, with a laugh.

"Whatever. Hell, your woman might like it when you take care of her."

"Here we go with this bullshit again," James snapped as the bartender set his drink in front of him.

"I'm just saying," Maurice said. "Her friend Serena Jacobs is a piece of work. Women like that run in packs."

"I know Jade. I know who she is and what she does. She's not responsible for her friends any more than you're responsible for your cheating-ass teammates. What if everyone subscribed to the notion that all you NFL guys cheat on your wives? Then what?"

Maurice held up his glass in mock salute. "Touché."

James took a sip of his drink and shook his head at his brother. "And you act like Jade and I are getting married. Despite what I feel for her, I won't be ready for marriage anytime soon."

Maurice clanked his glass against James's. "Thank the Lord! I was really thinking that you were going to tell me next week that you and this lady were going to get married."

"Man, that's way off in the future for me. Besides, you're the family man. I'm still a bachelor, and I'm loving the single life."

"That's what you say now," Maurice said. "But when the right one comes along, you'd give it up in a heartbeat."

"Only took you nine years to figure that out, huh?" James said, with a laugh.

"Whatever. Hell, when you're young and stupid, you do dumb things. You're not that young, bro."

"Are you trying to say I'm doing something stupid?"

Maurice shrugged his shoulders and then took another sip of his drink. "You and Jade met in Vegas, started having sex immediately, and then you made it seem as if you'd fallen deeply in love with her."

"I like Jade. I could see myself falling in love with her down the road," James admitted.

"She got you, man," Maurice said.

Before James could reply, two squealing women walked over to them. "I told you it was Maurice Goings. Oh my God, you look even better in person," the taller and bustier woman said.

"Thanks," Maurice said dryly.

The woman reached out and placed her hand on Maurice's thigh. "Can I please have your autograph? I love the Panthers!"

Maurice pushed her hand away and asked the bartender for a pen and a piece of paper.

"No," the woman said as she unbuttoned her blouse. "I want you to sign here." She pressed her body as close to him as she could. Then her friend snapped a photo. Maurice eased back against the bar.

"Ladies," James said, "have a nice night and move along."

The women turned and looked at James as if he were an alien. "Who are you?" they asked. "Do you play for the Panthers, too?"

"No, I'm head of security. Keep it moving," James said as he gave the women a gentle push.

As the women walked away, they mumbled under their breath about what an asshole James was.

Maurice rose to his feet and shook his head. "On that note, I'm going home."

"You know, I'm proud of you, Mo."

"Huh?"

"I remember when you didn't turn down groupie love."

Maurice shrugged. "I got real love at the crib. I'm not risking that."

James watched his brother walk away and thought about what he'd said. Was he ready, despite saying otherwise, to have real love at home?

CHAPTER 18

Fatigue started to set in as Jade crossed the state line into Georgia. Part of her was wishing that she'd taken James up on his offer to spend another night. But she knew if she'd stayed with him tonight, she'd be taking this drive tomorrow night. Besides, leaving his arms wasn't easy.

She stopped at the Waffle House at the first exit she came across to get a cup of coffee. People could say what they wanted about the food at the twenty-four-hour restaurant, but they had the strongest coffee on the interstate, and she needed a jolt. After getting her coffee, Jade got back on the road.

As she drove, she called Kandace to see if she was still awake.

"Are you in Fulton County yet?" Kandace asked.

"What happened to hello?"

"I'll take that as a no. You and James made up. I'm really happy about that."

"So am I. Kandace, I really like him, and it's kind of scary."

"Why? You deserve a good man. Lord knows

you've been with some losers lately. James seems different. I just wish he lived in Atlanta and had a single brother."

"Please, as much as you work, when do you have time for a man?" Jade asked.

"People make time for what they want to do. Right now, I'd love to be getting done," Kandace said, with a laugh.

"What kind of project are you working on?" Jade asked.

"Trying to find Devon Harris. Serena really needs to learn how to keep her damned mouth shut sometimes. She acts as if this thing with Stephen is her fight and not yours. Do you know how awkward it's going to be for me to contact Devon?"

"That thought crossed my mind when Serena said he'd be running our restaurant. Are you okay with this?"

"This is business. All that other stuff is the distant past. Black history, if you will."

"Kandace, I know you, and I know that if you had your way, you'd still be with him."

"How about we talk about your existing love life and leave my skeletons buried?"

"Whatever you say," Jade replied.

"What's the real deal with you and James? Is this going to work from such a distance? And what happens when you get busy with the restaurant and your CPA firm?"

"How about we cross that bridge when we get to it?"

"All right, Jade. I don't want to see you get hurt again, and I would hate to have to call some of the boys in the hood that I know in North Carolina."

"Please," Jade said, with a laugh. "You are about as hood as George Bush."

"Don't doubt my gangster," Kandace said. "Anyway, do you think you two are going to make this thing work?"

"I know we are. James is making it really easy for me to fall in love with him."

"Jade, you know I say this with love, but you're forever falling in love. I think you just like the idea of being in love."

"Well, if that isn't the pot calling the kettle black," Jade said.

"Whatever. There has been only one true love of my life, and we all know how that turned out."

"That was your own fault, and I thought we were leaving your skeletons buried," Jade replied.

"I did say that, didn't I?" Kandace said. "Back to you, though. How do you know that you and James are on the same page?"

"I guess I'll find out. We're taking this thing one day, one moment at a time. Can't I just love the moment?"

"Told you. You, my friend, are addicted to love. It's just about that feeling to you. Just remember the pain that can come from this."

"It doesn't always have to be that way," Jade said wistfully.

"Whatever, Cinderella. That fairy tale you're weaving, I hope it doesn't come undone."

"Who knows, this restaurant may be the start of your own fairy tale."

"On that note, I'm going to say good-bye," Kandace said. "How far away are you now?"

"I just crossed into Gwinnett County," Jade said. "I'll be home shortly."

"Drive safe," Kandace told her, then hung up.

Jade shook her head as she placed her cell phone on the passenger seat. Kandace was just as addicted to love as she claimed Jade was. That was why they got along so well, she surmised. And that was why they needed the friendship of the cynical twins Alicia and Serena. *Yin and yang*, she thought as she took the exit for I-285.

After she got home, took off her clothes, and crawled into bed, Jade dialed James's number.

"Hello," he said groggily.

"Did I wake you?" she asked.

"Nah, I was waiting for your call."

"You're such a bad liar."

"That's a good thing, isn't it?" James said, recalling the first conversation they had in Vegas.

"Funny," she said. "Well, I made it home safely."

"That's good to hear," he said. "I was starting to get worried about you."

"I've been home long enough to crawl into bed," she said as she bounced against the mattress.

"Umm, what are you wearing?" James asked.

"Did you seriously ask me that?" Jade said through laughter.

"Seems like a proper question to me with you being in bed and all. So, tell me, Ms. Lady. What are you wearing?"

Jade looked down at her black T-shirt and over-size boxers, then said, "Nothing at all."

"Really? Because I'm wearing the exact same thing."

"Yeah?" she said, her voice taking on a low purring quality.

"And if you were here, then we'd be making slow, passionate love. I'll bet that you're wet right now."

"Hot and wet, babe," she cooed. Before she even thought about it, her hand was between her thighs, stroking the wet folds of skin, longing for James's hardness. She moaned as her finger found her throbbing bud.

"How does it feel?" James asked. "How wet is it?"

"So wet. Feels so good," she said through staccato breathing.

"Just imagine me inside of you, you on top of me. Damn, I'm hard right now. Need you, want you so badly."

Jade could only moan in response as she sped up the movement of her hand. James's labored breathing told her that he was giving himself ecstasy as well. Her legs began to quake as she imagined that he was deep inside of her, touching every spot, giving her the pleasure and passion that she'd craved since their meeting in Vegas.

"Come for me," James moaned. "Let me hear it."

"James, James," she called out.

He groaned, hinting to Jade that he'd also reached his climax. She clutched her sheets with a smile on her face, and part of her expected James to be beside her.

Sighing, she said, "I've never done this before. Never."

"Well, I'm glad that I could talk you out of your cherry."

"Ha."

"Jade," he said.

"Yes?"

"You're a helluva woman."

"And you're a damned good man," she replied. "What time is it?"

"Time for a satisfied woman to go to bed. Don't forget about Maurice's party this weekend," James said.

"Are you sure it's all right for me to be there? Your brother still has an issue with me."

"Don't worry. After this party, Mo isn't going to have an issue with anyone."

"Sounds exciting," Jade said.

"It will be," he said. "Good night."

"Good night," she said. Jade knew her dreams were going to be filled with images of James. Sleep couldn't come fast enough.

When morning came, James nearly expected to find Jade wrapped in his sheets. All night he'd dreamed that they were doing all the things they'd talked about over the phone. Looking over at the alarm clock, he realized that if he didn't get out of bed soon, he was going to be late getting into the office. He and Amber had a new project to start working on with the city of Charlotte and one of their clients who had valuable land in the Fourth Ward. The real estate market in Charlotte was booming, and James couldn't be happier, but his real thrill came from Jade.

After showering and getting dressed, James headed to Starbucks to get a cup of coffee and a muffin. Then he dashed to the office. Amber met him at the door, with a worried look on her face.

"What's wrong, sunshine?" he asked his trusted assistant.

"There's a man here demanding to see you," she said in a hushed tone.

"Who is he?"

"Says his name is Stephen Carter, and he wants to talk about that restaurant we just sold."

James sipped his coffee. Stephen Carter was the last person he wanted to see, and he damned sure didn't want to give him an audience about the restaurant that Jade and her friends had outbid him on.

"Get rid of him," James said.

"It's not going to be that easy, Goings," Stephen said, appearing behind Amber. "What the hell are you doing?"

"Amber, excuse me for a moment," said James.

Amber quickly ducked out of the way, as if she could feel the sparks shooting between the men.

James brushed past Stephen, set his coffee and muffin on the edge of Amber's desk, and then he focused his gaze on Stephen. "Hell of a nerve coming here," James said.

"You're one to talk about someone having nerve. Chasing my sloppy seconds these days?"

"Five minutes, dude, and I'm not going to be able to control what happens to your punk ass."

Stephen stepped back. "Why don't you let go of the past? You sold my future to that bi—"

Before he knew it, James had reared back and clocked Stephen in the jaw with a right hook.

Stumbling backward, Stephen held his jaw. "You son of a bitch," he spat. Then he lunged at James, grabbing him around his neck.

James countered the move with a knee to Stephen's midsection. Stephen fell backward, clutching his stomach in pain. James stopped himself from stomping him while he was on the floor. He yanked Stephen up by his lapels.

"Get the hell out of my office, and don't show your face around here again," James hissed.

Stephen shook free of James's grasp. "You will be hearing from my attorney." He straightened his jacket and headed out the door. James looked down at his hand and saw that his knuckles were starting to swell. Amber returned to her desk and balked at the mess she saw.

"Are you all right?" she asked, her eyes wide in disbelief that James had gotten into a fight. "Who was that guy?"

"Someone who doesn't need to come in this office ever again. If you see him in the parking lot, call the police," James said in a growl.

Amber stepped back from him, surprised at the anger that he was showing. James had always been the calm diplomat.

He turned to his assistant and offered her a lopsided smile. "I'm sorry," he said. "That guy and I have a rocky past. He tried to cheat my mother in Atlanta after she'd done nothing but help his punk ass."

"Knew it had to be something, because this isn't like you."

"Why don't you go have some coffee or something while I clean this up?" James said. "I'll even pay." He pulled out his wallet and handed her a twenty-dollar bill.

Amber took the money and headed out the door to Starbucks. James looked at his overturned coffee cup and mashed-up muffin. He hated that he had let Stephen get the best of him. That was something that Maurice would've done. *Guess we're more alike than I want to admit,* he thought as he tossed the remnants of his breakfast in the trash.

As he was mopping up the coffee with a rag, Maurice walked in.

"What happened in here?" Maurice asked.

"Stephen Carter happened."

"What was that son of a bitch doing here?" Maurice asked hotly.

James focused his stare on Maurice and sighed as he picked up an overturned chair, then said, "He was here because of Jade."

"What does she have to do with . . . I forgot, they used to date. You have to wonder about a woman that would date—"

"Shut up, really," James said. "Because my fist isn't too swollen to punch you in the face, too."

Maurice folded his arms across his chest and shook his head. "I hate that I wasn't here to see thieving Stephen get what he deserved. Seriously, though, what did she see in him? Stephen's a liar and a fake. You claim she's a smart woman. How did she get—"

"I got two words for you," James interrupted. "Lauryn Michaels."

Maurice rolled his eyes. "When are you going to let that go?"

"As soon as you stop acting as if you've never made a mistake. That's what Jade did, and she admits it."

"Whatever. So, you two got into a fight over Jade, I take it?"

"Something like that," James admitted. He sighed

and told Maurice the entire story about Jade and her friends purchasing the restaurant that Stephen had wanted to take over in Charlotte.

"So, those women had a million dollars to spend on a restaurant that isn't even worth all of that? And they did it so Stephen couldn't bring his bland food to town? Umm, I think I'm starting to like Jade more and more." Maurice laughed. "Seems like she's making up for her lack of judgment."

"You *would* think something like that," James said as he took a seat on the edge of Amber's desk. "If she's over him, why the need for revenge?"

"Because some women are vindictive and evil. Maybe your dream woman is one of them," Maurice said.

"Whatever. He stole from her."

"Isn't that why my wife took her case? Kenya's actually going to Atlanta this afternoon."

"Maybe you should go with her," James suggested snidely.

Maurice slapped his hand against the desk and laughed. "You know I am, and I'm going to tell Ma all about your new girlfriend."

James pointed his finger in his brother's face. "You'd better not."

"I owe you. Who told Ma that Kenya and I got back together? Not me. It was you. Turnabout is fair play, dude."

James shook his head. "Hell no. I can imagine what you're going to say to Ma about Jade."

Maurice smiled. "I guess you'll find out when she calls you."

James tossed a pen at his brother, who caught it as if he were on the football field. "Don't play with me."

"I'm not going to say much. I mean, it's Ma."

"You just better not play the showgirl card again," James warned. "Why are you here, anyway?"

"I came to drop off these contracts from the city," Maurice said. "This morning I actually got up and did some work."

James took the folder from his brother's hands and looked over the paperwork. "I'm impressed. No wonder it's so damned cold outside."

"Shut up. Anyway, what are you going to do about Stephen? Because you know that jerk isn't going to just go away."

"I'm not worried about him," James said. "Besides, he's going to have his hands full with Jade and her crew."

CHAPTER 19

Jade walked into Kandace's office, smiling as if she'd won a huge Powerball jackpot.

"Maybe you need to spend more time in Charlotte with James," Kandace said when she noticed the look on her friend's face. "But I won't say that in front of your evil friend."

Jade waved her hand as if to swat away a fly. "I'm not concerned about what Serena thinks about me and James. He's special."

"Um, let's get out of here. I want something sweet and fattening," Kandace said, then patted her hip. "Even if I don't need it."

"Girl, please, you could stand to put a little meat on your bones."

"Says the chick with the perfect figure," Kandace joked. "There's this bakery in Sweet Auburn that makes delicious cinnamon buns that melt in your mouth."

"Really?" Jade said. "So, I guess that means you're driving."

"How about I'll pay your fare on MARTA? I'm not

losing my spot in the parking lot," Kandace said as she rose from her seat.

"Fine," Jade said. "But you should really try to drive more often. Then maybe you'd increase your skills."

"I know you're not talking. Didn't you come to a complete stop on the interstate a few days ago? What driving coach taught you that skill?"

"Whatever," Jade said. "I've been thinking about our restaurant today."

"Uh-huh," Kandace said as they stepped onto the elevator. "We're going to need a great general manager. Someone who's good with customers, chefs, and money."

"Let me guess. You're willing to move to Charlotte and run the place."

Jade smiled and nodded. "Yes, and before you say I'm following James, I want to point out that I was going to be hands-on when Stephen was opening a restaurant in Charlotte, too."

"Sure you were, but I doubt that you were going to move there."

"That's true, but it's not as if I have a job here. Why not? I can protect our investment and make sure we get the most bang for our buck."

"And you can bang James Goings as much as you like on the side," Kandace said, with a smile. "I think it's a good idea. But what about your CPA firm?"

"The only thing that came out of my relationship with Stephen is the fact that I know I love working in the restaurant industry."

"That's good," Kandace said. "At least we'll know that the person running our restaurant isn't going to rob us blind."

"That's right. We're going to split the profits, and we're going to make a lot of money," Jade said.

"We'd better. Not that I think this isn't a good investment, but that was all our money, which we've been saving for years. I hope that we make it back."

"We're going to make it all back. Charlotte's a growing city, and you know people don't cook anymore. If we make our restaurant down-home and upscale, we can appeal to the whole city."

Kandace nodded, impressed with Jade. "You have been thinking of something other than James. Good job."

"Anyway," Jade continued, "I'm going to Charlotte this weekend, and I'm going to spend a few days in town and look at some of the most successful restaurants in the city and see what they do best and what some of their weaknesses are."

"And while you're there, you're going to wrap yourself in James's arms and let him make mad, passionate love to you," Kandace said, as if she were reading from a script.

"Don't hate me because I have a man."

"A good man," Kandace said. "I like James. I feel like he's a good guy for you."

"That's good to hear. I'm glad one of my friends is happy for me," Jade said as they headed out the door.

Kandace and Jade made it to the MARTA station just as the train was pulling in. "Perfect timing," Kandace said as she paid their fares.

They got on the train and took the first pair of empty seats they found.

"So," Jade said, "have you found Devon?"

"Yes," Kandace said. "Or I found his people, who

are giving me the runaround. I can't help but wonder if he's just avoiding me."

"Maybe you should let Serena try and get in contact with him."

"And mix oil and water? I thought we wanted the man to run our kitchen. You know what? You're going to be the general manager. You get in contact with him. I'll give you his contact information, and you handle it."

"Fine," Jade said. "I've always liked Devon. What ever happened between you two?"

"I really don't want to have this conversation. Especially on the train."

Jade looked around and noticed that an older man in a seat near them was hanging on their every word. She nodded at the man, who quickly turned forward in his seat. Kandace and Jade broke out laughing.

"Too funny," Jade said.

"It's the South. People listen and voice their opinions, especially on the train."

"Well, we're not going to be on the train forever, so you buy the sweets, I'll buy the coffee, and you spill your guts."

"How about no to the gut spilling, but yes to the coffee?"

Jade shook her head and silently vowed to get to the bottom of Kandace's situation with Devon.

"Well, this is a surprise," Maryann said as Maurice and Kenya walked into the bakery. "What brings you two to Atlanta?"

"I'm working on a case here," Kenya said as she hugged her mother-in-law.

Maurice hugged his mother when the two women stepped apart from each other. "And you know, I wasn't going to let her come here alone," he said after kissing his mother's cheek.

"It's good to see you two, together and happy," Maryann said, with a wide smile on her face. "Mo, since you're here, why don't you take over the register for me so Kenya and I can talk?"

"I already know about the party this weekend," he said as the women headed for a table near the window.

"He's so nosy," Kenya said. "Can't keep anything from him." She gave her mother-in-law a wink.

Maryann scrunched up her face, and Kenya leaned into her. "He doesn't know about the baby yet," she whispered.

Kenya shook her head.

"Good."

Seconds later, after Maurice had taken his spot at the register, the bell chimed as Jade and Kandace walked into the bakery.

"I love this place," Kandace said. "In the morning you can barely get . . ."

"What?" Jade asked as she followed her friend's gaze.

"Isn't that your man's brother at the register?" Kandace whispered.

"Let's go someplace else," Jade said.

Before they could leave, Maurice spotted them at the door. "Jade?" he called out. "What a surprise."

Jade and Kandace walked to the register and

smiled at him. "It's more of a surprise to see you working," Jade said.

"My mother and my wife wanted to talk about me without me hearing it," he said.

Kandace grinned. "Your mother? Wow, I never had a clue that this was your mother's place. I come here all the time."

"These pastries are addictive," Maurice said. "I'm sorry. What's your name?"

"Kandace Davis," she said, extending her hand to him. "It's nice to meet you, but I got to tell you, I can't stand the way you light up the Falcons' secondary."

Maurice laughed. "Just doing my job," he said. "What can I get for you ladies?"

"Where's James?" Jade asked.

"In Charlotte," he said. "He was talking about you this morning."

Jade wanted to ask Maurice why he was being so nice to her, but she figured that he was just trying to put on an act for his mother.

"Can we get two of those big cinnamon buns?" Kandace asked. "And my girl is paying for two large cups of coffee." She nudged Jade in the ribs.

"All right," Maurice said. "And I'll take care of this."

"No, we're going to pay our own way," Jade said as she reached into her purse and pulled out her credit card. "This is for the buns and the coffee."

"Jade," Kandace said in a whisper. "What's wrong with you?"

"Nothing," Jade said as Maurice ran her credit card through the machine.

Maurice fixed their orders and handed them to the women. "Here you go," he said, then handed Jade the receipt for her signature.

She signed it quickly and offered Maurice a plastic smile. *Gold dig that,* she thought bitterly.

"Hey, Ma," Maurice called out. "Come meet James's girlfriend."

"What?" Maryann said, looking at the counter.

Jade's face heated up, as if someone had lit a match underneath her chin. "Maurice," she growled.

Maryann walked over to the counter and stood in front of Jade and Kandace. "Hello, ladies," she said.

"Hello," Kandace said as she broke off a piece of her pastry.

"Hi," Jade said.

"So," Maryann said, rocking back on her heels, "who's dating my son?"

Jade laughed nervously. "That would be me. I'm Jade Christian," she said.

"You're very pretty," Maryann said. "It's nice to meet you."

Kandace laughed. "Mrs. Goings, I love this shop, and these buns are just divine."

"Well, thank you, and you can call me Maryann," she said, but her eyes never left Jade's smiling face.

"I had no idea that you owned this place," Jade said. "I was hoping that James and I would see you together." She turned and shot an evil look at Maurice, who was smiling like the cat that ate the canary.

"Let me tell you something about my boys," Maryann said. "They like to tell each other's business. Do you know how I found out that Maurice and Kenya were back together? James came in here and told me over a batch of blueberry muffins."

Jade laughed, still nervous that she'd met James's mother without him. What if he didn't want his mother to know about them? And did James really call her his girlfriend, as Maurice had said?

Kenya walked over to Jade, with a smile on her face. "Don't let Maurice bother you," she said. "He's harmless."

"If you say so," Jade replied. "Are you here about the case?"

"Yes, I'm filing it with the clerk today if things don't go right with Stephen's lawyer. I'm going to try and broker a settlement. One thing I've learned about people is that they don't want a lot of bad publicity."

"Stephen probably isn't going to care," Jade remarked.

"You aren't talking about Stephen Carter, are you?" Maryann asked.

Jade nodded.

"That is one misguided cookie," Maryann said as she stepped behind the counter, relieving Maurice from his duties. "Can I get you ladies anything else? Kenya, you want to try one of my new creations, lemon-blueberry tart with vanilla icing?"

"That sounds good," Kenya said as she walked to the counter.

Jade and Kandace took a seat at an empty table near the window. "So, you really don't like Maurice, huh?" Kandace asked.

"He doesn't like me, either. Do you know that he had us investigated?"

"Investigated?" Kandace flashed a look at Maurice and shook her head. "What did he have us investigated for?"

"Because he thinks we're a band of gold diggers out to steal his brother's money and use the Goings name for our own purposes. That's why I didn't want to get these cinnamon buns for free. However, you will be giving me my money back," Jade said.

"Whatever," Kandace said as she took a big bite of her bun. "I don't turn down free food, so you're out of luck this time."

Jade rolled her eyes and took a small bite of her bun. The sweet pastry melted in her mouth, and she took an even bigger bite. "This is great," she mumbled between bites.

Kandace nodded. "That's why I'm a size ten now."

"And there's nothing wrong with your shape. What's really going on with you right now?" Jade asked.

"Nothing," Kandace said. "As a matter of fact, we'd better get going so that I can give you Devon's contact information and before I order another bun."

"I'm getting one to go," Jade said. "By the way, does this whole 'I hate my body' kick have anything to do with Devon?"

"Did I say anything about Devon? You go say good-bye to your 'mother-in-law,' and I'll meet you outside."

Jade drained the remainder of the coffee and headed to the register. Kenya was sitting at the counter, devouring a slice of tart and sipping a glass of milk.

"Leaving so soon?" Kenya asked.

"Yes, Kandace and I are trying to line up a celebrity chef for the restaurant. What we really need is to bring Mrs. Goings back with us," Jade said.

"My sons have been trying to get me to Charlotte since Maurice was picked by the Panthers, but I love

Atlanta too much to leave," Maryann said. "Want to try my tart?" She held a slice of the golden pastry out to Jade, who happily accepted the sample.

"This is delicious," said Jade as she chewed the crisp pastry.

"Thank you. I love baking and making new flavors," Maryann said. "So, how did you and James meet?"

"We were both on vacation in Las Vegas and ran into each other," Jade said, saving the more salacious details.

"Oh, well, that's interesting. My son hasn't told me a thing about you, though," Maryann confessed.

"Are you surprised?" Maurice asked as he fixed himself a cup of coffee. "James doesn't share anyone's business but mine. And he's been busy at work. You know, Jade is a businesswoman. She and her friends are opening a restaurant in Charlotte."

Jade shook her head as she looked at Maurice.

He continued talking. "Our company helped Jade and her people find a restaurant in the Cherry community."

"Maurice," Maryann said. "Boy, hush."

Jade was glad his mother had quieted him because she was a little afraid of what was going to come out of his mouth next. "Well," Jade said, "I have to get going. But I'd love to get a few of those cinnamon buns to go."

Maryann boxed up three buns for Jade and threw in two slices of the tart.

Jade looked at Maurice. "Why are you being so nice to me?" she whispered.

"Because my mother's here," he joked. "No, I can admit that I was wrong about you. Anyone that can beat Stephen Carter at his own game is all right in my book."

Jade folded her arms across her chest and eyed him suspiciously. "Really?"

Maurice leaned into her and whispered, "I hate that man more than James does, and my only regret is that I wasn't the one who kicked his ass this morning."

"What?" Jade asked.

"Jade," Maryann said, "here's your order."

Jade headed to the register, trying to wrap her mind around the fact that James had gotten into a fight with Stephen. What in the hell was Stephen doing in Charlotte, anyway? After paying for her order, Jade headed outside.

"Took you long enough," Kandace said. "They grilled you, didn't they?"

"No," Jade said. "I've got to call James, though. You go back to the office, and I'll meet you there."

"Is everything all right?" Kandace asked.

Jade nodded as she reached into her bag and pulled out her cell phone.

James leaned back in his leather chair, with his eyes closed and his hand buried in a bucket of ice. When his cell phone rang, he nearly turned the bucket over to grab the phone from the center of his desk.

"Yeah?" he said.

"Hello to you, too," Jade said.

"How are you doing?" James asked, sticking his hand deeper into the ice bucket.

"The question is, how are you doing? I heard that you were playing Mike Tyson today," she said.

"You heard what?"

"I was down in Sweet Auburn and ran into your mother and your brother, who told me that you and Stephen were fighting today."

"That damned Maurice," James muttered. "So you met my mother?"

"She's a nice woman and I love her cinnamon buns."

"What did Maurice tell her about you?"

"Only that you want to marry me and have lots of babies," she joked.

"What?" James grunted, sitting up in his chair and overturning the ice bucket.

"I'm joking," Jade said. "But did you really get into a fight with Stephen?"

"Yeah, and I have a swollen fist to prove it," he said. "The dude showed up at my office and . . ." James didn't want to tell Jade that the fight had been over her and the disrespectful things that he'd said about her.

"What?" she asked.

"We just don't get along, and some old feelings came up that caused me to deck that dude," he said. "I hate that I didn't get to introduce you to my mother."

"Your brother was nice about it. A little shocking, though."

"Maurice was nice? That's a first," James said, with a laugh. "We're still on for Saturday, right?"

"I wouldn't miss it, because I can't wait to see you. Just promise me, there will be no more fighting."

"As long as your boy stays in Fulton County, I won't be throwing any more punches."

"Good," she said. "Oh, and you should've told

me that your mother is such a great baker. I'm going to be coming down to Auburn Avenue every day for these cinnamon buns."

"Those things are good. Mo and I used to fight over them all the time. I tell you what. See if you can bring some of the cinnamon drizzle with you this weekend. I have an idea as to where it would taste delicious."

Jade laughed. "And just how am I going to ask your mother for that?"

"Easy," he replied, with a laugh.

"I've got to go. The train will be here soon."

When James said good-bye to Jade, he picked up his office phone and dialed the bakery so that he could take his lumps from his mother like a big boy. He knew that when his brother came back to town, he was going to get him for telling his mother about Jade.

CHAPTER 20

Two days after Kenya filed the lawsuit against Stephen, Jade was getting ready to head to Charlotte, armed with the icing from Maryann, confidence that Devon Harris was going to meet with her on Sunday, because he was in Charlotte with celebrity chef Marvin Woods, and a smug feeling, knowing that Stephen had been served and he was losing. Just as she packed her last piece of lingerie in her overnight bag, the intercom buzzed.

"Yes?" she said into the speaker, expecting to hear one of her girlfriends on the other end.

"Jade, it's Stephen. We need to talk."

"I have nothing to say to you," she barked into the speaker. "You can talk to my attorney."

"This is madness," he said. "If anyone should be suing someone, it should be me."

"What?"

"Do you really want me to stand out here talking about our business, or are you going to be mature and invite me in?"

"I'll come down there, because I'm on my way

out." Jade smoothed her hand across her black leather dress, which skimmed her knees; then she grabbed her bag and purse. She glanced at herself in the mirror as she headed for the door, then shook her head. She didn't give a damn what Stephen thought about her outfit or anything else. Why was he even here?

When she got out to the street, Jade was shocked to see Stephen with a black eye; then she remembered that he and James had fought earlier. She didn't hide her smug smile as she walked up to him.

"You have five minutes to say whatever you have to say," she spat.

"I don't even need that much time. I'm willing to give you the fifty thousand dollars you claim to have invested in my company in exchange for the property in Charlotte, and we'll be even."

"You're insane," Jade said, then attempted to push past him. "I'll see you in court."

Stephen grabbed her arm. "I have lawyers, too, and your little boyfriend isn't going to like it when I have him locked up for assault. It's funny that he was trying to defend your honor when you have none. But that's just like James. Always trying to play Captain Save a Ho."

Jade snatched her arm away from him and was tempted to punch him in his other eye. "You're such a sleazy bastard. I don't know what I ever saw in a slime like you."

Stephen shook his head. "You thought I was your meal ticket," he said. "You and that crew of yours are nothing but gold diggers. I know it, and that's why I got rid of you."

"The only gold digger I see is your thieving ass,"

Jade said, then stomped on his foot, putting all her weight on the stiletto heel of her boot. Stephen doubled over in pain, and Jade pushed him to the ground. Then she walked away as if she hadn't done anything wrong.

Stephen was going to be a problem, and as much as she didn't want to admit it, she had opened this can of worms when she decided to go after him. *James was right,* she thought as she climbed into her car. *It was never worth all this.*

James walked into the hotel ballroom where Kenya was decorating for Maurice's party. When he saw his sister-in-law standing on a stepladder, hanging a banner, he rushed to her side.

"What are you doing?" James asked as he lifted her from the stepladder.

"Decorating, since you're late."

"Superwoman, you know you could've waited." James hopped up on the stepladder and slapped the HAPPY BIRTHDAY, MAURICE banner in place.

"I thought you had gotten caught up with Jade or something. She's good for you, James," she said.

"What makes you say that?" he asked as he stepped off the stepladder.

"I haven't seen you smile this much in years. That's a beautiful thing when someone can touch your heart in that way."

"Jade is special. Who knew this was going to turn out like this?"

"So, will there be wedding bells soon?"

James shook his head and laughed. "Why do you

married women feel that it is your duty to marry off every single person within a ten-mile radius of you?"

"Whatever," Kenya said, then tossed a balloon at him. "I just want you to be as happy as I am."

"Well, marriage is not on my radar right now. And thankfully, Jade isn't one of those 'marry me now' women. We're taking our time and getting to know each other. There's no dash to the altar."

Kenya shrugged her shoulders. "If you say so. She is coming tonight, right?"

"Yes. Speaking of tonight, I got to go get the baby cake," James said as he made a dash for the door. "Don't try and hang anything else until I get back."

Kenya offered up a mock salute and continued blowing up balloons.

As soon as James got into the car, his cell phone rang. Grabbing the phone, he knew it was Jade before he said hello.

"I'm running late," she said.

"Where are you?"

"Greenville. I meant to be there before now, because I have a surprise for you."

"What's that?" he asked.

"Why would I tell you now?" she stated. "It sort of defeats the purpose of a surprise."

"You have a smart mouth for someone that needs a place to stay," he joked.

"Trust me, you're going to be more than willing to open your home and more to me."

"This must be one hell of a surprise."

Jade laughed. "Do you want me to meet you at your house or . . . Where is the party?"

"The Blake Hotel. Meet me at my house. I'm going

to get Kenya's surprise cake for Mo. Then I'll be home waiting for you."

"All right. I'll see you in a little bit," she said.

James couldn't get to the bakery fast enough. He wanted to make sure he dropped the cake off with his sister-in-law because he had the feeling that he was going to be late for the party.

About two hours later, after the baby cake was hidden and the ballroom decorated with silver and blue balloons, streamers, and banners, James arrived at his house at the same time Jade did.

He rose from the car and waited for Jade to exit hers. When she got out, James drank in her divine image, loving the short leather dress that she wore. The knee-high red boots set the black outfit off perfectly.

"Wow," he said. "I certainly hope you didn't stop on the way here."

"Why do you say that?"

"Because some man is somewhere having a hell of a fantasy about those legs, those boots, and this," James said as he pulled Jade against his body. He kissed her hard and deep. He cupped her round bottom, slipping his hand underneath her dress. He felt the silkiness of her skin and realized that she was wearing a thong. A shiver ran up his spine and caused his manhood to spring forward.

Jade stepped back from him, feeling his arousal. "We're never going to make it to the party if you kiss me like that again," she said throatily.

He brushed his lips against her in defiance. "I really don't care about a party right now," he growled.

"But I'm sure you want to be there for Kenya's surprise, right? And trust me, it's totally worth the wait."

James released her, then reached in the car to grab her overnight bag. "Speaking of surprises, where is mine?"

"After the party," she promised as they walked into the house. "I saw your mother yesterday. Those cinnamon buns are really good. I wonder if she'd allow us to sell her cinnamon buns on the weekends. Charlotte would be blessed with a little piece of Atlanta."

"We'll have to ask her about that next weekend," James said.

"Next weekend?"

"Yeah, I'm coming to town so that I can officially introduce you to my mother."

Jade smiled and didn't tell him that she and his mother had already become fast friends. She wondered if they'd be going out to dinner with his mother if Maurice hadn't spilled the beans. *Don't do this,* she told herself as James headed into the house. *You're having a good time. Don't read more into it.*

"All right. I'm going to get dressed," James said. Then he stole a quick kiss from Jade's plump lips.

As James dashed down the hall to his bedroom, Jade took a seat on the sofa, smiling about the package of icing she had tucked away in her bag. She couldn't wait until this party was over, because she wanted to feel James's arms wrapped around her and his lips against her neck. Closing her eyes, Jade thought about the moment she and James would walk through the door after the party and how she was going to change out of her dress and into a strapless, black lace teddy and matching three-inch pumps. Then she would pull out the icing, and they could take turns tasting it.

"Jade," James said, "you ready?"

She rose from the sofa and looked at him, drinking in his image. He was dressed in a pair of dark jeans, a collared white shirt, and a houndstooth sports coat. His look was sharp and classic. Jade could not wait until those clothes were out of her way.

"Yeah, let's go," she said.

They headed to the car and drove to the hotel in uptown Charlotte.

When James parked, Jade smiled. "This hotel is nice, but didn't it used to be something else?"

"Yeah, it was the Adam's Mark for years," he said as they exited the car. "Kenya has the ballroom decked out, and I'm sure that Maurice is in there, hamming it up."

Jade smiled. "It was really nice of Kenya to do all this for him. And I'm glad I got to see another side of your brother."

"Mo's all bark and no bite. He didn't even want this party, but when Kenya gives him his surprise, he's going to be very happy."

James placed his arm around Jade's waist and walked into the hotel. The party was in full swing as the couple entered the ballroom. Most of Maurice's offensive line was there with their wives or the flavor of the moment. Kenya and Maurice were tucked in a corner, sharing a kiss.

"They're sickening," James whispered to Jade.

"Someone sounds jealous," she said as she rubbed her hand across his chest. "I'll kiss you now if you want me to."

"Kiss me and we're out of here," James breathed against her ear.

Homer walked up to the happy couple just as

Jade was about to lay a kiss on James. "Well, well, well, if it isn't Ms. Cardsharp."

Jade turned around and faced Homer. "Still bitter, I see," she said, with a smile.

"Next time we play cards, I need you on my side," Homer replied.

"No, my brother," James said. "Jade's *my* ace. You got to get your own."

"Hater," Homer said. "This is a nice party. A little more subdued than a regular Mo bash."

"What do you expect from a boring married man?" Smitty, a wide receiver, asked when he walked up to Homer, James, and Jade. He leered at Jade, licking his lips as if she were on the buffet table. "And who are you?"

James was about to say something but shook his head instead.

Jade, on the other hand, said, "Someone you don't and will never know."

"Ooh," Homer said. "Smit, you want to pick that up?"

Scowling, a disgruntled Smitty asked, "Pick up what?"

"Your dignity," Homer bellowed.

James and Jade laughed before moving away from them. They headed for Kenya and Maurice.

"Get a room," James said as he slapped his brother on the knee.

"It's about time you got here," Kenya said as she and Maurice broke off their kiss.

"Happy birthday, bro," James said as Maurice stood up and they embraced.

"Yeah, man," Maurice said. "This is a great party."

Kenya stood up and smoothed her silver dress.

James smiled at her formfitting outfit and figured that she wore it because in the next few months, she wasn't going to be able to wear a dress like that. "James," she said, "I need you to get the thing."

James nodded and headed to the back, where he'd hidden the baby cake.

Kenya turned to Maurice and Jade. "I'm going onstage. You two play nice."

"I'm always nice," Maurice said, with a smile. He reached for his rum and Coke. "Having a good time, Jade?"

"The best," Jade told him.

"Thanks for coming. I really mean that. You seem to make my brother happy, and that's all I want for him."

"Is that so?" she asked. "I don't understand you. I mean, you've been pretty nasty to me, and this total one-eighty is catching me off guard."

"I was wrong," Maurice said. "I'll admit that. Forgive me if I have some trust issues when it comes to women."

"Well, you can't keep judging us by what one woman did," Jade said as she took a glass of champagne from a waiter's tray as he passed her.

"That's true, and thank God my brother doesn't think like me. He would've left a good thing in Vegas."

Jade tapped her glass against Maurice's. "Thank goodness." She was about to take a sip when the lights went up and everyone's attention was focused on Kenya, who had a microphone in her hand.

"Thank you all for coming to celebrate my husband's birthday," Kenya said. "He looks good for an old man."

The crowd laughed.

"This was supposed to be a surprise party, but if you know Mo, you know the brother is nosy and he found out about the party," Kenya revealed.

"Yeah!" Maurice called out and lifted his glass.

"But I know something you don't know, Mo," Kenya said. "As a matter of fact, come up here, darling."

Maurice bounded toward the stage and hopped up next to his wife. "What's up, babe?"

"I have a special present for you," Kenya told him.

James headed toward the stage, holding the box with the baby cake in it.

"Let me have it," Maurice said as he stole a quick kiss from Kenya's cheek.

James opened the box just as Kenya said, "I'm pregnant."

Maurice's mouth fell open, and then he scooped his wife up into his arms and hugged her tightly. James motioned for a waiter to come over and take the cake so that he could take a picture of his brother and sister-in-law.

Jade smiled as she watched the exchange between James, Maurice, and Kenya. They were really cute, and she wondered if James wanted all of this. Would he be as happy as Maurice if he was about to be a father? She shook her head. She and James weren't ready to do what Kenya and Maurice were doing. They weren't married, and that wouldn't be on the horizon anytime soon.

James crossed over to her and wrapped his arms around her waist. "Ready to go?" he whispered.

"That was really cute," Jade said. "What Kenya did."

"Uh-huh," he said as he brushed his lips against her neck. "So, you want some cake, or are we getting out of here?"

Jade turned around and smiled at James. "Why are you so ready to go?"

He took her hand and surreptitiously slipped it into his pants. "Because," he said.

When she felt his hardness, Jade was ready to leave as well. "I guess we'd better tell your brother and your sister-in-law good night," she said, with a smile on her face.

CHAPTER 21

Jade and James rushed back to his place, ready to get out of their clothes and into each other's arms.

"Where's my surprise?" he asked as they walked into the foyer.

She flashed him an alluring smile. "Wait right here," she said.

Jade dashed down the hall and into James's bedroom. She fished her teddy out of her overnight bag, then slipped out of her dress and stepped into the sexy black garment she'd purchased just for him. Then she reached into the side of the bag and removed the icing she'd gotten from his mother's bakery. Jade smiled as she looked at the squeeze bag and remembered the tale she'd told his mother about baking some buns of her own for James this weekend. There was no way she was going to tell Maryann Goings that she wanted to lick the sweet icing from her son's heavenly body.

"James," she cooed as she walked into the living room. His eyes widened as he drank in her image.

Her breasts sat up perfectly, and the black lace and satin made her caramel skin glow.

James crossed over to her and engulfed her in his arms. "Damn, baby," he said.

Jade held the icing up. "And here's your surprise," she said. She squeezed the bag, sending a line of icing down her chest. She stuck her finger in the white, creamy icing and held it out to James. He seductively licked the sweet icing from her index finger.

"Delicious," he said, then licked the line of icing from the middle of her chest.

Shivers ran up and down her spine as his tongue traveled down the center of her chest. With one hand, he pushed the top of her strapless teddy down, exposing her perky breasts. She squeezed icing across the tops of her breasts, then rubbed it down to her nipples as James hungrily eyed her. Slowly, he licked the icing from her bosom, sucking her nipples until all the sweetness was gone. Jade moaned, quaking as he alternated between breasts. Then he slipped his free hand between her legs and unsnapped the crotch. He entered her wetness with his finger, seeking out her throbbing bud. Jade moaned in delight as his finger found her pleasure point. He backed her against the wall and took the icing from her hands.

"This tastes a lot better on you than on any cinnamon bun," he said.

"I wonder what it tastes like on you," she whispered as she unbuttoned his shirt.

James squeezed a line of icing down the center of his chest as she pushed his shirt off his shoulders. She leaned into him and leisurely licked the creamy icing from his chest. Then she ran her tongue across his pecs, circling his nipples as he pushed her teddy down to the floor.

Now kissing his neck, Jade reached down and unsnapped and unzipped his fly and massaged his manhood through his silk boxers. He lifted her up and wrapped her legs around his waist.

"I need you," he whispered in her ear.

"You got me," she replied throatily.

With grace fueled by desire and need, James stepped out of his pants. His erection hung from the opening in the front of his boxers, ready to melt with Jade's wetness. Though he was tempted to enter her, to feel the heat of her body around him, he knew they had to be protected. So, instead, he lifted her hips to his lips, and with her back against the wall, he pressed his lips against the wet folds of skin that hid her desire. With his hot tongue lashing her sensitivity, Jade nearly lost it. Her legs trembled and she clawed at the wall.

James indulged in tasting her, as if she were the icing that they'd nibbled on earlier. He kissed slow and deep, darting his tongue in and out of her, all the while savoring her tangy juices as she came over and over again. Jade cried out, begging James to stop, because what she was feeling was beyond description, sinfully delightful. Her body went limp as he ignored her cries and continued lapping her juices. Finally, James ended his extended kiss and looked into Jade's satisfied face. When he lowered her to the floor, she stumbled a bit and wrapped her arms around his neck.

"You beat icing any day," he said as he cupped her bare bottom and pulled her against his hardness.

"Umm," she moaned, her throat too dry to speak.

James picked her up and carried her into the bedroom. Once he laid her against the sheets, he reached into his nightstand and retrieved a condom.

Jade looked up at James while he slid the latex barrier in place. Being with him was so easy, so comfortable, and everything unexpected. It was almost as if she was living that fairy-tale life that she'd dreamed about on those riverboats.

"Are you okay?" he asked once he caught her gaze.

"Yes, everything is fine." She stretched her arms out to him.

James lowered himself on the bed, wrapped up in Jade's embrace. He gently kissed her neck as she stroked his back lovingly. Jade parted her lips, inviting his tongue inside. She tasted her essence on his lips as she sucked his tongue, urging him to give her more. James responded to her kiss with his hands, wrapping them around her waist and pulling her hips against his. Their tongues bounced off each other's, jockeying for position in their passionate kiss. Jade spread her legs as she felt James's manhood throbbing against her thighs. She wanted him, needed him to be inside her. She wanted to melt with him, wanted their souls to become one as they rocked back and forth, giving each other untold pleasure. Was this happening too fast? Was she supposed to feel this way about him so soon after their meeting?

James thrust into her body, making her call out his name. He rotated his hips, touching every spot that made her scream. They fell into a sensual rhythm that was like a dance. Sweat covered their bodies as they rocked on.

"You feel so good," James groaned, nearly on the verge of climax.

Jade's only response was a moan, because she was in the middle of her third orgasm. Wrapping her legs around his waist, she gently nudged him so that he would roll over and give her a chance to take control. He held her hips, slowing her down to a gentle grind, which pushed him over the edge. He covered her nipples with his lips, then circled them with his tongue as she ground her body against his.

"Oh, James," she cried, reaching her own climax. She collapsed against his chest, closing her eyes as James held her. Their hearts seemed to be beating in tune. Jade didn't want to say it, but she'd fallen hard for James Goings. She was in love with this man.

"Are you sleeping?" he asked.

"No, I thought you were," she replied.

"Umm, not with all this in my arms." James tapped her bottom softly. "I like watching you sleep, watching you wake up, and watching you naked."

She playfully slapped his shoulder. "Just when I thought you were sentimental."

"I'm a man, so there's only so much sentimentality you're going to get from me."

"I have something to tell you," she said.

"What's that?"

I love you, she thought. But she said, "I don't want to freak you out, but I'm thinking about moving to Charlotte to run our restaurant."

James licked his lips, then smiled. "And why would that freak me out?"

"Because I don't want you to think that I'm trying to force you into something that you're not looking for or ready for."

"First of all, I can't be forced into anything. If I didn't want to be with you, we would've never made it past Vegas. Secondly, I have real feelings for you, and if you're going to be in town, that's going to save me a lot of money on gas."

"Let's be honest. What are we doing?" she asked. "I don't want to be hurt again."

"And I would never do anything to hurt you," he replied as he stroked her cheek. "You mean a lot to me."

Her heart leapt for joy at James's declaration. Granted, he didn't say those magic three words, but Jade was confident that they were heading in the right direction. She knew she could give him her heart and not worry about finding out about him and another woman in the Charlotte newspaper.

James made her feel safe, and that meant more to Jade than anything else. She wrapped her arms around him even tighter.

The next morning James did just what he'd told Jade he liked to do: he watched her as she slumbered against his sheets. He wondered if he should've told her last night that he was falling hard for her. *You mean a lot to me,* he thought. *What kind of crap is that? I'm lucky she didn't bolt out of the bed and leave. That is what you tell a friend, not the woman you're falling in love with.*

James had never been a man who wore his emotions on his sleeves. Confessing that he was falling head over heels for a woman wasn't something that he did. Love didn't last in his world. He'd seen what had happened to his parents, and even though

Maurice and Kenya seemed happy now, he remembered how much pain Kenya had been in when their relationship ended the first time.

Still, he didn't want to miss out on something special with Jade because of other people's mistakes. And then there was Stephen. Was she really over him?

We have time, he thought. *It's not as if I'm going to ask her to marry me tomorrow.*

Jade began to stir in the bed. He reached over and stroked her cheek; then her eyes fluttered open.

"Good morning, beautiful," he said.

"Morning yourself," she said as she stifled a yawn.

"Let's get dressed and grab some breakfast," he suggested.

Jade shook her head. "Let's stay naked and lie right here."

"You won't hear any arguments from me," he said as he kissed her cheek and nestled against her.

"Sorry. I'm just not a morning person," she said. "But you seem to enjoy the mornings."

James shrugged his shoulders. "It isn't that I enjoy the morning. Most days I don't have a reason to stay in bed." He squeezed her bottom. "Today is different, though."

Jade smiled and brushed her lips against his. "Really?"

"Oh yeah."

"So, you mean to tell me, you don't have women beating a path to your door?"

"It doesn't mean I let them in," he said, with a smirk. *And I don't let too many people spend the night.*

"I hear you, Mr. Goings."

"So, what are we going to do next weekend?" he asked.

"Next weekend?"

"Yeah, when I come to Atlanta."

She smiled brightly. "Anything you want," she said. "As long as it doesn't include a trip to Chez Marcel."

James groaned. "I wouldn't take a dog there," he said. "That bastard. Then again, maybe I do owe Stephen a debt of gratitude."

"What?" Jade asked, raising her right eyebrow. "What could you possibly have to thank him for?"

"For being the jackass who let you go," he said as he squeezed her waist. "But that doesn't mean I'm going to eat his cooking."

She laughed and kissed him again. "Well, when you put it that way, I should thank him, too."

"Really?"

"Uh-huh. Because had he not been a jackass, I would've never gone to Vegas, and I would've never run into you in that scandalous dress."

"That was a beautiful dress," he said. "As a matter of fact, where is it?"

She slapped him on the shoulder. "You're so bad."

"And you love it."

I love you, she thought again and nearly let those words slip from her lips. But she just smiled and nodded.

It was after eleven before they got out of bed, got dressed, and headed out of the house. Had it not been for Kenya's call, James and Jade would've stayed in bed all day, ordering pizza and Chinese food in between lovemaking sessions. But Kenya insisted that the couple join her and Maurice uptown for brunch.

"Your sister-in-law is nice, but I'm not sure your brother really wants me around," Jade said.

"Don't worry about Maurice. He's trying."

"Really?" she said, still smarting from the fact that he'd had a private investigator look into her past. It wasn't that she had something to hide, but it was such an invasion of privacy. Especially when she didn't want anything from James but his love.

"Mo is going to behave. Besides, that man is so happy to have a baby on the way, he'd have brunch with the devil in the hottest pit in hell without complaining."

"That's reassuring," she said.

"You know what I mean."

"Let's just hope he's as happy as you say, because I feel too good to let Maurice get to me this morning."

James kissed her on the cheek as they headed out the door. "Give the man a chance," he said. "Mo is really a nice guy."

Jade nodded but wasn't ready to totally agree with James.

They drove to Kenya and Maurice's uptown condo. Jade was impressed by the building as soon as they walked into the lobby.

"Expensive digs," she remarked as James waved to the doorman.

"That's what Charlotte does. It moves the poor out of uptown so that they can build these high-rises that only millionaires can afford."

"A page out of Atlanta's gentrification book," she said. "Why don't you live uptown?"

"I like to mow the lawn. What can I say?"

Jade imagined James outside in the summer, shirtless and sweaty, riding a John Deere mower. She wouldn't mind bringing him a cool drink of water or even working alongside him, planting a few rosebushes. Growing up, she'd always wanted a yard with lush green grass and blooming flowers. Even though she lived in a trendy neighborhood in Atlanta and didn't have a yard, she knew that when she moved to Charlotte, her place would have a big yard. Though she wouldn't be the one cutting the grass; she'd just plant flowers.

Kenya met the couple at the door of the penthouse. "I'm going to kill your brother," she said to James. "Good morning, Jade."

"What did he do now?" asked James.

"Just come in and watch," Kenya said.

Maurice bounded into the foyer. "Kenya, will you please sit down. You need to take it easy."

Kenya raised her eyebrows at James as if to say, "See what I mean?"

"Mo," James said, "she's pregnant, not an invalid."

Maurice glared at his brother. "Shut up. Hi, Jade."

"Hello," Jade said.

"Are you going to serve us brunch?" Kenya asked. "If so, then I will sit down."

"The food is on the table," Maurice said and pointed everyone toward the dining room.

James and Jade looked at each other and laughed. "Do you think they're going to make it nine months?" she asked.

"Nope," James replied.

"I can hear y'all," Maurice said as he pulled a chair out for Kenya. "What's wrong with me wanting my wife to be calm and relaxed?"

"Maurice, whatever," Kenya said in an exasperated sigh. "I just know that you better not show up at my job with your overprotectiveness."

"I make no promises," Maurice said as he doled out scrambled eggs and turkey bacon.

"You know what would set this brunch off?" Kenya said as Maurice handed her a plate.

"What's that?" James asked.

"Your mother's cinnamon buns. I love that icing," Kenya told them.

Jade, who was sipping orange juice, dropped her head and coughed as James glanced at her.

Kenya looked from James to Jade. "What?"

"Nothing," Jade said. "We love the icing, too."

"Why didn't Ma come last night?" Maurice asked.

"She said the new girl at the bakery had a family emergency," Kenya said. "But don't worry. She already knows that she's going to be a grandmother."

"I want to thank you two," James said. "You took the pressure off."

Maurice laughed. "Whatever," he said. "There was never any pressure on you, anyway."

"Here we go," Kenya said. Then she turned to Jade. "These two have a running competition on everything. It's been that way since we were little."

"So, you guys grew up together?" asked Jade.

Kenya nodded. "It's been a journey knowing these two. Are you originally from Atlanta?"

"No," Jade said. "I was born in Louisiana, but home was everywhere. My parents worked on riverboats."

"That sounds exciting," Kenya told her.

Jade offered her a fake smile and didn't reply. She didn't want to talk about her childhood and everything that she had missed. "Thank God for college," she finally said. "A riverboat life gets old quick."

Kenya bit into her bacon and shrugged. "I'm sure it did. So you went to school in Atlanta?"

Jade nodded. "Yes, Spelman College."

"I graduated from Clark Atlanta," Kenya said, then looked pointedly at Maurice. "Even though I didn't want to go to a college that had a scholarship named after my mother."

"Who's your mother?" Jade asked.

"Angela Taylor. She's an editor at the *AJC*."

"She spoke at Spelman once. She has a powerful presence," Jade said. "She's the reason my friends and I started our investment club. All these years later, it's paying off."

"That's right. You guys are opening a restaurant," replied Kenya.

Jade nodded. "We're actually trying to get Devon Harris to be our chef."

"I love his show," Kenya said. "Maurice, isn't he in town this weekend?"

Maurice rolled his eyes. "Yeah. Every night she watches this guy on TV, but do you think she cooks any of that stuff?"

James shook his head, and Kenya tossed a napkin at him. "Maurice didn't marry me for my cooking," she said, causing Jade to laugh.

After brunch Jade and James headed back to his place. While she knew she should've been reaching out to Devon, as she'd promised Kandace she would, Jade wanted and needed some more alone time with her man before she got down to business.

CHAPTER 22

As soon as Jade and James walked into his house, her cell phone rang. "Hello?" Jade said.

"Jade Christian?" a male voice said.

"Yes, and who's calling?"

"Devon Harris. I heard you've been trying to reach me."

Jade smiled and grabbed James's shoulder. "Devon, don't act like this is just a business call. How have you been, and why have your people been giving us the runaround?"

"That's my agent's way," Devon said, with a smile in his voice. "How are you and the girls doing?"

"Great, but you know we need your help," she said. James looked at her quizzically. "The chef," she mouthed to him.

"Do you have dinner plans?" Devon asked.

"I don't think so."

"Then you need to come by Mez, as my guest."

"Make it plus one and I'm there."

Devon groaned. "You're not still with Stephen Carter, are you?"

"You knew about that?" she asked. "But to answer your question, no."

"Great. Then I'll see you and your guest around eight, and we can talk," he said. "By the way, how's Kandace?"

Jade paused. How was she supposed to answer that? "Fine," she finally said.

"Tell her that I asked about her," he said.

"Why don't you just call her?" Jade probed.

"I have to go. See you at eight." He hung up before Jade could say anything else, causing her to believe even more strongly that Kandace and Devon had some serious unfinished business.

"Is everything all right?" James asked, noting Jade's furrowed brows.

"Yes," she said, offering him a smile. "That may have been the answer to my prayers."

"Here I thought I was the answer to your prayers."

She smacked him on his shoulder. "Silly. Do we have dinner plans?"

"Well, I was hoping that you were going to feed me," he said, with a wink. "But if you need to go out, go ahead."

"We've been invited to dinner," she said. "Devon Harris wants us to be his guests at Mez."

"All right," he said. "I've been meaning to try the food at the EpiCenter."

"Devon is working with Mr. Woods, and hopefully, he'll want to run his own kitchen."

James smiled, clearly impressed with Jade. "My little businesswoman is making moves."

"Well, I've got to make up for my lack of judgment with Stephen."

James wrapped his arms around her waist.

"Everything happens for a reason, and we all make mistakes."

She nodded and leaned into him. "You're right."

"But," he said, his voice simmering with sensuality, "we have a lot of time before dinner. We can get an early start on dessert."

"Let me get the icing," she replied, with a smile.

Hours later Jade and James emerged from the bed, satisfied and ready for dinner. She dressed in a formfitting pair of black slim-leg pants and a baby blue tuxedo shirt. James, seeing that Jade was looking very sexy, yet businesslike, decided that his jeans and sports coat weren't going to cut it.

"Let me be your arm candy tonight," he said as he pulled out a brown suit and coral shirt.

"Arm candy?"

"Yeah," he said, with a grin. "I look good and will make you look even better."

Jade ran her hand over James's arm. "I can't argue with that."

After James was dressed, they headed out to the popular eatery. What they didn't know was that the restaurant was hosting a private party that catered to the elite of Charlotte.

"It's a good thing I did change my clothes," James said after the maître d' checked their names off the list.

"Devon didn't tell me all this was going on," she said as they were led to a table in the center of the restaurant, which was marked CHEF'S TABLE.

The maître d' took the other chairs away, indicating

that Jade and James would be sitting alone. "Enjoy your meal," he said, then walked away.

The restaurant was dimly lit, giving an ambiance of romance. James slid his chair closer to Jade and placed his arm around her shoulder. "It looks like we have some competition," she said, referring to the restaurant.

"Are you guys going for an upscale type of restaurant or something more down-home?"

"It depends on Devon, Serena, Kandace, and Alicia. I'd like to make sure it's something that appeals to everyone."

James nodded. "Makes sense, and keep in mind, Cherry is an emerging neighborhood that has people from all walks of life."

A waiter walked over to the table and placed an array of appetizers in front of the couple. "Compliments of the chef," he said.

"Thanks," James said. He picked up a succulent piece of shrimp and held it out to Jade to bite.

"Umm," she moaned. "This is good."

James bit off a piece of the shrimp himself and agreed. "This guy is good."

Dinner came next, along with a bottle of chardonnay. James and Jade dined on grilled chicken breasts marinated in a cilantro-lime sauce, wild rice, and tender vegetables.

"I wonder what he can do with a steak," Jade mused as she sipped her wine.

"That's my girl," James said.

"Does this wine taste funny to you?" she asked as she set her glass down.

James sipped his wine and shrugged. "Tastes fine to me."

She waved for the waiter and requested a glass of water. Seconds later Devon Harris was walking toward their table, carrying a glass of water. "Ms. Christian, how are you?" he said as he set the water in front of her. Jade rose to her feet and gave the six-foot-two chef a quick hug.

"I'm very well. This is James Goings," she said. Devon extended his hand to James, and the two men shook.

"How was dinner?" Devon asked.

"Great," James said.

"Yes, it was," Jade said.

Devon smiled. "That's what I like to hear. Would you guys like to tour the kitchen after dessert?"

"Umm, James?" asked Jade.

James shrugged. "Why not?"

"All right," Devon said, smiling at the couple. "It's nice to meet you, James. I've got to get back."

"Nice fellow," James said once Devon was gone. "Doesn't look like a chef, though. The Bobcats could use him running the point."

She laughed. "I guess that's why his show is such a hit. People like looking at him."

"How do you two know each other?" James asked, with a hint of jealousy in his voice.

"He and Kandace used to date. I think they're still in love with each other, but they're fighting the feeling."

"A story as old as time," he said.

"You know how you men can be, and my friend is hardheaded."

"Do you think it's a good idea for them to work together? With all these feelings floating around?"

"He'll be working directly with me, and who

knows? This could be their chance. Second chance, if you will," Jade said.

"Maybe whatever broke them up means it's best that they stay apart."

"And did you tell your brother that when he and Kenya reconnected?"

"Checkmate," he said. "But everybody's story is different."

"What about our story?" she asked. "How will we go down?"

"I don't know," he said. "But I'm loving how it's playing out so far." He leaned over and kissed her on the cheek.

"Good answer," she said.

Moments later the waiter came over to the table with a molten chocolate cake and two forks. James whispered in Jade's ear, "Make sure we take some of this home, because I'd love to see how chocolate tastes on you."

"You are so bad," she replied, then asked the waiter for a to-go box.

Once they finished tasting the dessert and boxing it up, Jade headed for the kitchen, while James stayed at the table, listening to the jazz band.

"Where's your man?" Devon asked.

"He's not really interested in the kitchen," she said. "Besides, we need to talk."

"I know. So, you and the crew are opening up a restaurant?"

Jade nodded. "And we want the best."

"Are you sure it's a good idea for me to work for you guys? Our history isn't all peachy."

"Just so you know, it was Serena's idea to find

you. Kandace has been working really hard to get you, and I'm going to be the general manager."

"That's all nice to hear, but Serena, also known as the ice queen, hates my guts. Kandace, well, she just confuses the hell out of me, and Alicia, she's Serena's twin."

"Nothing to say about me?"

"You're nice, Jade, but I know how things are with you four."

"This is business and we need you. If for no other reason than to beat Stephen at his game."

"Aw," Devon said. "So, Mr. Wonderful has something to do with this restaurant venture. What did you ever see in that guy?"

"I ask myself that question all the time," Jade replied. "But this really isn't about him. You owe us."

Devon held his chin and peered at Jade. "One year."

"One year?"

"I will work with you guys for one year. We can get together and work out my salary. Then there is my TV show. If I'm working for you guys, then I need to be able to film my show in the restaurant, and I want to have some input in how the kitchen looks."

"All right, and you will have total control over the menu," Jade said.

"That goes without saying, buttercup."

"Please, don't call me that," she replied, with a laugh.

"So, what's the deal with you and James?"

She smiled. "Want to trade love stories?"

"There you go. We have nothing to trade."

She folded her arms across her chest and

rolled her eyes. "What happened between you and Kandace?"

"Ask her, because I don't know. One minute we're in love, and the next she's telling me she doesn't want to see me again. When you find out what happened, let me know." His voice was tinged with bitterness.

"Sorry," Jade said. "I had no idea."

Devon shrugged. "Give my business manager a call tomorrow, and let's meet before you leave town, say, one o'clock? Hey, don't you still live in Atlanta?"

"Yes, but when we open, I'm going to move here."

"And James lives in Atlanta?"

"No," she said, with a smile. "He lives here."

"It's good to know someone is getting a happy ending," he said wistfully.

Jade reached out and rubbed his shoulder with sisterly affection. "The book hasn't closed on you two yet," she said.

Devon offered her a melancholy smile. "If you say so," he replied.

"I'd better get back. Thank you so much for doing this."

"Tell Serena I said, 'What's up'?"

Jade walked back into the dining room and found James grooving to the smooth jazz band. She crept up behind him, bringing her lips to his ear.

"Excuse me, sir. Would you like to dance?" she whispered.

James turned around, with a wide smile on his lips. "Let's do it."

They took to the dance floor, walking hand in hand. James pulled Jade against his body, and they rocked their hips in a seductive dance that made them the stars of the show. The other dancers stepped aside and watched Jade and James slow dance in the middle of the floor. He spun her around with a flourish and then dipped her. Jade lifted her leg around James's waist as if she were a contestant on *Dancing with the Stars.* Some of the people around the couple started clapping as they continued to dance. Once the song ended, the crowd broke into a rousing round of applause. James and Jade took a bow and headed back to their table, hand in hand.

"I didn't know you had those kinds of moves," Jade said.

"Don't let the suit fool you," James replied, with a wink. She leaned into him, pressing her nose against his. He brushed his lips against hers and gently kissed her. "You want to get out of here?"

Jade nodded, and within seconds she and James were rushing out to his car.

The next morning Jade woke up before James. Her body tingled from the night of lovemaking that they'd shared. *Is this real?* she thought. *Can I really be this happy with him?* She gently stroked his arm and said a silent prayer that this thing with James wasn't an illusion and that he cared for her as much as she cared for him. Looking over at the alarm clock on his dresser, she realized that she needed to get out of bed and call Devon's manager so that they could set up a meeting. As she stole from the bed, James opened his eyes. "You leaving me, woman?" he said in a sleep-filled voice.

"Just to take care of some business. I need to make some calls."

He nodded and went back to sleep. Jade grabbed her cell phone and dialed Kandace before calling Devon's people.

"This better be an emergency," Kandace said. "It's way too early for you to be calling me when you should be in bed with your man."

"First of all, it's a little after seven. You should be getting ready for work."

"I took the day off. Don't you think I deserve it?"

"Yes, I do," Jade said. "Guess who I talked to last night?"

"Who?"

"Devon Harris. As a matter of fact, he invited James and me to be his guests for dinner at Mez. The things that man can do with food are just amazing."

"Uh-huh," Kandace said.

"He asked about you," she said.

"What did he say?"

"He said to call him," Jade fibbed. "Maybe you should come to Charlotte and join us for the meeting today."

"What time is the meeting?" Kandace asked, with a hint of excitement in her voice.

"One o'clock, so if you get out of bed and get ready, you can be here right on time."

"Where are you all meeting?"

"Ah, at James's office," Jade said, silently reminding herself that she needed to ask James if they could use his office.

"I don't know why I'm doing this, but I will be there before one."

"Great." Jade hung up the phone and headed

back into the bedroom. She realized she needed a place for this meeting. "James," she said, shaking his shoulder.

"Hmm?"

"Are you going into the office today?" she asked.

"I guess. Damn, lady, you trying to get rid of me?"

She shook her head and kissed him on the cheek. "I need a favor," she said. "Can I use your conference room today to meet with Devon and Kandace?"

"Sure," he said as he sat up in the bed. "But you're going to have to do something for me after your meeting."

"What's that?" she asked as she slipped back into bed with him.

James pulled her into his arms. "Meet me in my office when you're done, and leave your panties at the door."

"How did you know I was wearing a skirt today?"

He nodded toward the outfit she had laid out on the chair next to the dresser. "That's not exactly my style," he joked.

"Well, Mr. Goings, I think I'd be more than happy to meet you in your office," she said, then kissed him quickly on the lips. "I've got one more phone call to make." Jade leapt out of bed, nearly dragging James with her.

CHAPTER 23

James and Jade walked into his office around 12:30.

About two minutes later, Kandace burst through the door. "I'm here," she said.

"Good afternoon to you, too," Jade said to her friend.

James waved to her and headed into his office and closed the door.

Kandace looked toward the conference room. "Is he here?" she whispered.

"Not yet," Jade replied. "You look nice."

Kandace looked down at her fashionable gray pencil skirt and white ruffled blouse. "You like it?"

Jade nodded. "Very chic," she said as she rose to her feet, walked over to Kandace, and pulled the price tag from the blouse. "Very new, I see."

"You know me. Sometimes I need retail therapy. I was going to take this blouse back, but I figured I needed to look my best today," Kandace said.

"You always do," a silky voice said from behind her. Kandace and Jade turned around and found

Devon standing in the doorway, with a basket of goodies in his hands.

"You're early," Jade said.

"Yeah," he said as he walked in. "I thought I was going to get lost, so I left a little too soon."

Kandace smiled at him but didn't say anything. Jade took Devon's basket and headed into the conference room. Neither Kandace nor Devon moved.

Jade took a muffin from the basket. "We need coffee," she called out. "I'm leaving to go get some."

Still, Kandace and Devon stood in the middle of the floor, not saying a word. Jade walked out to the entrance and asked Amber where she could find a Starbucks.

"I'll go for you," Amber said. "It's not a problem."

"No," Jade said, with a smile. "I think I need to leave the chef alone with Kandace while I get some lattes. Do you want something, and what's James's favorite drink?"

Amber smiled and told Jade that James was a regular-coffee man and he didn't like sugar in his coffee, just three packs of Splenda.

"And he gets his coffee from the gas station some times, doesn't he?" Jade questioned, with a laugh.

"He sure does."

"Thanks, Amber," Jade said, then headed out the door, even though part of her wanted to stay near Kandace and Devon to see what was going on with the two of them.

"Hey," James called out after Jade. "Where are you going without me?"

"Starbucks. Devon brought some muffins, and I figured coffee would go great with them."

"I hope you're getting decaf, because those two outside of my office don't need caffeine."

"What's going on up there?" she asked.

James shrugged. "A lot of finger pointing, some name calling, and a bunch of questions. What? Are they divorced or something?"

"They never made it down the aisle," she said. "They were close, but something happened and Devon went to Paris and Kandace started the marketing firm after she went away for a few months."

James shook his head. "It's a good thing you're going to handle the day-to-day operations, because I think those two would kill each other."

Jade fought the urge to go upstairs and eavesdrop. She just prayed Devon would still want to work for the restaurant.

After getting the coffees, James and Jade headed back to the office, wondering if the place would still be standing. It was, but Kandace and Devon hovered in separate corners of the conference room like wary warriors.

"Here's some coffee for you guys," Jade said timidly.

"This isn't going to work," Devon said as he took a cup from the center of the table. "I'm sorry, Jade, but I can't go into business with you."

"That's right," Kandace snapped. "You're the liar that I always knew you were."

"Kandace, let it go. I made a mistake and you want to hold it against me after all these years?"

James cleared his throat. "Guys, I have clients coming in, and this isn't the time or place for your personal war."

"There is no war," Devon said coldly. "Jade, sorry I wasted your time."

Jade cleared her throat. "Devon, look, we need you and—"

"Don't you dare beg him!" Kandace exclaimed.

Devon slammed his coffee cup on the table. "You know what? I know you need me," he said to Jade but looked pointedly at Kandace. "But some people can't let go of the past. I'm sorry I cheated on you."

"Devon, you promised me a year," Jade said. "Please, if for no other reason than to beat Stephen at his own game."

James shuddered, then stepped out of the room.

Jade immediately regretted saying anything about Stephen. "Come on. You two need to think about this from a business aspect. Kandace, we won't find a better chef." Jade turned to Devon. "Kandace won't even be here that much."

"I won't be here at all," Kandace snapped, then stormed out of the conference room.

"Why did you tell her I wanted her to be here?" Devon asked.

"Because I know you two still have feelings for each other, and whatever happened between the two of you is in the past. Can't you just move on from it?"

"You don't understand, and I'm not going to try and explain it. Just stay out of my personal life from now on. My business manager will be here with contracts shortly." Devon blew past Jade, leaving her confused but happy that he was still going to run the kitchen.

* * *

James sat in his office—pissed off. He'd thought that Jade had gotten over trying to get revenge on Stephen, yet she was pulling more people into her web. He flipped through a file on his desk, not focusing on the words on the papers. It was one thing for Jade and her friends to open the restaurant because they wanted to cash in on Charlotte's growth, but she was still on this revenge kick, and he questioned whether he was a distraction for her and if she was truly over Stephen.

A knock at his door broke into his thoughts. "Yeah," he called out.

The door opened and Jade walked in.

"Hey," she said.

He nodded in acknowledgment.

"Is something wrong?" she questioned.

"No, just busy. Did your meeting turn out to your satisfaction?" he asked, sarcasm peppering his voice.

"Kind of," she said, then leaned against the desk.

"Jade, I have work I need to take care of."

She stepped back from the desk, with a confused look on her face. "I thought . . ."

"Something just came up," James said.

"Are you upset with me?" she asked, with her arms folded across her chest.

James slammed his file on the desk. "Don't I have a reason to be? Beat Stephen at his own game? What am I supposed to think? This guy came here and I defended you, but you still have this urge to get back at him. Why is that?"

"Are we really going there again?" she asked in an exasperated voice.

"Why don't you go in the conference room with your friend? I have work to do," he said dismissively.

"How about I just leave, period," Jade snapped. "For whatever reason, you won't take my word about Stephen. Do you really think . . . Forget it, James." She stormed out of the office, and part of him wanted to go after her, but he had his own anger to work out.

After a few minutes, James left the office and headed back to his place, hoping that Jade was there. However, when he arrived home, Jade's car was gone. James rushed inside, knowing that her things would still be there because she didn't have a key.

Maybe she'll come back, he thought but didn't call her.

Jade drove aimlessly around Charlotte. She had no idea where to go or if she should head back to James's office and demand that he give her his house key so that she could get her stuff and leave. Why couldn't he just get Stephen out of his head? She didn't want anything to do with that man; she just wanted her money and a successful restaurant. Was that so wrong?

Jade looked out the window and saw SouthPark Mall. She was lost and had no clue how to get back to James's place. The last thing she wanted to do was call him, so she called Kandace instead.

"What do you want?" her friend snapped.

"I'm sorry about everything."

"Sure you are. What were you thinking? What was *I* thinking? Devon and I have run our course, and there's no way we're getting back together."

"Why not?"

"Because I said so, damn it. I'm surprised you and James aren't doing that thing you do."

"James and I aren't talking right now. For whatever reason, he can't get past the Stephen thing."

"Great. Everything is falling apart," Kandace said. "Are you coming back to Atlanta anytime soon?"

"Yeah. As soon as I get my things from James's. I refuse to set myself up to be hurt again, so it's best that we just stop doing whatever it is we're doing." Though Jade said the words, she didn't believe them, and she wasn't ready to leave James behind when she knew she'd fallen head over heels in love with him.

"This love addiction is worse than heroin. Maybe we need to take a page from Serena's book and just say screw it."

Sighing, Jade agreed. "You know what? He can send me my clothes. I'm hitting the highway and heading back to the A. From now on, when I come to Charlotte, it's going to be strictly business."

"Sure," Kandace said. "You're just going to let a misunderstanding end your relationship?"

"I can't keep fighting the same battle with him. For whatever reason, he keeps thinking that I'm either using him for a rebound romance or that I'm harboring some secret feelings for that asshole Stephen."

"Well, I'm in Gastonia, at the Waffle House. Do you want me to wait for you?" Kandace asked.

"Yeah, and order me a patty melt with extra onions. I should be there in about thirty minutes."

When Jade arrived at the restaurant in Gastonia some twenty minutes later, she found Kandace sitting at the counter, eating a piece of pie. When Kandace saw her friend walk in, she waved for the cook to start the patty melt.

"You got here quickly."

Jade shrugged. "I had no reason to stick around Charlotte. I guess I'll go back next month to start talking to some contractors about the renovations."

"Are you still going to move there?"

"Yes. I said I was going to run the place. I'm just not going to sell my home in Atlanta in a hurry."

Kandace nodded. "I don't blame you for that."

A waitress walked over to the women and refilled Kandace's coffee cup. "What can I get you to drink, hon?" she asked Jade.

"A Coke will be great," Jade replied. When the waitress left, Jade turned to Kandace. "It's time for you to spill."

"What?"

"That scene with you and Devon was pretty intense. What happened between the two of you?"

Kandace sighed and shook her head. "It's really stupid, but I've been holding a grudge for ten years. I was supposed to be by Devon's side in Paris. Instead, I found out about him and Jolisa Covington."

"Ugh, not her."

Kandace nodded. "That's what I saw when I went to his house after graduation and his father was so happy that I caught them. Devon Sr. never thought I was good enough for his son. I can't say that I was sorry to hear that she didn't go to Paris either. I thought I could let it go and seeing him today was supposed to be about burying the hatchet."

"So, what went wrong?"

Kandace shrugged as she sipped her coffee. "Seeing him brought all of those old feelings back."

"Is it that you want another chance with him?" Jade asked as the waitress set her Coke on the counter.

"Absolutely not. Seeing him threw me for a loop, because Devon is still fine, but I need something new in my life. This restaurant is a step in the right direction and since you are the GM, I don't have to deal with Devon."

"So, throwing everything away is the answer?"

Kandace sighed. "For me, yes. I can't speak for you and James. He makes you happy. Are you sure this is something you guys can't work out?"

"I don't know," she said as she glanced at her cell phone. It wasn't lost on Jade that James hadn't called her. *Maybe it's for the best,* she thought. *We should've left it all in Vegas, anyway.*

CHAPTER 24

One month later

Jade woke up feeling as if she had butterflies floating in her stomach. She leapt from the bed and threw up dinner and everything else that was in her system. Chalking it up to the fact that she had eaten a big steak and a pint of Ben & Jerry's Chunky Monkey before going to bed, Jade rinsed her mouth out and crawled back into bed. She was not looking forward to what she had to do in the morning. Going back to Charlotte and overseeing the renovations on the restaurant meant that she'd eventually run into James, who she hadn't talked to in a month.

Ever since the argument in his office, they'd cut off all ties. There had been moments in the last month where she'd dialed nine of the ten digits of his phone number, but she'd hang up before dialing the last digit. He could've easily called her, and if he could go a month without talking to her, then what they had shared wasn't as important to him as it was to her.

To hell with James. I don't have to see him. Nor do I have to talk to him, she thought as she pulled the covers up to her chin. But moments later she was throwing up again. *What is wrong with me? Maybe it's just nerves.*

It was after 2:00 a.m. before her stomach settled down and she was able to go back to sleep. But sleep didn't last long. Her alarm clock blared at 5:45 a.m., and she dragged herself out of bed. Serena was meeting her at 6:30 with some ideas for the contractors. Part of her wished her dour friend was taking the trip to Charlotte with her. But Serena had made it clear at dinner that this was Jade's bed to lie in alone.

"I don't want to say I told you so," Serena had said. "But . . ."

"Please, I don't need to hear you right now," Jade had replied.

"Well, had you listened a month ago, you wouldn't be sitting here with tears in your eyes."

I hate it when that heifer is right, Jade thought as she stepped into the shower.

James stared at his phone before he finally picked it up and dialed Jade's number. The last thirty days without her had been hell. But she was in Atlanta, and for all he knew, she and Stephen could've reconciled. James slammed the phone down as he imagined her and Stephen wrapped up in each other's arms in her bed. *This is bullshit,* he thought as he rose from his desk and stood by the window. James didn't even hear Maurice walk into his office.

"Yo, man, what's going on with you?" Maurice

asked as he walked up behind his brother and grabbed his shoulder.

James slapped his hand away. "Why are you here?"

"Because you missed a meeting this morning, and that's not like you."

"Things happen," James said.

"Does this have anything to do with Jade?"

"How's Kenya doing? Is she starting to show yet?"

"Don't try to change the damned subject," Maurice snapped. "You stay buried in this office, I haven't heard you talk about her, and I haven't seen her around. And your attitude of late is that of a man who's not getting any."

"Mo, you weren't too thrilled with Jade, anyway, so why are you acting concerned?"

Maurice shrugged his shoulders. "Maybe I've seen the light. Jade seems good for you. Who am I to judge the woman?"

"Like I was looking for your approval in the first place," James barked. "But it's moot, anyway. For thirty days I haven't heard from her, so maybe what I thought was something serious wasn't."

"Have you called her?" Maurice asked pointedly. "The phone works both ways. You should keep that in mind."

"What was the meeting about?" James asked, glossing over what his brother had said.

"I handled it, but back to you. Are you trying to push the woman away?"

"When in the hell did you become Jade's cheerleader?" James slammed his hand against the back of his desk chair. "It's obviously over, and I don't want to talk about it, damn it."

Maurice backed away as if he were getting away

from an opposing linebacker. "Fine. We've been selected by the Urban League to receive a trailblazer award for the development in Wesley Heights. The ceremony is in three weeks. That's what the meeting was about."

James nodded. "You get the award, and I'll cheer you on from a distance."

"Actually, you're the one receiving the award. I told the committee that it's your work that keeps us involved in a lot of good things, so you can't get out of going. Besides, it will be a great chance for you to take your mind off—"

"Don't say it," James said, throwing his hand up.

"This is what I'm talking about. Don't give up on her if this is what you really want."

James didn't even want to argue the point further, but it wasn't about what he wanted anymore. Obviously, Jade had made her decision. And he was going to abide by it. If there was anything between them, she would have to prove it. He wasn't going to chase her, and he damned sure wasn't going to beg—even if it meant he'd be miserable.

How did it all go so wrong? I was ready to tell that woman that I loved her and she was still hung up on Stephen—a man who has no respect for her. James dropped into his chair and glanced up at his brother.

"Why are you still here?" he asked Maurice.

"Because you're worrying me. James, stop being so damned stubborn, and call her."

"Why don't I just wait nine years?"

Maurice shook his head. "I know misery loves company, but I'm too happy to stand here trying to save your love life. I'm out."

Maurice headed out the door, and James propped

his feet up on his desk, pondering if he should reach out to Jade. Maurice did have a point. James wanted her more than he was willing to admit. He missed everything about her: the sound of her voice, the feel of her skin, and the taste of her lips. James picked up the phone and dialed Jade's number. The call went straight to voice mail, and he hung up without leaving a message, wondering if she was screening her calls.

"Give me my phone, Serena!" Jade shouted as she drove into the Charlotte city limits. She was now wishing her friend had stayed home.

"Why? So you can get all caught up in James again? You haven't heard from him in a month. Why is it so important to talk to him now? We're going to Charlotte for business, not for you and James to have a reconciliation."

"You don't have the right to . . . Just give me my damned phone."

Serena folded her arms across her chest and shook her head. "I don't think so. Not until after the meeting with these contractors. As soon as they see women walk in the room, they are going to think that we're clueless."

Jade rolled her eyes. "Why do you think all men are out to get you?" she asked.

"Because they are," Serena said flatly. "And I don't want this to turn into one of your speeches about the right man being out there for me. Can we just get through this meeting, come up with some plans? And we need to name the place. Serena's has a nice ring." She laughed to inform Jade she was only joking. "Have you thought about what we should name the restaurant? What does Charlotte identify itself with?"

"I don't know," Jade said.

"Are you still moving here?"

"What choice do I have? I said I was going to manage this restaurant, and I'm going to keep my word. This is business."

Serena smiled tersely. "I hope that you plan on calling James after the meeting, because I am tired of you moping about this man. Besides, he's not that bad, and I don't understand why you haven't called him in a month."

Jade looked at Serena as if she were possessed by an alien. "What did you say?"

"You heard me. It's been a month. You could've called him."

"No. Did I hear you say he's not that bad?"

Serena shrugged. "Whatever. I just know that I'm tired of you acting as if the world has come to an end because you two haven't talked."

"He doesn't want to talk to me, because he hasn't called me," Jade said. "Not counting the call that you made me miss."

Serena rapped her hand on Jade's forehead. "Are you slow? Is there a brain in there?"

"Shut up," Jade said. "So, you really think I should call him?"

"Yes, as long as you shut up about that man!" Serena said as Jade pulled into the restaurant's parking lot.

Once they walked into the restaurant, Serena and Jade realized that they had a lot of work to do. The interior of the building was moldy and cold.

The smell of the damp wood and mold seemed to slap Jade in the face. Closing her eyes, she dashed outside, nearly knocking two contractors over, and threw up in the bushes near the entrance.

One of the hulky contractors walked over to Jade and placed his hand on her shoulder. "Ma'am," he asked, "are you all right?"

Wiping her mouth with the handkerchief he offered, Jade nodded. "I'm fine," she said. "This isn't how I wanted to meet you."

"Come again?" he asked.

"You're Antonio Billups, right?" She looked at the man, taking in every inch of his chocolate, muscular, six-foot-four-inch frame.

Billups smiled, showing a mouth full of pearly whites. "Guilty. Serena Jacobs?"

"No, Jade Christian," she said. "Serena's inside."

He nodded. "Are you sure we don't need to reschedule this meeting?"

"I'll be fine. I had something for dinner that didn't agree with me. I'm going to head to the gas station and clean up," she said. Though Jade had no choice, she didn't think leaving Serena alone with the contractors was good for business. The plan was for them to be sugar and spice. Without the sugar to balance the spice, Jade feared that the contractors would walk out without even making an offer.

She drove to the gas station, walked into the bathroom, and washed her hands, then rinsed her mouth with water. Jade knew that her nausea didn't have anything to do with dinner. A thought flashed in her mind, and she pulled out her cell phone, then scrolled down to the calendar function.

My God! she thought. *I'm late. Could I be pregnant?*

Jade shook nervously as she thought about the possibility of carrying a child. James's child. Just as she was about to drop her phone back into her purse, it rang. Looking down at the caller ID, she saw it was James. She hit the talk button.

"Hello, Jade," James said.

"Hi."

"I still have your things at my house," he said.

Genius! You didn't call her about her damned clothes.

"Really? So, is that why you're calling me?" she asked. Her voice had a hint of annoyance.

"No," he admitted. "I miss you. Maybe I was wrong to jump to conclusions about you still having this thing for Stephen."

"It took you a month to figure that out?" she said sarcastically.

"I didn't hear from you, either," he said. "But that's not the point. I'm trying to apologize."

"You're not doing a good job of it," she said.

James sighed and pushed back from his desk. Jade was right; he wasn't doing a good job at it. "All right. Let me come to Atlanta tonight and apologize in person."

"Well, I'm not in Atlanta," she said. "I'm actually in Charlotte, about to meet with some contractors."

A slow smile spread across his face. "Is it possible for us to see each other?"

"Yes, I'll call you when we're done with the meeting."

"All right," he said. "I look forward to it."

When they hung up the phone, James called Ruth's Chris Steak House and made a dinner reservation. Then he headed out to the florist and bought two dozen red roses. Just as he was about to sign the card, his cell phone rang.

"Yeah?" he said after seeing that it was his brother.

"James, I was just in the Cherry neighborhood, and I saw your girl. Maybe you should—"

"We're having dinner tonight."

"Good," said Maurice.

"What were you doing over there?" James asked.

"Trying to find my wife some Chunky Monkey ice cream."

James laughed. "The Ben and Jerry's store is in South Park," he said.

"That's what that is?" Maurice replied, with a laugh. "I walked into the Circle K, and the clerk looked at me as if I was speaking a foreign language. Let me get to the south side and get back to her office before she has a fit."

"I'm surprised you still allow her to work," James said.

"When have I ever been able to stop Kenya from doing what she wants to do?"

"How about never? Let me go. I've got to finish up some work before I head out."

James had to figure out how he was going to make up with Jade and get her back into his life. He knew the first thing he was going to have to do was trust her and let go of his suspicions about her and Stephen.

Jade ambled into the restaurant, somewhat afraid of what she was going to find. What she didn't expect was to hear laughter and see Serena smiling at Antonio Billups and his partner.

"There you are," Serena said when she spotted Jade. "Mr. Billups said you weren't feeling well."

Once again, Jade was shocked at her friend's demeanor. "I'm fine."

"Great," Serena said, clasping her hands together. "We have contractors and Mr. Billups. . . ."

"Please, call me Antonio. Mr. Billups is my father," Antonio said in a smooth voice.

"Only if you call me Serena," Serena said, her tone playful.

Jade smiled but held her breath because she felt her stomach bubbling again owing to the moldy smell in the building. "When can you get started on the work?" Jade asked.

"I'm going to get the contract drawn up, and we can get started at the end of the week," Antonio said to Jade, but his attention was on Serena.

"Wonderful. Can we get out of here?" Jade asked. "The smell in here is just overwhelming."

The group headed out into fresh air, and Jade was thankful that she hadn't vomited again.

"Serena," Antonio said, extending his hand to her, "it was a pleasure meeting you." He turned to Jade and smiled. "I hope you feel better, ma'am."

"Thanks, Antonio," said Jade.

Once Jade and Serena were alone, Jade turned to her friend. "Did I just see the ice queen flirting?"

"Did you see that man?" Serena shook her head as if she'd just bitten into a succulent piece of chocolate. "Just five minutes alone with him, ooh!"

"When are you going to stop treating men like sex objects?"

"As soon as they do the same. He's going to give us a good deal, he said his family had a home in this neighborhood, and he's glad to see it coming back to life." Serena ran her fingers through her hair. "I'd love to see how it feels to fall asleep in those arms."

"And what happens when you wake up a month later with a late period?"

Serena slapped her hand against her thigh. "Tell me that you're speaking hypothetically," she said. "You're not pregnant, are you?"

Jade shrugged her shoulders. "It explains a lot. I've been sick for no reason, and I checked my calendar. My period is late."

"Let's find a drugstore and get a pregnancy test. If you are pregnant, are you going to keep it?"

Jade closed her eyes. "Whatever decision I make, James and I are going to make it together," she finally said.

"Are you sure it's James's child?" Serena asked quietly.

Jade rolled her eyes. "Yes. If I were pregnant by Stephen, I'd be showing by now. You know we hadn't been sleeping together toward the end."

Serena nodded and folded her arms underneath her breasts. "I don't envy you," she said. "Have you talked to him?"

"Yes. We're supposed to be meeting for dinner. Do you mind staying overnight?"

A slick smile spread across Serena's face. "I sure don't. As a matter of fact, I'm going to call Antonio and discuss our contract."

Jade grabbed her friend's shoulder. "Please don't do anything to mess things up with him. They say he's one of the best contractors in town, and you know how hard it is to find honest contractors."

"Trust me, I'm not going to do anything but talk

to the man," Serena said. "We have a lot invested in this unnamed restaurant."

Jade rolled her eyes. "We're going to come up with a name, all right. Let's go see if we can find a room in Uptown."

"Uptown? You're sounding like a native already," Serena joked as they got into the car.

CHAPTER 25

Jade called James around six and told him that she and Serena were staying at the Westin and she'd be ready to meet him for dinner around 7:30. What she didn't tell him was that she was waiting to see if her over-the-counter pregnancy test was going to turn blue. The first test she'd taken had given her the plus sign, meaning that she was pregnant. The second test had had the two pink lines, meaning that she was pregnant. With mixed emotions, she waited for the last test to make a prediction.

Serena knocked on the bathroom door. "What's the verdict?"

Jade opened the door and walked out with the blue test and held it out to Serena. "This is not good."

"Jade, what are you going to do?"

Crossing over to one of the beds, Jade plopped down and shook her head. "I guess I'm going to have to tell James."

"But the test could be wrong."

"All of them? I took three of them. Same result."

Serena sat down beside her friend and put her

arm around her shoulders. "You know, whatever happens, we're going to have your back. Alicia, Kandace, and I want this restaurant to succeed, but if you want to be a mommy, then we'll just hire a—"

"Wait a minute. I'm still going to manage the restaurant, and if I do have this baby, I'm sure that there are day cares and things that will make it possible for me to work *and* take care of my child."

"And what's James going to do while you're trying to be supermom?"

Jade shrugged. "Who knows what his reaction is going to be? He may not even want a baby."

Serena shook her head and hugged her friend again. "Like I said, we got your back."

"I'd better get ready for dinner," Jade said as she walked into the bathroom.

Serena was already on the phone, calling Alicia and Kandace.

James walked into the lobby of the Westin Hotel at 7:20. He wanted to see Jade as soon as she walked off the elevator. Things had been so much simpler in Vegas, he recalled. But now he had feelings invested in this woman, and the last thing he wanted was to be hurt because she wasn't over Stephen or something crazy like that. *I need to stop expecting the worst,* he thought as he heard the chime of the elevator. Moments later Jade was walking toward him, with a worried look on her face. James took note of the black dress she wore and the matching leather pumps. Though the outfit was alluring, something about the look on her face troubled him.

"Are you all right?" James asked after saying hello.

"Yes, I'm fine," she said quietly.

James raised an eyebrow at her. "You're sure? You have the look of a woman carrying the weight of the world on her shoulders."

Jade stared at him for a moment. "I'm a little confused, James. Are we supposed to be picking up where we left off, or do we forget what happened the last time we were together?"

"I made a mistake and I'm sorry, but I'm not the only one who should be apologizing. You just left, with no word about where you were going or anything."

"And you were so worried about me that it took you a month—thirty days—to call me?" she snapped.

"I called," James said. "But I kept getting voice mail. Obviously, you were too busy to talk." His statement lingered in the air like an accusation. "But you know what? You didn't dial my number, either, Jade."

"I didn't think I had a reason to. James, you have got to understand, I'm a one-man woman, and you are the man I want and need in my life," she said. "Tell me you believe that."

He reached out and stroked her smooth cheek. "I do," he replied. "Let me be honest with you. This is new to me, and maybe I was trying to deny what's been happening for a long time."

"What's that?" she asked.

"That I'm falling in love with you, and it drives me crazy to think that I could lose you or that someone else will kiss you, touch you, or make love to you," he said emphatically. "And I take back what I said. I'm not falling in love with you. I'm already there."

Jade melted in his arms. "I love you, too," she murmured. "But I'm just as gun shy as you are."

"Maybe we just need to stop being shy and just pull the damned trigger," James said, then brushed his lips against hers.

She fell into his kiss, her body reacting to the expert touch of his hands. But they broke off the kiss before they were carried away by passion.

"We have dinner reservations," he said. "But we could always go back to my place."

"No," she said, with a grin. "But we can have dessert at your place."

It was James's turn to smile. "I think there might be some icing in the refrigerator."

All through dinner, Jade tried not to focus on the three pregnancy tests she'd taken. James had said he loved her, and so if the tests were accurate and she was pregnant, they would be able to work things out, wouldn't they?

"You're quiet," James observed.

"Just enjoying my last meal at Ruth's Chris."

"Last meal?"

"Yes, because once the restaurant opens, you're not going to eat here, either."

James smiled and leaned across the table. "I know what I'd like to eat." His voice had a hint of seduction dancing in it. "What do you think it is?"

Jade reached up and stroked his cheek. "You're so bad," she said. "And I'm going to enjoy my steak."

"All right," he said, easing back from her. "But I can't wait to get you home."

Jade smiled and wondered if she should enjoy her

reunion with James before dropping the bomb on him that she might be pregnant. As they finished up their meal, Jade decided to wait until she got confirmation from her doctor before telling James that she thought they were going to be parents.

"Do me a favor," she said as they walked out of the restaurant. "Take me to the hotel so that I can get a change of clothes."

"All right," he said. "I'll wait for you in the lobby, because I'm sure Serena isn't going to be happy to see me."

Jade laughed. "Actually, today she might be."

"And believe it or not, Maurice missed you."

"That I find hard to believe," she said, with a dismissive laugh.

"It's just as believable as Serena being happy to see me," James said.

"I guess we've been making the people around us pretty damned miserable," she said.

James nodded in agreement as the valet brought his car around.

Jade slid into the passenger side of the car as James tipped the young valet. Then James got into the car. "All right," he said. "Let's get out of here and into my sheets."

She winked at him and refused to think about anything except the pleasure that James was going to give her as soon as they got to his place. But first, she needed to pack a few things.

James dropped her off in front of the hotel, and she headed for the room. When she made it upstairs and opened the door, Jade's mouth dropped. Serena and Antonio Billups were locked in a passionate embrace near the glass doors.

Jade cleared her throat loudly, causing the duo to break off their kiss. "Sorry to interrupt," she said when they turned and looked at her.

"Jade, I didn't expect you back so soon," Serena said, her face flushed with embarrassment.

"I'd better go," Antonio said.

"No," Jade said. "I'm just grabbing my bag. Serena, love, we'll talk tomorrow." She grabbed her bag and headed out the door. As soon as she reached the lobby, Jade called Serena's cell.

"Yes," Serena answered breathlessly.

"Please tell me that you aren't doing what I think you're doing!"

"Look, we're adults. There is nothing wrong with mixing a little business and pleasure. Besides, I had no idea that—"

"That you would get caught? Can you at least wait until the renovations are complete before you start mixing?"

"I have to go. Remember checkout is at eleven," Serena said before hanging up.

Jade shook her head as she walked over to James.

"What's wrong?" he asked.

"The world is truly spinning out of control," she said.

James furrowed his brows. "Huh?"

"It's nothing. Serena's just acting really strangely." Jade linked her arm with James's. "But that's not important. We have dessert to get to."

He licked his lips and smiled at her. "That's right."

The couple got into the car and headed out to James's house. Jade closed her eyes and allowed her mind to go to a day when she and James would pull into his driveway with a beautiful little girl in

their backseat, fast asleep. Jade figured that James
would race to the backseat to lift his little angel
from the car seat. Jade would grab the diaper bag
and open the front door quietly as to not wake the
baby. Once inside, however, the baby would wake
up and start cooing at her loving daddy.

"Hey," James said, breaking into Jade's fantasy.
"Are you sure that you're all right?"

"Yes, I'm fine," she said as they pulled into his
driveway.

"Still shocked by your friend?" James asked,
probing.

Jade nodded, hoping to mask the real reason for
her silence.

He wrapped his arm around her waist after she got
out of the car. "Jade," he whispered, "I missed you."

She twirled around and brought her lips on top
of his, hungrily kissing him. James lifted her into his
arms as he backed up to the porch. Gingerly, he
stepped up the three brick steps, still kissing her and
savoring the taste of her tongue. He dropped down
on the wrought-iron chair, with Jade still wrapped
around his body. He probed the depths of her mouth
with his tongue as he slipped his hand underneath
her dress. Jade moaned as his fingers pushed aside
her panties and entered the wet folds of flesh between her thighs. She pressed her hips into his probing fingers, quietly urging him to find that spot to
make her scream. James heeded her silent request
and found her throbbing bud of sensuality. Arching
her back, she nearly climaxed as he moved his finger
back and forth, up and down, and in a circle. Her
moans turned to screams as he used his free hand to
stroke her bottom. Every nerve in her body was

standing on end, so every time he touched her, she was near the brink.

Neither of them cared about being outside. James had enough privacy shrubs planted that no one would see them unless they drove up the driveway. So, when James pulled her dress over her head, Jade went along with the flow and clawed at the buttons on his shirt. He unsnapped her bra and let the straps fall down her smooth shoulders. She pushed his shirt off and brushed her lips across his chest while easing down his torso. She flicked her tongue across his navel as she reached for the button fly of his slacks. She made quick work of unbuttoning and unzipping his slacks, and then she slipped her hand inside, stroking his manhood, which was already hard. Dipping lower, she brought her lips over the tip of his hardness, taking him deep into her mouth.

James moaned as she bobbed up and down. He buried his hands in her silky hair as she brought him close to climax. Pulling away from her, he once again lifted her and carried her inside. They didn't make it to the bedroom, as James placed her on the sofa, kicked out of his slacks and then lowered himself on top of her. He made short order of removing her lace panties. Jade wrapped her legs around his waist as he reached into a pocket of his discarded slacks and retrieved a condom. She closed her eyes as he slid the sheath in place. Her mind went back to the one time they hadn't used protection. Why had they been so irresponsible, and how were they going to deal with the consequences of their actions?

Jade tensed up momentarily.

James looked down at her. "What's wrong?" he asked.

"Nothing," she said. "I want you."

She stroked his cheek and pressed her hips into his. James plunged into her, delving into her wetness and crying out her name. Jade gyrated her hips, falling into rhythm with James and moaning as he hit her spot over and over again. She pressed her mouth into his shoulder, gently biting him as the effect of an orgasm gnawed at her senses.

James groaned as he spent himself. He focused on Jade, who sank back into the cushions with her eyes closed. He stroked her leg and smiled. "Let's go to bed," he said as he rose to his feet.

"Uh," she groaned, "give me a second."

He bent down and picked her up. "Come on. I think we both need some sleep."

Once they were in bed, Jade snuggled up next to James, resting her head against his chest, but she didn't fall asleep. Nervousness flowed through her body as she thought about telling James that she was pregnant. *What if he doesn't want children? What are you going to do then?* Jade rolled over onto her side, with her back facing James. Seconds later he had his arm around her waist.

"I'm not even going to ask what's wrong, because you're going to say nothing," he said, his voice thick with sleep.

"There isn't anything wrong," she said.

"Uh-huh," he said, leaning his head against her shoulder. "Relax and go to sleep, all right?"

"Yes, sir," she said, patting his cheek gently. Jade closed her eyes, but sleep didn't come easily. Her torturous dreams were filled with images of James rejecting her and their child.

The next morning James was up early, with a smile on his face. He went into the kitchen to prepare Jade a simple breakfast in bed. Despite what she'd said all night, he knew something was wrong. Maybe it was the stress of starting the restaurant; maybe there was something going on in Atlanta that she didn't want to talk about.

As he cracked eggs, James tried to shut his mind off to the doubt that was creeping in. Part of him couldn't help but wonder if she and Stephen did try to see if they could work out their problems. *Stop it*, he chided himself silently as he flipped the eggs in the pan.

After the eggs were done, he brewed a pot of coffee and dropped some bread in the toaster. He topped off their breakfast with a couple of links of turkey sausage and placed their plates on a tray. He crept back into the bedroom and watched Jade as she slumbered. She looked like an angel against the white cotton sheets. He was happy that she was getting some rest after she'd tossed and turned all night, and he almost felt guilty about waking her up to eat. Still, watching her made him think about what it would feel like to wake up every morning with her by his side. Was he really ready to settle down and get married?

Jade had awakened feelings in him that no other woman had. He craved her presence, yearned for her touch, and was aroused by the sound of her voice. Staring at her in this moment, he saw the other half of himself and the woman that he'd wait at the altar for. Setting the tray on the nightstand, James eased into the bed, beside her, and brushed his lips across her cheek. "Wake up, Sleeping Beauty," he said.

Like butterfly wings, her eyes fluttered open. "Is it morning already?" she grumbled.

"Yes, and I made breakfast, so you don't have to get up." James held a buttery triangle of toast to her lips.

Jade didn't take a bite; instead, she bolted from the bed as if she had been stung by a bee and dashed into the bathroom. James sniffed the bread, wondering if the butter was spoiled. Placing the toast back on the plate, he crossed over to the bathroom and knocked on the door.

"Jade, are you all right?"

All he got in response to his query was the sound of Jade vomiting. Part of him wanted to kick the door in. What had made her sick? Just as he was about to open the door, Jade walked out, with a lopsided grin on her face. "What a way to start the morning," she remarked.

"Are you sick?"

She shook her head. "Not exactly."

"So, was it the food or my morning breath?"

Jade sucked her bottom lip between her teeth and closed her eyes.

James drew her into his arms. "Baby, what's wrong?"

She shook her head and blinked rapidly before saying, "I don't know for sure. When I get home, I'm going to the doctor."

"Is this what's been troubling you?"

"Yes," she said quietly.

"It's probably just a bug or something. You'll be fine, and I tell you, I feel like going to Atlanta, if you'll have me. I do owe you a visit."

She smiled, but the smile didn't reach her eyes. "All right. When?"

"This morning. Just let me call the office and clear my calendar. We can go have dinner with my mother, depending on what your doctor says."

"You don't have to come today," she said nervously. "Besides, I'm sure you don't want to sit in a doctor's office, waiting on me."

James stepped back from her. "What's the real deal?" he asked.

Closing her eyes, she blurted out, "I think I might be pregnant."

James nearly lost his balance as her words sank in. "Pre-pregnant? Do you know for sure?"

"No, that's why I'm going to the doctor. I took three home pregnancy tests, and they all had the same result."

"All right," James said, taking a deep breath. "Why don't we just find out who Kenya's doctor is and see if we can get an appointment so that you don't have to drive back to Atlanta with this on your mind?"

A look of relief spread across Jade's face. "Thanks," she said.

"You know that if you are pregnant, there's only one thing for us to do."

She narrowed her eyes at him. "And just what is that?"

James folded his arms across his chest. "Get married."

Jade nearly swooned at James's suggestion. "What did you say?"

"I think you heard me."

She inhaled and ran her hand over her face. "James . . ."

"I'm old-fashioned, and if there is a baby, I'm going to take care of my responsibilities."

"That doesn't mean you have to marry me. How long will we be together before you start regretting giving up your life because . . ."

James lifted her chin and looked directly into her eyes. "I'm not giving up anything. I'm going to be able to go to sleep with you every night, wake up with you every morning, and you're giving me a gift that—"

"That you may not want," Jade said. "How can we get married when we barely know each other?"

"I know I want to be a major part of my child's life, and the best way to do that is to be married to his or her mother."

Jade pushed him in the chest. "Sounds so romantic," she said sarcastically. "When I get married, I don't want it to be out of some sense of obligation. Because you and I both know you wouldn't be proposing marriage if we didn't think I was pregnant."

"All right. Fine," he said. "I'm going to call Kenya and see about getting you an appointment with her doctor."

Jade couldn't continue her argument, because a wave of nausea washed over her and she ran back to the bathroom. *What are you doing?* she thought as she hugged the toilet. *If James wants to marry you, why are you fighting him on it? Do you really want to be another baby's mother? He didn't even ask you if the child was his. He just wanted to step up to the plate.*

Jade rose to her feet and rinsed her mouth and held on to the sink.

"Jade," James called out, "are you all right in there?"

"I'm fine," she replied as she walked out of the bathroom. "James, I'm sorry."

"About what?"

"Bringing all this confusion into your life," she said. "I understand you want to do the right thing, but don't feel—"

"You didn't make this baby alone," he said. "And you're not going to raise it alone. Kenya's doctor can see you at one thirty."

She nodded and looked at the clock on the wall. "I'd better call Serena."

CHAPTER 26

Jade watched James as they drove to the doctor's office. She was happy that Serena had agreed to take her car back to Atlanta and that James had agreed to take her home as soon as she was ready to go. What was she going to do if her suspicions turned out to be true? Would she and James really get married, and if they did, would the marriage last?

"We're here," James said as he pulled up to the Carolinas Medical Center facility.

Jade got out of the car, then walked slowly.

James slowed his pace and waited for her. "Jade," he said, "baby, everything is going to be fine." It was almost as if he could read her nervousness.

She smiled at him tentatively as he held the door open for her. "I know. I'm just a little scared."

"Why?" he inquired.

She shrugged her shoulders and, with a pensive look on her face, said, "I'm not sure I can do this. If there is a baby, how do I know I'm going to be a good mother? It's not like I grew up with the best parents in the world. They spent most of my childhood fighting like cats and dogs and cheating on each other, as if it was some kind of sport."

James hugged her gently as they took a seat in the waiting room. "We're not our parents," he said. "My father was the biggest asshole that ever lived. I promised myself if I ever got married and had children, I'd be there for them in ways that my father wasn't there for my mother and me."

"What if we fail at this and do something to damage our child?" she mused. "I don't know if . . ."

"What are you saying?" he asked. "Do you want to have this child?"

"Yes, of course, but I can't help but wonder about these things."

"I'm here to support you, and when we get married, I'm not going to be one of those dads who expect you to do everything. We're going to be partners in every sense of the word."

Jade turned away from him, willing the tears in her eyes to just stay there. She'd dreamed of being proposed to, and there was champagne, roses, and chocolate. Not the feeling of an obligation or a duty to a baby. What about real love? What about desire?

James stroked her back. "Jade?"

"Yes?" she said, wiping her eyes before facing James.

"What's the matter?"

She opened her mouth, about to say the things that she'd been thinking, but a nurse walked into the waiting room and called her name. She and James stood up quickly, nearly bumping heads, and walked over to the nurse. "Follow me," the nurse said, smiling at them.

As they walked into the examination room, James

kissed Jade's hand. His touch said that everything was going to be all right. But Jade wondered how long it would be before he stopped touching her, period. This wasn't a bygone era where they were supposed to get married because she was pregnant.

The nurse took Jade's temperature and blood pressure, then said, "The doctor will be in momentarily."

"Thanks," Jade replied.

James took her hand in his and stroked it with his thumb. "Nervous?"

"That's one way to describe it," she said softly.

"Once we find out what's going on, then we can move forward," he said.

"Where are we going? Is marriage really the right thing if I am pregnant?"

Before James could respond, the doctor walked in. "Good afternoon," he said.

James and Jade responded to his greeting.

The bushy-haired doctor smiled at them. "So, you two think that there's a baby? Excited?"

Jade smiled nervously and nodded.

"Well," the doctor said, "I'm going to need to take some blood and do a pelvic exam. When I do the exam, sir, I'm going to need you to leave the room."

"All right," James said. He looked at Jade, who had a tense look on her face.

A female nurse walked into the examination room to assist the doctor. James waited until the blood was drawn and then left the room. As soon as he walked out of the room, his cell phone rang.

"Hello?" he said.

"Tell me why you and Jade needed Kenya's OB's number?" Maurice asked.

"Damn. Do you two tell each other everything?"

"James, you didn't get her pregnant, did you?"

"So what if I did?" James growled. "I don't see how it's any of your business."

"All right," Maurice said. "I know I said I was going to give Jade a fair shake. But this whole pregnancy thing is a little suspicious."

"I'm going to hang up on you before I say something that I might regret in a month or so."

"What if she is pregnant?"

"Then I'm going to do the right thing."

"Which is?"

"Marry her and be a father to my child."

"Have you lost your damned mind?" Maurice boomed. "How in the hell are you going to marry a woman you've known for about two months?"

"How long did you know Lauryn before you asked her to marry you? Look how that turned out."

"Okay. How long are you going to throw my mistake in my face? I'm trying to stop you from making one," said Maurice.

"I love her," James said.

"And if you keep saying it, you might convince yourself," Maurice shot back.

James pressed the end button on the phone and shook his head.

Jade closed her eyes as the doctor began the pelvic exam. A part of her wanted to have James's child and the life he'd been telling her they'd have as husband and wife. She knew that their son or daughter would grow up feeling protected, unlike the way she had. But what kind of marriage would they really have? Would the fire between them fizzle at some point? Would James just look at her as an obligation?

"All right, Miss Christian," the doctor said. "We're done. I can have your results in a few hours and will give you a call."

Jade sat up on the table and nodded. "I put my cell phone number on my form," she said.

"Okay. Well, you can get dressed and head out," replied the doctor. "Do you want me to send your husband back in?"

"He's not . . . yes," she said.

The doctor nodded, and he and the nurse left the examination room. Jade released a sigh and pulled her cell phone out to call Serena. She figured her friend should've made it back to Atlanta already.

"Are you knocked up?" Serena asked.

"Hello to you, too," Jade said.

"I'm hoping you're calling me to tell me that you're not pregnant."

"I don't know," Jade said. "But if I am, James wants to get married." Silence greeted her from the other end of the phone. "Serena?"

"I hope you said no. What does he think this is? The fifties? People don't just get married because there's a baby involved."

Jade sighed, knowing she had called the wrong person. "Whatever," she said.

"My God, you're considering it!" Serena shrieked. "Are you insane?"

"So what if I am? You know how I grew up," Jade said. "If I'm pregnant, I don't want my child to be faced with what I went through growing up."

"And marrying a near stranger is going to make your child's life better?"

"I've got to go," Jade said as James walked into the room. She hung up the phone over Serena's protest and hopped off the table.

"What did he say?" James asked.

"The test results should be back in a few hours," she said.

"Want to go get something to eat?" he asked.

She nodded. "That's fine. I just want to get—," she began, but her cell phone started to chirp. She was surprised that it wasn't Serena and curious that it was Kandace. She held her finger up to James as she answered the call. "Hello."

"Hey," Kandace said. "You know, Serena told us that you think you're pregnant."

"I figured that," Jade replied.

"Did you tell James?"

"Yes."

"Good."

"Uh, James and I are about to leave the doctor's office," Jade said, alerting her friend that she couldn't really talk.

"I love you, Jade, and I wouldn't try to tell you what to do, but make this decision with James," Kandace said sagely.

"I will," Jade said. "And thanks."

"Call me later, okay?"

"I will," Jade said. She hung up the phone and turned to James. "Let's go."

"Everything all right?"

"Yeah," she said. "You know news spreads fast."

"Your girls?"

Jade nodded as they headed to the lobby. "Let's just eat and not talk about them or anything else."

"Avoiding the subject isn't going to make it go away," he said.

She rolled her eyes as they walked out of the building. "I know this. But do we have to think about it every second and every moment?"

"Fine," he said, not wanting to argue with her.

"James," she said, "I don't want to make this a bigger issue than it needs to be."

"I don't think it gets much bigger than a baby," he said flatly as they got into the car.

"I know that, but we don't even know if there is a baby yet and . . ."

"And if there is a baby, I stand by what I said. I want to marry you."

"And if there isn't a baby, then what? Do I still get the ring and the wedding?" Jade snapped. "I told you, I don't want you to marry me out of an obligation to our child."

"Would you rather I walk away so you and your friends can talk about what a bastard I am? What the hell do you want from me, Jade?"

"Nothing," she said. "Nothing at all."

James focused on the road, not responding to Jade. Anger surged through his system. How could she sit there and say she didn't want anything from him when he was offering her everything?

They pulled up to the restaurant and James slammed out of the car, leaving Jade sitting on the passenger side, with a blank look on her face.

Moments later she walked into the restaurant and took a seat across from James at the booth he'd chosen in the rear of the dining area.

"James," she said, her voice low. "When I said what I said, it wasn't—"

"Did the doctor call?" he asked as he picked up the menu.

"No. James, please," she said, grabbing his hand. "Listen to me."

"What, Jade? What do you have to say now that you haven't already said?"

She closed her eyes and placed her hands flat on the table. "James, I don't want us to make a mistake," she said quietly. "I don't want you to feel as if you're giving up your life because we both made mistakes."

"*I* made the mistake," he said. "I should've been more careful and protected us every time we made . . . had sex. But don't fault me for wanting to give my child something I didn't have."

"Don't you think I want our child to have a better childhood than I had?" Jade said. "But what kind of life are we going to have if we . . ."

"Do you think I would've asked you to marry me if I didn't think our relationship would work?" James asked. "It wasn't like I hated you when we made this child."

"If there is a child."

"And if there isn't a child, do you think I'm going to take away my proposal?"

Her eyes stretched to the size of silver dollars. "What are you saying?"

"I'm saying that I love you, whether you're pregnant or not," James said. "But if this isn't what you want, let me know."

She looked away from him. Of course this was what she wanted, but did he want this as well? Granted,

James was saying all the right things, but were they true and lasting?

"I'm not . . . I don't know what . . . James, are you sure? When I get married, I want it to be forever," she said.

"And you think I don't? What kind of man do you think I am? Do you really think I would ask you to marry me and not want it to last? Child or no child, I want you in my life today, tomorrow, forever."

The tears that welled up in her eyes this time were tears of joy. "James, if you mean it, then yes, I will marry you," she said.

James leaned across the table and kissed her lips gently. "Thank you," he said, then kissed her again, this time with passion and fire that made her knees buckle.

They broke off the kiss as the waitress walked up to the table and cleared her throat. "Are you two ready to order?" she asked, with a sly smile on her face.

James winked at the waitress and asked for a few minutes to look over the menu.

CHAPTER 27

After eating a down-home lunch of fried chicken, collard greens, and corn bread, James and Jade headed back to his place, still waiting on the call from the doctor's office.

When they pulled into the driveway, James's cell phone rang. "Yeah?" he said into the phone.

"James, it's Kenya. Is Jade still with you?"

"Yes. Why? What's going on?"

"I have news about her case against Stephen, and I misplaced her cell phone number," she said.

"Hold on," James said. He handed his phone to Jade. "It's Kenya. She has news about your case." He parked the car and got out to give Jade privacy to talk with her attorney.

He was about to walk up the front steps and open the door when he heard Maurice speeding into the driveway. James waited at the top of the steps as his brother barreled toward him.

"Well, is she pregnant?" Maurice asked.

"Maurice, go home," James said.

"No. Don't you think you need to—"

"Need to what?" Jade asked when she got out of the car.

"Jade," Maurice said, plastering a smile on his face, "I guess congratulations are in order?"

"I'm going inside," she said, rolling her eyes at Maurice.

"Wait," Maurice said. "I want both of you to hear this."

James folded his arms across his chest and looked at his brother. "I'm sure this is going to be rich," he said.

"I'm sorry," Maurice said. "Jade, I've been judging you unfairly, and if my brother loves you, who am I to say anything about it?"

"So, you've finally realized that it's my life and I can do with it what I want," James snapped.

"I realize that I've been an asshole to both of you. Jade, I truly apologize," Maurice said.

She raised an eyebrow. "Do you mean it?"

Maurice nodded. "Kenya informed me that I'm not doing any favors to the family by acting like an asshole."

"Jade and I are getting married," James said. "And it's not simply for the sake of our child."

Maurice nodded. "Do you know for sure that you two are having a baby?"

As if on cue, Jade's cell phone rang. "Hello," she said.

"Ms. Christian, this is Nurse Neill from the doctor's office, and I have news for you."

"Okay," Jade said breathlessly.

"Congratulations. You're pregnant. You're going to need to see your regular obstetrician to get an ultrasound and a due date," the nurse said.

"All right," Jade said, then hung up the phone, with mixed emotions.

James and Maurice looked at her and begged with their eyes to know the news.

"So?" James asked after a few moments of silence passed.

"We're having a baby," she said quietly.

James turned around and pulled her into his arms. He gently kissed her on the cheek. "Are you all right?"

She nodded and placed her hand against his chest. "I'm going inside," she whispered.

Maurice walked up the steps and stood near his brother. "Good news?"

"Go home," James said. "Jade and I need a moment alone. And let *me* tell Ma that I'm getting married."

Maurice threw his hands up. "All right. But I meant what I said."

"All right. Whatever." James walked inside and closed the door in his brother's face.

Jade sat on the sofa, trying to digest all the information that she'd received in the last five minutes. First, Kenya had told her that Stephen had filed a countersuit against her, claiming that she'd used inside information to purchase the building in Charlotte, and that he was suing her for 1.5 million dollars. And on top of that, she had got the confirmation that she was indeed pregnant. As James crossed over to her, she tried to smile.

He took her hands in his and kissed them.

"So, that call from Kenya wasn't good news?" he asked knowingly.

"The bastard's suing me for over a million dollars," Jade said. "I can't believe he has the nerve."

"He's an asshole. That's just who Stephen is."

"This is too much," she said. "I don't want to battle this thing out with him in court. Not now."

"We'll figure something out," James said. "Don't even worry about it right now."

"I have to get back to Atlanta and let the girls know. I got them into this mess, and I'm going to have to get them out of it."

"You want to leave now?" he asked.

Jade nodded. "The sooner I let them know about Stephen's countersuit, the better. We're going to have to stand together on this if we're ever going to get this restaurant opened."

"I can't believe he's suing you when it was your money that helped him get where he is, slimy son of a bitch."

Jade smiled despite herself. Her future husband had her back, and that was all the affirmation she needed to know that she was going to make it through all this—the pregnancy and Stephen's lawsuit.

Kenya had told her that all they needed to do was answer the countersuit and prove that Stephen had used her money to research the restaurant's location.

Leaning against James, she closed her eyes and exhaled. "Maybe I don't have to hurry back to Atlanta. I want to get some rest."

James led her to the bedroom and watched her as she stretched out on the bed. Within minutes, she was asleep, and he crept out of the bedroom and grabbed the phone. He wanted to end this thing with Stephen before it got too far out of hand, and if he had to offer the bastard an olive branch, then he would do it. James prayed he wouldn't have to beat him over the head with that same branch.

He dialed 411 and asked for Stephen's number in Atlanta. The operator gave him the number and told him that for an additional seventy-five cents, the number could be automatically dialed. James opted for it, because he didn't want to write the son of a bitch's telephone number down.

"This is Stephen," a man said when he answered the phone.

"Stephen, it's James Goings."

"What the hell do you want?"

"You need to end this thing with Jade."

Stephen laughed. "I'm not ending a thing. She started this war when she filed that suit against me and stole my restaurant. Forget her and don't call me, trying to play hero."

"Listen to me for once in your sorry damned life. Why don't you try to do the right thing?" James snarled. "You know that you wouldn't have the success that you do if you hadn't stolen from women, including my mother."

"Not that again. Will you let it go? Don't be mad at me because I have a booming restaurant and your mother is stuck in the slums, running a bakery that she doesn't even own."

I should hang up this phone, because he's two seconds from getting cursed out. Who in the hell does he think he is? "Look," James said. "If things are going so well for you, why don't you just give Jade her investment back and let this thing go? She's moved on. Why don't you do the same?"

Stephen laughed again. "You think you got something real special, don't you? If I decided right now that I wanted her back, I could have her."

It was James's turn to laugh. "This isn't some pissing contest over a woman who loves me. It's about you doing the right thing."

"James, you and that bitch can go to hell. I'll see her in court, unless I decide to go to her house tonight and get an out-of-court settlement, if you know what I mean."

James slammed the phone down because if Stephen said another disrespectful thing, he was going to drive to Atlanta and give him another beat down. Turning around with a scowl on his face, he saw Jade standing behind him.

"I wish you hadn't done that," she said.

"What?"

"Called Stephen. James, you know how he is, and that call is only going to make matters worse," she said.

"First of all, I don't want you to worry about that and to go through added stress because of that. . . ."

"You're stressing me right now," she said, closing her hands over her ears. "Seriously, James, this thing with Stephen has been a problem for us since we met, and I don't need you to get involved now."

"And I don't want you to get so worked up over him that something happens to you or the baby."

She shook her head. "I'm pregnant. I'm not an invalid. Isn't that what you told Maurice about Kenya?"

"Will you calm down?" James said evenly. "I'm not trying to stress you, but Stephen is—"

"My problem and Kenya and I will handle it. Please don't go behind my back in the name of helping me," she said, then stomped back to the bedroom.

I can't win for losing, he thought as he followed her. James reached out and grabbed her elbow. "Do you want me to apologize for trying to make things right? Because I'm not."

"What?"

"We're getting married, we're going to have a partnership, and if I see something is going to hurt you, then I'm not going to stand by and watch it happen. Do you think I'm sorry for wanting to protect you? Well, I'm not."

She looked at him, not saying a word. Though she wanted to be angry, Jade realized that this was just what she'd wanted all her life. She wanted to be protected, and she wanted someone to look out for her best interests. However, now that it looked as if she had it, she didn't know how to handle it.

"Jade," he said.

"What?"

"I love you, and I want you to know that we're not always going to agree, but I'm always going to have your back. If that means calling an asshole like Stephen and trying to appeal to his human side, then I'm going to do it."

She couldn't fight anymore, and she opened her arms to him, beckoning him to embrace her. James hugged her tightly, pulling her against his chest. Then he gently kissed her lips, all the while whispering how much he loved her. A lone tear slid down her cheek.

"I love you, too," she replied before he kissed her again.

This time it was fiery, the kind of kiss that made her weak. When his hands slipped up the back of her blouse, she melted against him. His touch made everything seem all right, made her forget that there was a world outside. It was love, it was special, and it was going to be this way forever. Hungrily, she responded to his probing kiss, and her tongue touched his as he pulled her closer to him. Then they fell against the bed. Jade straddled his body, breaking off the kiss long enough to unzip his pants while he unbuttoned her blouse. He slipped her bra straps from her shoulders as she ground against his stiff manhood. James leaned in, outlining her erect nipples with his tongue. Moaning, she sped up her grinding, then pulled him inside her wetness.

James released a guttural groan as she enveloped him in her warmth. She rode him so hard and so fast that he grabbed her hips just to keep pace. He thrust his pelvis forward, hitting her in the center of her G-spot. Jade shuddered with growing desire. Stretching her arms above her head, she cried out his name as she arched her back and took his full length deeper inside her. James pressed deeper, holding her hips steady as he lost himself inside her wetness, feeling as if he were swimming in a heated pond on the most beautiful place on earth. Jade gripped his shoulders as her body shook. Neither of them wanted the feeling to end or the passion to diminish. They slowed their pace, gently rocking back and forth, riding a wave of ecstasy that ebbed like the waning tide of the sea. James kissed her, softly capturing her lips like an elusive butterfly.

"I love you," he whispered in between kisses.

Breathlessly, she replied, "I love you, too."

Finally, they reached their climax, collapsing in each other's arms. He sought out her lips again, tracing their lushness with the tip of his tongue.

Jade smiled. "Stop," she said playfully. "That tickles."

James laughed and pulled her closer. "I guess we need to think about getting you home."

"And I was starting to think of this bed as home," she said, then kissed him on the cheek.

"It will be as soon as we move your stuff from Atlanta, and we have to tell my mother about the upcoming wedding and the baby," he said.

She snuggled closer to him and sighed. "I love you so much," she said.

"Same here, baby," he said. Then they both drifted off to sleep.

The ringing of James's phone woke him and Jade around eleven that night. Groggily, James rolled over and picked up the phone. "Hello?"

"James, it's Serena."

"How did you get my home number?" he asked.

"That's not important. Do you know where Jade is?"

"She's asleep."

"Can you wake her up, please? It's important." Serena's voice sounded desperate, and James felt compelled to wake Jade.

"It's Serena," he said as he held the phone out to a confused-looking Jade.

"Yeah?" Jade said when she took the handset.

"I was talking to one of the editors at the *AJC* at dinner, and he said there is going to be a front-page story about Stephen's lawsuit against you in tomorrow's paper."

"What?" Jade answered, bolting straight up in the bed. "How did . . . Is there any way your editor friend can stop the story?"

"No," Serena said. "I tried. I told him that he should at least get your side before running the story, and he said he spoke with your attorney, who said, 'No comment.' Why didn't she just say something or have them call you? Do you know her mother is the executive editor of the paper? If she can't get that story killed, maybe you need a new attorney."

"Calm down, Serena," Jade said, then yawned. "Sometimes it's best to keep quiet."

"You do realize how this is making you and us look?"

"Stephen and I are going to court, and we're going to handle this. I don't care what lies he's telling the media. But right now I'm going back to sleep, and maybe you ought to do the same."

"Whatever," Serena said. "When are you coming back to Atlanta to clean up this mess?"

"I'll be there in the morning, after I meet with Kenya."

"All right," Serena said. "And tell James I'm sorry that I called his home phone."

"Okay," Jade said, then handed the phone back to James.

"What's wrong?" he asked as he hung up the phone.

"Stephen went to the press with the lawsuit, and there's going to be a huge story in the *AJC* tomorrow."

James uttered a bombastic curse and shook his head. "What does he hope to accomplish?"

Lying back in the bed and in James's arms, she shrugged. "Can we just deal with it tomorrow?" She planted a sweet kiss on his chest. "Let's go back to sleep."

The next morning James and Jade got an early start heading to Atlanta. They stopped off for coffee and doughnuts at Krispy Kreme, and then it was full steam ahead.

"Too bad we couldn't wait for some of your mother's cinnamon buns," she said as she crumpled half of her glazed doughnut in a napkin.

"You just want the icing," James joked.

"Dripping all over you," she replied, with a smile.

"Funny," he said. "But you know I can arrange that."

Jade smiled and curled up in the seat. James glanced at her as she closed her eyes, and smiled. He would do anything to protect Jade and their child. Stephen wasn't going to get away with trying to embarrass her, and James wasn't going to sit by idly and let her be hurt by his lies.

Whatever it takes to keep her safe, I'm going to do it, he thought, fully focusing on the road.

CHAPTER 28

James and Jade arrived in Atlanta about 9:30. The first thing Jade did was make James stop at the first gas station that sold the *Atlanta Journal-Constitution*. She plopped fifty cents on the counter after picking up a copy of the paper, and there it was on the front page: RESTAURATEUR CLAIMS EX-LOVER OUT TO RUIN HIS BUSINESS.

"You mean to tell me there's no other news going on in Atlanta," she mumbled as she read the story back in the car. It read like a fictional tome. According to the paper, Jade was a vindictive and scorned lover who had once worked for Stephen, and when the relationship was over, she'd used insider information to block his expansion attempt and sued him for a gift she'd given him.

That son of a bitch, she thought as she balled up the paper.

"That bad?" James asked.

She nodded and squinted her eyes. "I just wish he would fall off the face of the earth."

"So do I."

Jade stopped short of asking him how they could make it happen. Instead, she just uncrumpled the paper and continued reading the story. Each paragraph made her anger grow like a wildfire.

"I can't believe this," she said. "That ass claims that I'm suing him because our relationship ended with him finding his true soul mate. As if I give a damn about him and Miss Plastic. This is an embarrassment. I can't believe a reputable paper would've printed this nonsense." Jade rolled the window down and tossed the paper out. "It's as if I just read the *National Enquirer* or something."

"You know, littering is a crime," James said. "Forget what he said in that paper. We know the truth, and after this court case, so will everyone else."

"I hope Kenya can make this go away."

"I bet she can. She's a hell of an attorney. And trust me, Stephen has no idea as to what he's stepped in."

Jade smiled, imagining Stephen losing in court and her reputation being restored.

"Jade?" James said.

"Hmm?"

"I asked you if you wanted to head home first or go to my mom's bakery."

"We can go to the bakery first. Maybe a few of your mom's treats will put me in a better mood."

James grinned and shot her a seductive glance that told her he knew how to fix her attitude. She smacked him on the shoulder as she read his racy thoughts.

"What did I do?" he asked, with a smile.

"I know what you were thinking," she said, and before she could say more, her cell phone rang. "Hello?"

"Jade, it's Kenya. I'm so sorry about that story in the *AJC*. I have a good mind to sue them for libel, but my mother would kill me."

"I'm in Atlanta now. This is getting out of hand," Jade replied.

"I know. But we're going to win, because Stephen laid out his case in the press, and it doesn't match what he said in the suit. He's going to regret that story. So, do me a favor and avoid him at all costs."

"You don't have to tell me twice," Jade replied.

"Do me a favor and relay that message to James," Kenya said knowingly.

Jade looked over at her man and smiled. "I'll let him know," she said.

"Let me know what?" James asked when she'd placed her phone back in her pocket.

"To stay away from Stephen. Kenya's orders."

James mumbled under his breath and then said, "Let's hope I don't accidentally on purpose run into him fist first."

"James!" Jade exclaimed.

"Kidding, only kidding," he said unconvincingly.

"Sure you are." She shook her head. "Promise me that you're going to be cool."

"All I can do is try," he replied.

James pulled up to the bakery and was surprised to see a line of people standing at the entrance. "I wonder what's going on," he said as he put the car in park.

"I don't know," Jade said, "but can we bottle some of it and take it back to Charlotte when we open the restaurant?"

He laughed as they got out of the car. He pushed through the crowd to get to the door, and he pulled on it, finding that it was locked. He looked inside and saw his mother sitting at one of the tables, with her head down. James banged on the door, calling out his mother's name. Maryann turned and looked at the door. Slowly, she walked over to the entrance and unlocked the door. She ushered James and Jade in, then told the other patrons that the bakery was closed until further notice.

"Ma, what's going on?" James asked after she'd relocked the door.

"Stephen Carter purchased this building," Maryann said. Then she walked behind the counter and handed James the letter she'd received from Stephen's attorney. "He's shutting me down."

James read the letter and his blood boiled. "How in the hell did this happen?"

"The owners of the building wanted to make some quick cash, and Stephen came by with an offer," Maryann explained. "That little bastard."

"I'm so sorry," Jade said softly.

Maryann shook her head. "It's all right. I'm going to relocate my bakery, and Stephen can have this building. It's falling apart, anyway, and I hope when he walks in, it crumbles on his head."

"No, Ma, I'm not going to stand for this," James said as he pulled out his cell phone and dialed the attorney's number on the letterhead.

"Timothy Harrington's office. How may I help you?" the woman who answered the phone asked.

"I need to speak to Mr. Harrington about a letter he sent to my client on behalf of Stephen Carter," James said.

"Hold on please."

Seconds later Timothy Harrington was saying hello.

"Mr. Harrington, James Goings. What is this letter that you sent to Maryann Goings about the purchase of her bakery?"

"Well, if you read the letter, it says that the building was purchased and we want the premises cleared within thirty days. What's there to question?"

"The question is, how can you represent an asshole that would throw a woman out of her establishment and close down a neighborhood staple?" Anger peppered James's tone.

"Sir, I don't have to take this abuse from you," Harrington said.

"But you're going to represent trash like Carter, and you don't think what he's doing is abuse?"

"Just hang up the phone, James," Maryann said in an exasperated voice. "I don't feel like fighting with Stephen and his lawyer."

James hung up and crossed over to his mother. "Mo and I will find you another place to open up a bakery right here in Sweet Auburn," he said as he enveloped her in a hug.

Maryann sighed. "Good luck on that. Do you know how much real estate is going for around here these days? Since the buppies and yuppies started moving in, Sweet Auburn isn't what it used to be."

"Those buppies and yuppies love your bakery," James said, "and Stephen knows that."

"He's jealous," Jade said, "because no one is standing in line for his dried-out food and fake ambiance. This is so like him. I don't even know where he got the money to even buy this building. He was on the verge of bankruptcy when I loaned him money."

James shook his head. "He must have found another fool to give him some money," he spat.

Jade nodded in agreement. "I've been that fool," she muttered.

"I'm going to stop feeling sorry for myself and open these doors while I still can," Maryann said as she wiped her hands against her thighs. "Stephen is going to get his."

James didn't say a word as his mother turned the lights on in the bakery.

Jade walked over to him and wrapped her arm around his waist. "Are you all right?" she asked.

"Hell no. I know why he's doing this, and he's not going to get away with it."

"This is my fault," Jade said.

"Not totally, but I told you this whole revenge thing wasn't worth it. This is the kind of shit I was talking about," he responded.

Jade dropped her arm from around him. "What are we going to do?"

"I'm going to take care of Stephen, one way or another," he said angrily, and then he stormed out of the bakery.

"Where is he going in such a hurry?" Maryann asked Jade.

"I think something bad is going to happen," Jade replied as she pulled out her cell phone and called Maurice.

James got into his car and headed to Stephen's restaurant. He wanted answers and he wanted blood. He double-parked his car in front of Stephen's building, not caring about the citation that he was sure to get if parking enforcement came by, and he hopped out, then stormed into the restaurant, which had just opened for lunch.

"Sir, how may I help you?" the hostess asked.

"Get Stephen out here right now," James bellowed.

"Do you have an appointment?"

James pushed past her and headed for the rear of the restaurant. He found Stephen's office and burst through the door. Stephen, who was sitting at his desk, on the phone, dropped the receiver and looked up at James, who was standing over him with his fist reared back. Before Stephen could react, James had clocked him in the face, knocking him out of his chair.

"You slimy son of a bitch! How dare you involve my mother in your bullshit!" James pounded away on him, unleashing a string of curses, which vibrated throughout the restaurant. Stephen was helpless to defend himself as his mouth filled with blood. James pulled back from him when Stephen's body went limp. "Get up, bastard!" he demanded.

Stephen didn't move immediately. Slowly, he tried to rise to his feet, holding on to the edge of his desk. He spat out a mouthful of blood and glared at James. "You're going to jail." He attempted to pick up the phone and dial 911, but James slapped the phone from his hands.

"You and Jade can fight all you want, but when you involve my mother, you have to deal with me."

"To hell with Jade and your mother. You wanted to get in the fight. Now deal with the consequences," Stephen said through labored breaths.

James rushed him and grabbed him by the collar.

"Check this out, bastard," he bellowed. "You're going to find my mother a new location for her bakery, or I'm going to break every bone in your damned body." He pushed Stephen into his chair and glared at him. "You have twenty-four hours."

"Do you think you're in any position to dictate anything to me?" Stephen coughed and spat blood into a handkerchief.

"Do you think I'm playing with you?" James asked.

"How effective do you think you're going to be from jail?"

"Twenty-four hours, or you'd better press charges and hope the Atlanta police can find me."

A security officer walked into the office. "Mr. Carter, is everything all right?"

James pushed past the rent-a-cop and headed out the door. Getting into his car, he headed back to the Sweet Auburn Bakery. He didn't notice that he had bloodstains on his shirt and his hands were swollen. The moment he walked into the bakery, Jade and Maryann rushed toward him.

"Where have you been and what happened?" they asked in concert.

Jade grabbed his hands and looked at the blood on his shirt. "James," she said.

"I lost my cool, but everything is fine," he said, shaking out of her grasp.

"James, you're not doing me any favors by fighting with Stephen," Maryann said. "I know that you and this man don't get along, but this isn't how we're going to handle this thing."

He looked down at his hands and the blood on his shirt. "All right. I messed up," James said.

"You're damned right you did," Maryann said.

"Beating that man isn't going to change a thing. Go clean yourself up." She stalked away from him.

Jade shook her head and hid her tears from James. His anger was scaring her, and she knew the only thing she could do to make things better was to drop her lawsuit against Stephen and try to end this war.

"Jade," Maryann said. "I hope you're not too put off by my son's behavior. He's always been very protective of me, and it has a lot to do with the hell his father put me through when he was growing up. James is highly protective of the people he loves."

"I know," Jade said quietly.

"But I don't condone violence. We've had enough of that in our lifetime," Maryann said. "I pray this thing doesn't get out of hand. Why is Stephen even doing this?"

Jade looked at her and started to say it was her fault, but James walked out of the bathroom and over to the women. "I'm sorry if I caused either of you to worry," he said calmly.

Maryann hugged her son. "You know, Stephen isn't your father."

"Ma," he said.

"Just remember that," Maryann added.

Customers began trickling into the bakery, asking Maryann why she hadn't been open earlier. She didn't pull any punches and told her loyal customers that her building had been purchased by Stephen Carter.

"The guy who was in the paper this morning?" a woman asked. "I've been to his restaurant, and it's horrible. Why does he want this building?"

Maryann shrugged her shoulders. "We're closing in thirty days," she said.

"That's a damned shame," the woman said as she took a huge bite of her pastry. "Do you have a Web site? Because I'd order these all day online."

Maryann smiled. "That's a great idea."

The woman continued munching on her pastry as Jade walked over to Maryann. "You know, you could always sell your stuff in the restaurant my friends and I are opening in Charlotte."

"My sons have been trying to get me to North Carolina for the longest time. I guess this is the—"

The door to the bakery flung open, and Maurice stormed inside. "Where's James?" he asked when he spotted Jade.

"He's in the back," Jade said. "Maurice, you really need to talk to him."

Maurice looked over at his mother and then grabbed Jade's arm. "Is this about Stephen?"

"Yes," Jade admitted.

"I knew you were trouble. Stephen wasn't worrying about my mother or this place until you and your friends started this war with him," Maurice stormed.

"Let go of me," Jade said as she jerked away from him. "I know this is hard on your mother, but I can make it right."

"What are you going to do? Leave us the hell alone? But you can't do that, since you got yourself knocked up," Maurice bellowed.

"What did you say?" Maryann asked. She turned and looked at Jade. "Are you pregnant?"

At that moment James walked to the front. "Maurice, what are you doing here?"

Maryann slammed her hand against the counter. "Wait a damned minute. Jade, are you pregnant?"

James glared at Maurice as Jade said, "Yes. That's one of the things that we came here to tell you."

"Pregnànt? Wow," Maryann said.

"And we're getting married," James said. "But this is not how I wanted you to find out."

"Well, this makes what you did even more reprehensible," Maryann said. "If you're getting ready to start a family, why are you acting like Mike Tyson?"

"What did he do?" Maurice asked.

"Got into a fight with Stephen Carter," Maryann reported.

"Again?" Maurice said.

"Again?" Maryann asked.

"Stephen came to my office in Charlotte, and we had an altercation," James explained.

"All because Jade and her friends started this thing with Stephen," Maurice blurted out.

"That's not fair," Jade said. "I wanted my money back and—"

"The only person to blame in this situation is Stephen. Jade's about to be a part of our family, and I don't want any more fighting today," Maryann said, waving her hands, and then returned to her customers.

Jade turned and walked toward the door.

"Jade!" James called out.

Jade ignored him and walked outside; then she called Kandace to come and pick her up.

CHAPTER 29

By the time Jade got into the car with Kandace, she had cried a bucket of tears. "I can't believe everything is such a mess," she said in between her sobs.

"I knew Stephen was dirty, but to go after James's mother? That's low even for him."

"Well, James's brother is trying to put all the blame on me," Jade said as she wiped her eyes. "And James just stood there, not saying a word. It's as if he agrees with him."

"Did James say that he blamed you?"

Jade shook her head. "Then," Kandace continued, "why in the hell are you running away like he told you to go to hell? I wonder about you sometimes."

"What do you mean by that?"

"I mean you shouldn't have been so quick to run out of there," Kandace said.

"But James just stood there while Maurice said all those ugly things."

"Really?" Kandace asked. "Or did you run out of there before you let him say anything? You have to realize that you're carrying his child, and it's not just about your hurt feelings."

Jade squeezed her eyes shut. "You're right."

"I know I am. I've always been the smart one."

"All right. Turn the car around," Jade said. "It's time for me to stand up to Maurice once and for all."

Kandace smiled. "And when baby Goings is old enough to understand, Godmommy Kandace is going to tell him or her all about the day she saved his or her family," she said, then made an illegal U-turn and headed back to the bakery.

James slammed inside the bakery and grabbed his brother's arm, dragging him to the back while their mother was checking out a line of customers. "What the hell is wrong with you?" James boomed.

"What are you talking about? That bi—"

James grabbed Maurice by the collar. "I have beaten one man today. Don't become the second one. Jade is going to be my wife, and you will respect her. She isn't the one who's forcing Ma out of here."

"Let go of me," Maurice said, pushing away from his brother. "Stephen wouldn't care about this building if it wasn't for her."

"And you blaming my pregnant fiancée is going to change matters how?" James demanded.

"All right, all right," Maurice said, throwing his hands up. "I was mad and lashed out. Jade called me because she was afraid that you were going to kill Stephen or end up in jail. I guess I shouldn't have gone off on her."

"You think?" James snapped. "Jade is the mother of my child, and I love her more than anything. Maybe I shouldn't have gone over there and beaten the hell out of Stephen, but I won't let you disrespect her. I will not have you making her cry because you have your ass on your shoulders. Stay away from her—us—until you can treat her with respect."

"Look, Jade has got you involved in this crap with Stephen, and you're not even acting like yourself."

"I'm protecting the woman I love, just like you did when you went after Lauryn."

"That was different, because Lauryn tried to kill Kenya," Maurice agreed.

"And Stephen is messing with my future wife and my mother."

"You need to check yourself, because you're acting like him. How long is it going to be before you're taking your anger out on Jade?"

James dropped his head. "I would never do that."

"She was scared when she called me."

"And that's a call I should've never made," Jade said from the door. "I didn't know you were going to come here and blame me for everything."

Maurice and James turned to face her. "I'm sorry about that," Maurice admitted sincerely. "I was wrong, and I shouldn't have said this is your fault. Stephen is the one who's forcing my mother out of here."

"I'm going to try and end this," Jade said. "I'm going to call Kenya and have her drop the lawsuit against Stephen, and maybe he will stop harassing your mom."

"And then he'll own this building!" James blurted. "No, you keep the lawsuit going, and we will figure the rest of this out."

"Do I get to have a say in what happens?" she asked.

"Yes," James said and jabbed Maurice in the stomach with his elbow.

"Of course," Maurice added.

"Then let me do this. Your mother has been

nothing but kind to me, unlike some other people."
She looked pointedly at Maurice, who turned away
from her glare. "I want to help."

"All right," Maurice said. "If you want to help,
then help us. Help us find someplace else for Ma to
open her bakery, and that's it. Stephen owes you,
and Kenya's working hard on the case. We're going
to stick behind you on this."

Jade nodded, but in the back of her mind she
wondered if Maurice meant what he'd said.

"All right," Maryann said from the door. "Have
you all cleared up all your drama? I hope you know
that I could hear you all up front."

Maurice walked over to his mother and hugged
her. "Sorry," he said.

"I know I taught you better than this. You're
going to be nicer to Jade, because she is family,"
Maryann ordered.

Jade smiled brightly. "Mrs. Goings," she said.

Maryann held up her hand. "Now, Stephen can
have this building. It's too small for all the people
that come here, and one of my customers had a great
idea, I can make a Sweet Auburn Bakery Web site
and ship my products all over the world. I don't need
this building to keep my dream alive. And with all the
grandchildren coming, I'm going to need to be close
to them, so you boys have your wish. I'm finally
moving to Charlotte, and Stephen can go to hell."

Hours later James and Jade were sitting on the
sofa in her Buckhead penthouse. She dabbed his
swollen knuckles with peroxide while they waited
for a delivery of Chinese food for their dinner.

"James," she said while bandaging his hand with gauze, "why are you so angry?"

"What? Babe, I'm not angry," he said, snuggling closer to her.

"Your actions today say otherwise. Don't you think the way you went after Stephen and the way you spoke to Maurice were a little over the top?"

"I let my temper get the best of me, but that's only because I don't like people messing with my mother or you, and that's what Stephen is doing."

"What about your brother?" she asked. "Maurice doesn't like me."

"Maurice was just overreacting, but he's straight now."

"Because you threatened him."

"Quiet as it's kept, I'm pretty sure my football-playing brother could beat my ass. So, my threats don't matter much."

Jade kissed him on the forehead.

He cast his eyes upward at her. "Jade," he said, "I hope you don't think that I'm violent and that I'm ever going to do something to hurt you."

"I don't think that, but I don't want you to get hurt or end up in jail because of this. I know Stephen isn't going to let this thing go."

"He will, if he values . . . Let's just say Stephen and I came to an understanding, and he knows what he has to do tomorrow."

"What do you mean?" she asked.

James grabbed her hand. "Don't worry about it. I know my mother, and she loves Atlanta. She may say she'd be happy with the Web site and moving to Charlotte, but she's going to want to come back to her life here, and I'm going to ensure that she has one."

"How?" Jade asked, easing her hand out of his.

"By finding her another building. I put in a call this afternoon and found out who holds the loan that Stephen got to get the property. Maurice and I can easily purchase the loan."

"I thought you two wanted this thing to be over?"

"There are certain things that you don't mess with, and a man's mother is one of them."

"James," she intoned, "what am I going to do with you?"

"Love me."

Jade bent over to kiss him sweetly on the lips. Hungrily, James devoured her lips as they kissed with their faces oriented in opposite directions. Before they got carried away with passion, the doorbell rang. Reluctantly, they broke apart, and James bounded to the door, thinking that it was their dinner. Seconds later Serena, Alicia, and Kandace burst into the living room.

"So," Alicia said, "are you all right?"

"And what are we going to do about that article?" Serena asked. Her voice was a lot calmer than Jade had expected.

Kandace sat on the sofa, beside her friend, and wrapped her arms around her shoulders. "I'm glad you came to your senses."

"Why are you all here?" Jade asked, looking at them, confused by their presence.

Moments later James walked into the room with two bags of food. "I didn't order enough for everyone," he said.

"That's fine," Alicia replied. "We're not going to be here much longer. I guess congratulations are in order."

"Where's the ring, James?" Serena asked, with a smile.

"The ring?" he asked.

"Now, you know we know you proposed," Kandace said.

"I haven't gotten her a ring yet, but it's coming, ladies," James said, grinning at them.

"Nothing less than two carats," Alicia said. "And the stone should have exceptional clarity."

James set the bags of food on the coffee table and folded his arms across his chest. "Do you have a picture of said ring?" he asked, half expecting Alicia to pull a picture from her purse.

"No, but if you need me to go shopping with you, let me know," Alicia volunteered.

"Hey," Jade said. "I'm hungry, and I'm tired of you all talking around me. Kenya and I are going to release a statement to rebut Stephen's damned article, and that's all we need to do."

"When is the work going to get started on the restaurant?" Serena asked. "I can go back to Charlotte with you and have a more hands-on role in the design process."

Jade looked up at her friend. She wanted to say, "I know what you want to get your hands on," but she remained silent for a moment. "That's fine," she finally said. "Now, are we done?"

James took the bags of food and headed into the kitchen, as if he knew the ladies needed some private time to talk.

"You know, it's all over town that James beat the living hell out of Stephen," Alicia said.

Jade peeked around the corner to make sure James was out of earshot. "Is he going to press charges?"

"Not that I know of, but this is making it really hard to attract some investors for our venture. Thank goodness Devon Harris is still on board," Alicia said, looking pointedly at Kandace.

"Whatever," Kandace said, rolling her eyes.

"You can 'whatever' all you want. We have a lot of money tied up in this restaurant, and you three—including you, Serena—have seemed to be focused on other things. Can we please get back to business?" Alicia asked.

"What am I focused on?" Serena asked, pretending to be innocent.

"Please don't play me like I'm stupid," Alicia said. "There's no way you and that contractor have to talk on the phone that much."

Serena rolled her eyes and turned to Jade. "We're going to leave now," she said. "James, we're done talking about you."

The women laughed at Serena as they headed out the door. They couldn't remember when their friend had been so lighthearted; something was definitely going on.

James walked into the living room with a steaming plate of rice and sesame chicken. "Everything all right in the inner circle?" he asked as he handed Jade the plate.

"As all right as it's going to be. Serena is sleeping with our contractor, and she thinks no one knows."

"So, is that why she's been so nice lately? I'm all for it," James joked.

Jade popped him on the shoulder. "Serena could be making a huge mistake. We've got enough problems on this project as it is. She's not going to make things easier if she does what she normally does when it comes to men."

"And what's that?" James asked as he sat down beside Jade.

"You know that old Hall and Oats song 'Maneater'? That's always been Serena's theme."

James dipped a fork in the food and held it up to Jade's lips. "How about you eat this and we let Serena do what she does and deal with it later?"

She took a bite of the food and silently agreed not to talk about Serena for the rest of the night. Still, she had to wonder if Serena's relationship with the contractor was going to cause a delay in the restaurant's opening. Taking a look at James, Jade decided that she needed to keep her thoughts to herself and contently eat her dinner.

After dinner Jade gave James the tour of her home. He was struck by the way she'd decorated the place in rich colors, like reds, browns, and yellows. But it was her bedroom that reflected her personality the most. The walls were the color of green jade and trimmed in silver. A queen-size bed with oak posts sat in the middle of the room. The bedding was gold and trimmed in jade. It looked like a room fit for a queen.

James smiled as he took a seat on the edge of the bed. "You sure you didn't miss your calling as an interior decorator?"

"I wish I could take credit for this place, but the walls were already painted when I moved in. There was a fire in the building on New Year's Eve a few years back, and the prices dropped."

"Who owns this place?"

"Jill Alexander. She's some computer guru or something, with money, like Oprah. I read about her in *Essence* once. I was hoping some of her good fortune would rub off on me."

"Has it?"

Jade sauntered over to James and wrapped her arms around his neck. "What do you think? I got you. Who cares about anything else?"

He pulled her into his lap. "I hope you remember that when you're getting up at three in the morning to feed James Jr."

"Our son is not going to be little J.J.," she quipped. "Maybe we can name him Braxton. And if it's a girl, we can name her something pretty, like Aisha."

"Well, if we do have a daughter, I hope she's just as beautiful as her mother," James said.

Smiling, she leaned into him and planted a kiss on his lips. "I hope you're not going to be one of those overprotective fathers, grilling all the guys our little girl dates."

"Of course not, because she's not dating until she's forty." James lifted Jade from his lap and laid her on her back on the bed. "And I'm sure you're going to be one of those mothers who cuts the girls our son dates a lot of slack."

"As long as they meet the standards that I think women who want to date my son should meet, then they won't have a problem with me," she said as she wrapped her leg around James's waist.

"I can see it now," James joked. Then he leaned in and kissed Jade's slender neck. "This bed has to come to Charlotte."

"Why?"

"It's so comfortable," he said. "And it's you. I want my house to be as much your home as it is mine."

"It already feels like home there," she said, with a wistful tone to her voice.

"What's wrong?"

"Nothing," she said. "I just haven't had a place

that feels like home in my life, and with everything that's going on, I don't want to lose you and what we have."

"You won't," he said. "I love you, love being with you, and I can't wait to make you my wife."

"James," she whispered as he leaned in to her and kissed her lips gently.

The kiss quickly became deeper and more passionate. It was as if they were becoming one in the embrace. With quick hands, James slipped Jade's blouse from her shoulders, kissing each smooth section of skin he exposed. Jade unzipped his slacks as he moved up and down her body, tasting and teasing her with every kiss.

She had some teasing of her own to do as she slipped her hands inside his open fly and stroked his manhood. James moaned as he continued to kiss her neck. Deciding to play her game, he slipped his hand between her legs and stroked her inner thighs softly before entering her with his index finger. He parted her wet folds of flesh, seeking her hot bud of sensuality. It was Jade's turn to moan as he found her pleasure spot.

"James," she breathed as he inched down her body, his erection slipping from her hand.

He replaced his finger inside her with his tongue. Jade gripped his head, urging him to give her more as he lapped at her juices. He wrapped his tongue around her throbbing bud and began to suck gently. Jade screamed his name in pleasure as she felt the edges of an orgasm attacking her senses. James didn't stop. He wanted to taste her desire, and when she came, it was as if he'd been caught in a rainstorm. Pulling back, he looked up at her, his heart full of love, yearning, and passion for her. He needed her as much as she needed his love. Jade was his home, his love, and his life.

He quickly kicked out of his slacks as Jade lifted his shirt and pulled it over his head. "I need you," he said breathlessly.

She parted her legs, granting him full access to her valley of desire. He plunged into her wetness, enjoyed the heat building there. She pressed her hips into his, crying out in joy. They ground against each other, sweat beading on their bodies as they danced their intimate dance. James held her close, brushing his lips against her forehead. Jade shivered and tightened her grip on him. He shuddered as the waves of an orgasm attacked his senses.

"I love you," she moaned over and over again.

"My love, my love," he repeated in her ear as he spent himself inside her.

They lay in each other's arms, gently kissing one another.

"Yes, this bed is coming to Charlotte with us," he said. "We're going to make a lot of memories in it."

Jade smiled and stretched against him. "We just made one. I can't wait to see what we do next."

Their next act was to go to sleep.

CHAPTER 30

The next morning James's cell phone woke the sleeping couple. "Yeah," he said after finding the phone on the floor.

"It's Stephen."

"What the hell do you want?"

"The bank called me this morning, and it seems that someone purchased my loan."

James sat up in the bed. *Maurice, boy, you work fast.* "And this sounds like a personal problem."

"There's no way I can buy your mother another building. My money is tied up in other things."

"I told you that you had twenty-four hours to make things right. But I'm in a good mood today," James said. "And you have another choice."

"What's that?"

"Drop this thing with Jade, and go back to the paper and admit that you used her," James said.

"She sued me. She started this!"

"And it's time for you to be a man and end it," James said hostilely. "I'll make your life a living hell if you don't. The whole loan thing is just the beginning."

"You and your piece of trash brother did this to me all for that—"

"Stephen, you better choose your words carefully," James said, cutting him off. "Jade is going to be my wife, and I'm not going to let scum like you take advantage of her."

"That bitch took advantage of me! That restaurant in Charlotte should be mine," Stephen spat. "I'm not dropping a damned thing."

"You sure about that? I hear your restaurant is mortgaged to the hilt. Wouldn't it be something if Jade opened a restaurant in Charlotte and Atlanta?"

"You can't do that," Stephen growled.

"Stephen, you're one bill away from being bankrupt. I can make that happen sooner than you think."

"This is blackmail."

"No, it's not. It's a fact. Jade is willing to drop her lawsuit, provided that you give her what you owe. There's no way a loser like you could've operated a restaurant without her help and money."

"You and Jade can go to hell!"

"By the time I'm finished with you, you're going to think you're there. I'll expect a decision by noon. Once we head back to Charlotte, all bets are off."

"I don't have to take this shit," Stephen said.

"No, you don't. You can keep trying to fight it. But Maurice and I have more than enough money to slowly buy everything you hold dear. Especially that shitty restaurant."

Stephen sighed into the phone. "Fine. I've devoted enough of my time to this mess," he said. "You and that tramp win. But know this. If you're filled with steam and you're thinking about coming back to my restaurant to cause more problems, I will have you locked up."

"One more thing. If I go to jail, you're going to lose everything. But as a show of good faith, I'll never set foot in your damned restaurant again." James ended the call and rose from the bed.

"I guess that was Stephen," Jade said sleepily.

"So you heard that?"

"Most of it," she replied, sitting up in the bed. "Do you really think it's over?"

"It's in Stephen's best interest to let this stuff go," James said as he took a seat on the bed, beside Jade. "We've got enough going on without having that bastard causing problems for your and your business venture."

"But what about your mother?" she asked.

James pulled Jade into his arms. "Don't worry about any of that. As a matter of fact, let's get dressed and go have breakfast with her. Then we need to go shopping."

"Shopping?" she asked, with a gleam in her eyes. "You're speaking my language."

"Great."

"But," she said, snuggling closer to him, "before we go anywhere . . ." Jade slipped her hand between his legs, and James was instantly aroused.

It was nearly noon before Jade and James emerged from the bed, showered, dressed, and headed to Maryann's bakery. When they arrived at the building, it was crowded with people, as if today were the last day the Sweet Auburn Bakery would be open. Jade and James pushed through the crowd and searched for an empty table. When they found one, close to the bathroom, James deposited Jade in a seat and headed to the counter to talk to his mother.

"It's pretty busy in here, isn't it?" James said as he slipped beside her.

"Once the word got out that I was closing this place, people just started coming and haven't stopped. There was a line of about fifty folks when I got here this morning," she said excitedly.

"Are you sure you want to give this up?" James asked as he began to fill the orders his mother was passing his way.

"What choice do I have? If I stay here, I can imagine what you're going to do to Stephen. Besides, both of my sons are having babies. Do you really think I'm going to miss the chance to spoil two little ones?" Maryann slid some cash in the register as the last person in line placed their order for a slice of pecan pie and a half dozen cinnamon buns.

As James fixed the order, he put a few buns aside for himself and Jade, since that was one of the reasons why they'd got out of bed. Maryann shook her head as she watched her son pilfer the sweets.

"I could've made some more," she said.

"It's all right," he replied, then gave his mother a quick kiss on the cheek. "You need to get off your feet. Maybe you moving to Charlotte will be a good thing. You work way too hard, when you don't have to."

"James, you and your brother have been trying to protect me since you were little boys. When are you both going to learn that Mama can take care of herself? Those wives of y'alls don't know what they've gotten themselves into," she said, with a chuckle. Maryann looked at Jade, who was sending a text message on her cell phone. "I really like her, so don't take this the wrong way, but are you sure you want to marry her?"

"More than anything else in my life," he said. "I know we don't have the history that Mo and Kenya have, but I love Jade more than I ever thought I'd love anyone."

"So, if she wasn't pregnant, would you still marry her?" Maryann asked.

James paused and pondered the question as he looked at Jade. In the few months that he'd known her, his life had been fuller, richer, and vibrant. He couldn't imagine not having her at his side, not being able to touch her and feel her arms around him as they went to sleep together.

Unlike so many other women he'd met since Maurice was drafted in the NFL, Jade didn't want anything from him other than his love, and she had it today and forever.

Turning to his mother, he smiled and said, "I would still marry her, Ma. She has brought more than just a child into my life. She reminds me a lot of you."

Maryann's right eyebrow shot up. "Really?"

"Yes," James said, pinching off a piece of one of the cinnamon buns and popping it in his mouth. "She has that same stubborn, independent streak that you have."

"Boy, don't think you're too big for me to take you over my knee! I'm not that Carter boy. I'll knock you out. Why don't you go feed that woman?"

James gave his mother another peck on the cheek before taking the rolls over to Jade.

"I thought you forgot about me," Jade said when he set the plate in front of her.

"That I could never do," he said.

She leaned across the table and stroked his cheek. "Me either," she said before planting a light kiss on his lips.

"All right, you two," Maryann said as she walked over to the table, with a cup of coffee for James and a glass of milk for Jade. "People are going to think you two are in love if you don't stop."

"Thank you for the milk," Jade said as she looked enviously at James's steaming cup of coffee.

"I've got to take care of my grandbaby and his or her mother." Maryann was about to sit down with Jade and James, but just then another crush of customers entered the bakery.

"People really love your mom and her treats," Jade said. "She can always use our kitchen if she does want to do the Web-based business."

"*Our* kitchen? As in that small room in my house with a stove that I rarely use?"

"No, silly, the kitchen at the restaurant. From the looks of things, she's going to be filling a lot of orders."

"Well," he said after taking a huge bite of his cinnamon bun, "we'd better get out of here before she puts us to work."

Jade took another bite of her cinnamon bun and didn't make an effort to move. "Do you think I'm going to rush through this piece of heaven because you're lazy?" She rolled her eyes and continued eating.

James sipped his coffee, chuckling at her. Jade was his match in every way. He couldn't wait to spend forever with her. "All right. When you're finished eating, we're going shopping."

"That's not going to make me speed up," she said as she took another leisurely bite.

James smiled and took the last bite of his cinnamon bun.

Jade smiled at James and finished her bun. "Let's go," she said as she wiped her mouth with the edge of her napkin.

Jade and James rose to their feet and headed to the register to tell Maryann good-bye.

"You two be good," Maryann said as she waved good-bye to the couple.

"I'll try to keep him in line," Jade quipped. Then they walked out the door. Once they were outside, Jade suggested that they take the train.

"All right," James said. "Do you think you're going to miss all this?"

"No," she said. "I'm leaving Atlanta but gaining something even better."

"And what would that be?" he asked.

"A life with you. And no more two-eighty-five congestion."

James wrapped his arms around Jade's waist and lifted her in the air. "I'm glad you feel that way," he said before putting her down. "I'm sure your friends are going to miss you."

"They're going to be just fine," she said. "Besides, they're going to be spending a lot of time in Charlotte."

"From the looks of things, Serena might be joining

you there," James said. "Since she's messing with that guy."

"Our contractor, and I'm hoping she doesn't mess up our business relationship with him. Or if she's going to break his heart, I hope she'll do it after the restaurant is renovated."

"You never know. This contractor might tame your friend."

"You talk about her as if she's a horse or something," Jade said as they walked to the MARTA station.

James shrugged his shoulders, not really knowing what to think of Serena.

The train arrived at the Lenox station, and Jade and James headed for the mall. She shook her head as they pushed through the crowd of workers heading back to their offices following their lunch hour. Holding James's hand, she smiled.

"I've always wanted to be one of these people," she confessed.

"One of what people?" he asked.

"The kind who shop during office hours."

"Oh," he said, pulling her closer as they headed for the Cartier store.

Jade raised her eyebrows as they walked into the high-end jewelry store. "You know, this is going to sound strange, but I'm not big on diamonds."

"Really?"

She nodded.

"I thought it would be corny to get you a jade ring," he said, with a laugh. "Besides, your girls made it seem as if nothing but two carats would do."

She bumped her hip against his. "You know me better than that."

James reached into his pocket and pulled out a velvet box. "I sure do," he said as he opened the box, revealing a red jade, white sapphire, and chocolate diamond ring. It had a white gold setting.

Jade was stunned at the beauty and uniqueness of the ring. She ran her finger across the pear-shaped red stone. "Where? When did you get this?"

"The day after I asked you to be my wife." James slipped the ring on her finger, and it fit perfectly.

"It's beautiful," she said, with tears pooling in her eyes. "James, if you had the ring already, then why are we here?"

He waved for the clerk.

"Good afternoon," the woman said. "How may I help you today?"

"You have a custom order for James Goings that I need to pick up."

"All right. Give me one moment to get it," the woman said, then disappeared behind the counter.

Moments later she returned with a box and handed it to James. He opened the rectangular-shaped box, displaying a platinum necklace with a red jade and diamond pendant that matched Jade's engagement ring.

"Oh my God," Jade said. "It's beautiful."

"Not half as beautiful as the woman who will be wearing it," James said as he removed the necklace from the box and placed it around her neck.

The clerk smiled at the couple. James took a step back and looked at Jade. She was a vision. He handed his credit card to the clerk without taking his eyes off Jade.

"James, you're spoiling me," Jade said as she hugged him.

"I figured this trip was going to be taxing, and I set this up to put a smile on your face." He took her face in his hands and kissed her gently. "Did it work?" he asked.

"Yes, yes, it did. But being with you keeps me smiling," Jade said.

After James was given his credit card back and he signed the receipt, he and Jade rushed back to the train station so that they could make it back to her place and she could properly thank him for the gift.

As they took their seats on the train, James wrapped his arm around her waist. "We need to set a wedding date," he said.

"I was thinking about that," she said. "We don't have to make a big production of it."

"Music to my ears. Big weddings don't go over real big in my family," he said, with a laugh, referring to Maurice's incident at the altar.

"Then let's go back to where it all started," she said. "Let's get married in Vegas this weekend."

James smiled broadly. "I like the way you think," he said. "We're getting married in Vegas."

CHAPTER 31

If James and Jade thought they were going to be able to skip off to Las Vegas and get married without anyone knowing, they should've never told Maryann their plans. Before the couple had booked seats on a weekend flight to Vegas, Maurice and Kenya knew about the proposed wedding.

"He's truly lost his mind," Maurice told his wife after hanging up with his mother.

"Who's lost his mind?"

"James. He and Jade are eloping."

"Are you still criticizing Jade? They are going to have a baby, Mo. You need to stop. . . ."

"No, I'm glad they're getting married, but he isn't doing it without me standing there and giving him a shit-eating grin," Maurice said. "Who would've thought that my brother would be following in my footsteps?"

Kenya hugged Maurice tightly. "My man is growing up. So, what are we going to do?"

He licked his lips and lifted his wife up. "Before or after I get you out of these clothes?"

Kenya slapped her husband on his shoulder. "You are so bad. And after you get me out of these clothes, what are we going to do?"

"We're going to Vegas, baby," Maurice said as he carried her into their bedroom.

James looked down at his watch. "If we're going to make our flight, you're going to have to hurry up," he called to the closed bathroom door.

"I'm coming," Jade replied. Seconds later she opened the door, dressed in a tracksuit, with her make-up bag on her shoulder. "Are you telling me that I'm not worth waiting for?"

"I think you are, but the TSA might not agree." James took her bag and headed out to the car.

Jade took one last look at herself in the mirror; she was ready to do this. She was ready to become Mrs. James Goings. She couldn't help but remember what had happened the first time they were in Vegas together. *Who would've thought that I would be walking down the aisle and into the arms of a man like James,* she thought as she headed out the door.

"You're ready?" James asked as he opened the car door for her.

"More than you'll ever know," she replied as she slipped into the car.

James sped to the airport, hoping and praying that they didn't have to get screened. Traffic on Interstate 85 South was uncharacteristically light, and they made it to Hartsfield-Jackson Airport with plenty of time to spare.

"You rushed me for nothing," Jade said as they breezed through the security checkpoints.

"Nah, I rushed you because I'm ready to get on this plane and make it official."

They took a seat in the boarding area. "Getting here early isn't going to make that pilot take off any sooner," Jade said as she snuggled up next to James.

"Do I need to call somebody?" he joked.

Leaning her head against his shoulder, she smiled and shook her head. "We'll be fine."

About ten minutes later they began boarding the plane.

"Maybe we should've invited Maurice and Kenya," Jade said after they were secure in their seats.

"It's too late now. What about your girls? Aren't they going to be a little salty because you didn't tell them you're running off to make me the happiest man in the world?"

"Serena will have something to say, Alicia probably won't say much, and Kandace is just going to want all the details."

James wrapped his arm around Jade's shoulders as the plane was readied for takeoff. "So how are we going to do this? Drive-through chapel or an Elvis impersonator for a minister?"

"Do I look like Britney Spears?" Jade asked, jabbing him in his ribs playfully.

"Not at all, but I'm sure if we shaved your head, you two might look like sisters."

"Don't quit your day job, because you're not funny," she said.

James kissed her on her forehead. "Whatever," he replied.

As the plane lifted into the air, Jade snuggled closer to James and drifted off to sleep. He looked down at her and smiled. Little did she know, he had a beautiful ceremony planned at the chapel of the Las Vegas Hilton. Neiman Marcus was sending over a few gowns for her to try on and a tuxedo for James.

He slid his hand across Jade's still flat belly. He couldn't wait for the day when it swelled with their child. It didn't matter if it was a girl or a boy as long as the baby was healthy. He knew that the child would have a happier childhood than he or Jade had had.

As he drifted off to sleep, he dreamed of the day that their child would be born.

Jade woke up as the flight attendants walked through the cabin, offering snacks. She grinned at her sleeping fiancé. How did she get so lucky? she wondered. She ran her hand across his lap and thought about spending the rest of her life wrapped in his love. James made her believe that forever was possible, made her believe that happily ever after was in her grasp. Inhaling, she hoped that the plane would land soon, because she could not wait to say "I do" to James Goings.

Hours later the plane began its descent into Las Vegas. James woke up, fastened his seat belt, and smiled at Jade.

"You have one last chance to change your mind," he quipped.

"I thought about it while you were sleeping, but I couldn't find the parachute," she shot back. "You're not going to get rid of me that easily."

"Good," he said. "Because that's the last thing I want."

The captain announced that it was sunny and eighty-two degrees in Vegas.

James turned to Jade as the plane taxied to a landing. "You don't have any condoms tucked in your purse this time, do you?"

She pinched his bicep. "Whatever."

"Hey," he said, throwing his hands up, "the last time we were here . . ."

"I was being influenced by women who thought getting over one man meant finding a new one," she joked.

"Did it work?"

She winked at him. "What do you think?"

Once they'd landed and retrieved their baggage, James and Jade headed to the rental car desk to secure a car for the weekend. He rented a red Ford Mustang convertible so that he and Jade could cruise the Strip in style.

"I always wanted one of these," he said when they located the car. "Maurice and Kenya have two."

"I wonder how a car seat would fit in the back of one of these," Jade mused as she slid into the passenger seat.

"That's a good question," he said as he started the engine and listened for the roar of the horses. "Aw yeah." James pressed the gas and took off from the curb.

Jade gripped her seat belt. "Yeah, you don't need one of these," she said as they pulled out onto the Strip.

He slowed the car down and smiled at her. "If you wanted me to slow down, all you had to do was say so."

They pulled up to the Hilton, and Jade got out

of the car to check in while James found a spot to park the car. She walked up to the counter and gave the clerk James's name.

"I have special instructions for you," the clerk said after typing his name in the computer. "You're Jade, right?"

"Yes, I am," Jade replied.

The clerk handed her a key card. "This is your room. We'll check Mr. Goings into his room when he gets here."

"There are two rooms?"

"Just following instructions," the clerk said.

Jade shrugged her shoulders, took the key card, and headed to her room. When she got up to the room, she found Kenya waiting for her. "What are you doing here?" she asked as she crossed the room to hug Kenya.

"Did you and James really think you were going to get away with it?" Kenya asked.

"How did you find out that we were getting married here?" Jade asked, with a smile on her face.

"Maryann called as soon as you guys told her that you were going to elope, or as Mo said, 'Return to the scene of the crime.'"

"Your husband," Jade snorted.

"I know he hasn't been the easiest person to get along with, but he's come around. When he heard that James was going to get married, he was so excited and he wanted to be here. He knows that you're good for James."

"And he's good for me," Jade said. "James is the best thing that's ever happened to me."

Kenya hugged her soon-to-be sister-in-law. "That's good to know." She took a step back from Jade, with a warm smile on her face. "Now, let's get you ready to marry that man of yours."

Jade placed her hand on Kenya's shoulder. "Thanks for being here. I was so nervous."

"I know what you mean, but when you see him standing up there, waiting for you, nervousness is the last thing that you're going to feel."

Jade nodded. "I know."

The women headed for the settee by the mirror, and Kenya started fixing Jade's hair.

James paced the floor in his hotel room. Where was his tuxedo, and more importantly, was Jade facing the same problems he was?

"This is not how today was supposed to go," he mumbled.

"And just how was it supposed to go?" Maurice asked as he walked into the room.

"The hell? What are you doing here?" James asked in surprise.

"Saving you from making the biggest mistake of your life," Maurice said.

James frowned and shook his head. "I don't need this today," he said. "I love Jade, and I'm sick and tired of you—"

Maurice held up the garment bag that he had behind his back. "The mistake that you were making was that ugly-ass suit," he said as he held the garment bag out to his brother.

"What's this?" James asked as he took the garment bag from Maurice's hands.

"Open it," Maurice said.

James unzipped the garment bag and revealed a

black Hugo Boss tuxedo with diamond cuff links in the shape of a G. "Mo," James said. "This is . . ."

"A lot better than that ugly suit you had picked out yourself. Did you really think I was going to allow your wedding to proceed without me being here?"

"How did you find out?"

"Ma. She called me as soon as you and Jade left the bakery."

James laid the tuxedo on the bed and hugged his brother tightly. "I'm glad you're here."

"So am I. Because you were going to have some ugly wedding photos without me."

James punched his brother on the shoulder. "Leave it to you to make my wedding all about you."

"Uh-huh," Maurice said. "And Ma will be here in an hour, too."

"Thanks, man."

"I've finally realized that Jade is a good woman, and she's the kind of person that you need in your life. She loves you and you love her, too. That's just what you need. Hell, we all need someone to love. I have that with Kenya, and you're going to have that with Jade and the baby."

James smiled. "Yeah. You're right. Let me get dressed. I got a wedding to attend."

About an hour later Maurice and James were heading up to the fifteenth floor of the Hilton. James reached into the pocket of his jacket and pulled out a platinum wedding band with three diamonds in the center. Smiling, he handed the ring to Maurice.

"Since you're here, you might as well stand up as my best man," James said.

"Wow. I feel so honored," Maurice quipped. "It took you long enough to ask."

"Hell, I'm still trying to get over the shock of you being here and supporting this."

"I was pretty hard on her," Maurice said pensively. "I admit, I was wrong. But what about this whole situation with Stephen? Is that over and done with, or will I be bailing you out of jail?"

"That's done. He dropped his lawsuit and agrees that he has no claim on the restaurant in Charlotte. I'm sure before she moves to Charlotte, Jade's going to have her money back from Stephen," James declared.

"All right. Do I even want to know how this deal was brokered?"

"A lot of threats and that's about it. And the fact that Stephen knows we can make his life a living hell. It didn't take long for him to decide to do the right thing."

Maurice chuckled. "I bet it didn't. How long do you think Ma is going to stay in Charlotte?"

"Probably until the grandkids are grown," James said.

"We have to make sure these babies have an easier time growing up than we did," Maurice said. "I worry about whether I'm going to be a good enough father."

"I know, we damned sure didn't have a good role model in that department," James said. "But you know what? As much as we love these women, just imagine how much more we're going to love these children. I just hope and pray that Jade has a boy."

"I'm saying the same prayer for Kenya. I don't

think I could handle having a daughter knowing what I know about the games men play."

"Especially since you invented a few of them," James joked as the doors to the elevator opened.

"Whatever."

They entered the chapel, which was decorated in gold and white. The lights were dim, and candles flickered near the altar. Maryann was sitting in the front row, already dabbing her eyes with a white handkerchief.

"Ma, are you all right?" James asked.

Maryann rose to her feet and hugged him, then pinched his shoulder. "Yes, I'm all right. But I can't believe you and Jade were going to try and do this without the family."

"I didn't know you all would want to make the trip up here," James said.

Maryann shook her head. "I can't wait to welcome her into the family. She's good for you, and she's going to keep you out of trouble."

Maurice pushed James aside and hugged his mother. "How was your flight, Ma?"

"It was fine," she said. "I'm glad you finally decided to give the girl a chance and stop being so damned judgmental."

"Ma," Maurice said, furrowing his brows. "Isn't this a church?"

She smacked him on the shoulder. "Whatever, boy. Where's Kenya?"

"Helping Jade get ready. They should be up here shortly," Maurice said, then turned to James. "Unless Jade came to her senses and changed her mind."

"Why would I do a thing like that?" Jade asked from the doorway.

James's breath caught in his chest as he took in the vision that was Jade in her formfitting off-white gown. The strapless gown showed off her sexy shoulders and brought out the highlights in her skin. With her hair pinned up and a few curls framing her face, she looked like a queen. James wanted to skip directly to the "you may kiss the bride" part.

"Wow," he finally said. "You're beautiful."

Jade smiled demurely. "And you look great yourself," she said as she crossed over to him.

Moments later the reverend walked into the chapel. "Hello, everybody," he said. "Are we ready to begin?"

Jade and James looked deeply into one another's eyes before saying in chorus, "We're ready."

The ceremony was short and to the point. But when it was time to kiss the new Mrs. Goings, James didn't rush it. He pulled his wife into his arms and brushed his lips against hers. Then he devoured her lips as if they were the most luscious fruit he'd ever tasted. She wrapped her arms around his neck, losing herself in their kiss and melting against his body.

Maurice and Kenya, who stood on either side of the couple, tapped them on their shoulders.

"You two have the rest of your lives for this," Maurice said, spurring the couple to break off their passionate embrace.

"The rest of our lives," Jade said.

"That's right," James said.

Maryann walked up to the couple and held her arms out to Jade. "Welcome to the family, baby," she said. "You are a beautiful bride. Now, if you two will excuse me, I'm going down to the casino to press my luck."

"Ma," James and Maurice said in unison, "you be careful down there."

Maryann waved her hands at her sons and headed out the door.

Kenya walked up to Maurice and linked her arm with his. "I know what I want to play," she said. "And it's not on the casino floor."

"All right. See you later," Maurice said as he and Kenya made their exit.

"Mrs. Goings," James said, "let's get our honeymoon started."

"I'm ready, Mr. Goings."

James lifted his bride into his arms and looked into her eyes. "I love you so much," he said.

"I love you, too," Jade said. "Too much to describe."

Kissing her lips gently, James silently swore that he'd love her forever.

EPILOGUE

Grand opening day

The television cameras were poised to record the moment that the doors of Hometown Delights opened. But the general manager was nowhere to be found. Maurice smiled at the reporters. He'd told Jade and James that he'd cut the ribbon and make sure all of Charlotte knew about her business, but he wasn't doing a damned thing until she showed up.

Serena walked over to him, her hands on her hips and a scowl on her face. "Where is your sister-in-law?" she demanded.

"Not here," he said. "They will be here."

Kandace walked up to them and placed her hand on Serena's shoulder. "Maybe she had the baby."

"It would be just like her to give birth and not tell us," Alicia said as she joined the group.

The three women looked at Maurice and rolled their eyes playfully.

"Ladies," he said. "Had I known one of your phone numbers, I would've gotten you to Vegas. But, hey, I almost didn't make the wedding myself."

"Mighty funny that you were in all the pictures," Kandace said.

"And speaking of babies, didn't you and your wife just welcome a bundle of joy into the world?" Serena asked.

"Yes, Nairobi LaRae Goings. She's at home with Kenya and her grandmothers," Maurice informed them.

"Her mother's name is Kenya, and her name is Nairobi. That's interesting," Alicia said. "I wonder how many people will understand the significance of that?"

"Not many," Maurice said.

"Here they come," Kandace said, pointing at James and a very pregnant Jade as they walked toward the entrance of the restaurant.

"Hey, sorry we're late," James said. "Somebody couldn't figure out what to wear."

Jade glanced down at her black trapeze dress. "I don't want to look as big as this building on camera," she said.

"Baby, you're not fat," James said. "You're pregnant and totally beautiful. I dare anyone to say different." He looked pointedly at Maurice, who threw his hands up.

"I love pregnant women," Maurice said and then leaned into his sister-in-law and gave her a kiss on the cheek. "James is right. You are beautiful. Now, can we cut this ribbon so that I can get back to the women in my life?"

"How is little Nairobi?" Jade asked as she rubbed her belly. "I wish her cousin would hurry up and join her."

Serena rolled her eyes. "Are we ever going to open this damned place?" she asked.

"You got a hot date or something?" Jade asked.

Serena shook her head. "No. I have to get back to Atlanta before . . . Oh my God, what's he doing here?"

Jade looked over at Antonio and shook her head. "I thought you two were . . ." She stopped talking when she saw a buxom woman grab his hand. "Whoa."

"Whatever. He's free to do what he wants to do. Maybe she wants to be tied down. I certainly do not," Serena said as she tore her eyes away from Antonio, who was staring her down.

Jade turned to James. "Please tell me that this is going to go off without a hitch," she whispered.

James kissed her on her plump cheek. "It will. Mo's going to cut the ribbon, you're going to say 'Welcome,' and we're getting out of here so that you can put your feet up and have my son."

"How do you know it's a boy?" Jade quizzed.

"Because it is. I put in a special order with God," James quipped. "Come on. Let's get up front and get this party started."

Charlotte's mayor arrived just as Alicia handed Maurice a pair of giant scissors to cut the yellow ribbon at the door.

"Are we ready now?" Jade asked as she joined Maurice, the mayor, Alicia, Kandace, and Serena at the front of the restaurant.

"If someone will get Kandace off the phone, we'll be ready."

Jade clutched her stomach as the baby pummeled her with a succession of kicks. "We're going to have to do this without her."

James leaned into her. "Are you all right?"

"If this is a boy, he has soccer in his future," Jade said as the baby kicked her again.

"Are you going into labor?" James asked.

Jade shook her head. "Not until these doors open," she said.

James tapped Maurice on the shoulder. "Let's get this thing started before she has the baby on the doorsteps," James said.

Maurice walked up to the podium, and the crowd began to cheer for the Super Bowl MVP. "Thanks for joining me and the ladies who are about to open your new favorite restaurant, Hometown Delights. Food Network's Devon Harris and his staff have been cooking all day, and I don't know about y'all, but I'm ready to eat!" Maurice held up the scissors, and the crowd began cheering again.

James, however, was focused on his wife, who was grimacing in pain. "Babe," he said.

"My water just broke," Jade said. James scooped her up in his arms and dashed toward their car.

Maurice handed the scissors to the mayor. "Help me out, dude. Cut the ribbon. I'm about to be an uncle."

Maurice caught up with James and Jade. "Hey, my car is closer, and I'll come get you from right here."

"All right," James replied, his gaze never leaving Jade's face. "You all right?"

Jade closed her eyes and moaned. "No, I'm not all right," she replied hotly. "I'm in labor."

Seconds later Maurice pulled up in his Mercedes SUV. James loaded Jade into the backseat. "Breathe, baby," he said. "Remember yoga breaths, through your nose."

She grabbed James by the collar. "Would you

shut up!" As a contraction struck, she gripped his collar tighter. "Oh my God! It hurts so bad."

"Mo, hurry up, man!" James shouted when Jade loosened her grip on his shirt.

"Going as fast as I can," Maurice said, glancing at them in the rearview mirror. "She got the kung-fu grip, too, I see."

Jade gritted her teeth as she felt another contraction.

"Did you call her doctor?" Maurice asked.

"What?" James said.

"Call the doctor. Let him know we're on the way to the hospital," Maurice said.

"Right, right," James said as he pulled out his cell phone and dialed the doctor's number. "Dr. Harris, James Goings. My wife, her water broke, and we're on our way to the hospital."

"All right, James," the doctor said calmly. "I'll meet you all at the emergency-room entrance, and then we'll go up to the maternity ward."

"Okay." James hung up the phone and turned back to Jade. "How are you?" He stroked her sweaty forehead.

She took a breath and closed her eyes. "Kenya didn't tell me that it was going to feel like this."

"Just breathe. Remember those yoga classes we took?" James turned to his brother. "Can you move a little faster?"

"This car doesn't fly. There's traffic in front of me, dude," Maurice said. "We'll be there in five minutes."

Jade grunted. The contractions were coming every three minutes. She silently prayed that the baby wouldn't make his or her grand entrance in the back of her brother-in-law's SUV.

James stroked the back of his wife's hand. The

baby was due tomorrow, and he had told her that they shouldn't go to the grand opening of the restaurant, but Jade wasn't going to stay away. "How are you feeling?" he asked.

"Like there's something kicking and screaming inside me," she moaned.

"We're here," Maurice said as he pulled up to the emergency room of Presbyterian Hospital.

James hopped out of the car and grabbed a wheelchair from the entrance while Maurice gingerly lifted Jade from the backseat.

"Jade," James said, "breathe slowly."

Jade dug her nails into Maurice's neck as another contraction hit her.

Maurice quickly deposited her in the wheelchair and placed his hand on his neck, checking for blood. "Damn, why do women get superhuman strength when they deliver children?"

James shrugged his shoulders as he wheeled his wife into the hospital.

Two hours later James and Jade welcomed their son, Jaden James Goings, into the world. Jade lay back in the bed, holding the nine-pound-three-ounce baby boy against her chest. James stood over her, smiling down at her and at his son. The little boy was a mixture of his parents: his coloring was like James's, and he had his mother's black hair.

The door opened, and Serena, Alicia, Kandace, Kenya, Maurice, and Maryann walked in.

"Ooh, look at my grandson," Maryann squealed as she walked over to Jade. "He looks so much like his father." She gently stroked his cheek, and Jaden's eyes fluttered open.

"He knows who Grandma is," Maurice said.

"Jade, how are you?" Kenya asked as everyone else cooed over the baby. "Once you give birth, everyone forgets about you."

Jade smiled. "This feels so unreal. You don't even remember the pain once you're holding this little one."

"I can't believe you're somebody's mother," Alicia said. "But you look like you're going to be so good at it."

"Are you crying?" Serena asked Alicia. "My goodness, all of you are getting soft on me."

Alicia wiped her eyes. "I'm really happy for Jade and James. That's all."

"It's okay," Jade said in a quiet voice as her mother-in-law took the baby from her arms. "Serena has a soft spot, too, and the day someone finds it, we're all going to be crying."

Kandace laughed. "Yeah, right."

"You have a beautiful family," Alicia said.

"And if it wasn't for us taking you to Vegas, all of this would've never happened," Serena added.

Jade looked up at James and smiled.

He leaned down and kissed her on her forehead. "I love you, baby," he said.

"I love you more," Jade replied.

"Okay. We're out of here. I'm going to stick around and fill in as the general manager until you're back on your feet," Serena said.

Jade raised an eyebrow at her friend. "And I'm sure this has nothing to do with Antonio."

"Who's that?" Serena said as she bolted out the door. Kandace blew Jade a kiss and followed Serena.

Alicia gave Jade a quick hug and a kiss. "I love you, girl. Take care of that beautiful little boy."

Jade nodded. "I will."

Shortly after Jade's friends left, Maurice, Kenya, and Maryann said good-bye as well, leaving James and Jade alone with their son.

Jade wrapped her arms around the little boy. "Are boys supposed to be beautiful?" she asked her husband as he eased into the bed, beside her.

"Only when they're babies. Then they become handsome, and rugged when they grow up." He gently tweaked the sleeping baby's nose.

It didn't take long for Jade to drift off to sleep. James slipped off the bed, took the little boy from her arms, and held him against his chest. "Jaden, you're a lucky little boy," he whispered. "You know that? You have the best mommy and daddy in the world. There's going to be so much love surrounding you. There's your crazy uncle Mo and auntie Kenya and your little cousin, Nairobi. And your grandma is going to spoil you and Nairobi like it's nobody's business."

Jaden sucked his fist and looked up at his father as if he understood just what he was saying to him. James kissed his son's forehead, then placed him in the bassinet and watched him until he went to sleep. James had never felt such peace and such responsibility. Turning back to his sleeping wife, he got back in the bed with her and snuggled close to her. This was perfect. This was the payoff from his ultimate gamble in Vegas, and he'd hit the jackpot.

NFL superstar Maurice Goings
meets his match in

Let's Get It On

Available now wherever books are sold.

CHAPTER 1

Nine years ago:
Johnson C. Smith University, Charlotte, North Carolina

Kenya Taylor didn't like surprises, yet she was in for a big one as she walked across the lush green campus of Johnson C. Smith University. Despite the fact that it was late October, the sun beamed brightly, and the temperature had soared to around seventy degrees. She was tempted to pull off her soft leather jacket. But knowing her luck, it would be thirty-five degrees tomorrow, and then she'd be sick with the flu.

With her work-study check in her pocket and another A plus in her political science class, Kenya was ready to celebrate with her boyfriend, Maurice Goings. The high-school sweethearts had come to college together and beat the odds of most couples like them. They were still together. Most of the others had broken up a few months after arriving on campus. Not Maurice and Kenya.

At least, not yet.

She approached his dorm room, with a smile on

her lips. Thoughts of the night they'd spent together simply holding each other made her happy, though moments like that were beginning to happen less frequently. She understood he had other things to do and didn't make a big fuss about it.

Maurice was a star football player, and every girl on campus wanted him, but Kenya trusted him and was confident that their love could withstand any temptation. Without knocking, as she'd done on several other occasions, Kenya walked into his dorm room.

"Baby," she said. Then the rest of her words froze in her mouth. The sight before her was indescribable. Maurice wasn't doing this to her. This was a nightmare.

"Oh, yeah, big daddy," Lauryn Michaels screamed as she rode Maurice as if he were a prized stallion.

Grasping the wall, Kenya swallowed the bitter bile rushing up her throat and settling in her mouth. Tears threatened to fall from her eyes. All she wanted to do was slip out of the room and forget what she'd seen. Holding on to the edge of the wall, she spun around to leave the room, but as she made her exit, she knocked over a stack of Maurice's books. The couple turned and looked toward the door. As tempted as she was to pounce on them, she didn't.

"How could you do this to me?" she said, shaking her head.

Maurice and Lauryn untangled their bodies, and he rose from the bed, stumbling to cover his nakedness.

"I didn't mean for you to find out like this, Kenya," he said as he crossed over to her. Kenya shrank away from him as he reached out to touch her arm.

"You, you . . ." Words failed Kenya as she looked at the smirk on Lauryn's face. "She doesn't care about you! She doesn't even know you! It's funny, now that you have NFL scouts looking at you, every skank on campus wants to latch on to you, and you're too blind to even see it."

Maurice ran his hand over his face. "Kenya, I don't know how to tell you this, but I love Lauryn, and I want to be with her. I'm glad it's out in the open, because this sneaking around hasn't been fair to you, me, or her."

"You love her? How can you even . . ." With closed fists, Kenya pounded his sculpted chest, hoping to reach his heart and break it as he'd broken hers.

"Don't do this," he said as he grabbed her wrists. "You're making a fool of yourself. People grow apart, babe, and that's what happened with us. What we had was high school and—"

"He needed a real woman, not a little, fat girl," Lauryn called out from the bed. "He has me, and you're dismissed."

Maurice turned to Lauryn. "Stay out of this," he said.

Kenya stepped away from him. "You know what? You two can have each other. I hope you're happy with your choice, Mo."

Storming out of the room, Kenya refused to give either of them the satisfaction of seeing her tears. She'd only loved Maurice Goings since she was a freshman in high school. She'd only helped him study for exams that he had to pass so that he would be eligible to play for the Golden Bulls' football team. She'd only given him her heart and her virginity, and all she'd gotten in return was the ultimate betrayal.

Sorrow, anger, hurt, and disappointment flowed through her body like the blood in her veins. *Grown apart? Had we grown apart when I wrote your damned research paper? Had we grown apart when I stayed up all night, helping you grasp the concepts of calculus?* she thought bitterly.

Kenya rushed into her dorm room and flung herself across the bed. Her roommate and best friend, Imani, looked up from her computer.

"What's wrong, *chica?*" Imani asked, noticing her friend's tears.

"Nothing."

"What are you crying about? Failed a quiz?" She laughed, then returned to typing, expecting a quirky comeback from her roommate.

"Leave me alone." Kenya buried her face in her pillow.

Rising to her feet, Imani crossed over to her friend and sat on the edge of the bed. "Kenya, all jokes aside, what's going on? Did something serious happen?"

Kenya focused her teary-eyed gaze on Imani. "Remember when we met freshman year and I told you my boyfriend and I came here together and that we were so in love? I said that we'd probably walk down the aisle to get our degrees and then get married."

Imani nodded. "And I said it wouldn't last past second semester, and look, we're about to graduate, and you two are still together. That wedding is probably going to happen soon."

Kenya shook her head. "Never. It's not going to happen." Her voice was barely above a whisper.

"What?"

Sniffing and wiping her eyes with the back of her hand, Kenya exhaled loudly. "Maurice and I broke up because he's sticking it to that slut Lauryn Michaels."

Imani shook her head and pulled Kenya into a sisterly embrace. "Girl, forget him. You can do so much better than a low-down cheating dog. And if he's sleeping with Lauryn, he'll be in the clinic soon. There aren't too many guys on campus who haven't had the pleasure of her company. If he has a car and money to spend, you can guess who was in love with him."

"But I still love Mo. It's not like I can turn off what I feel for him because he was in bed with *her*. I wish it worked that way. And as wrong as it is, I want to rip the weave right out of that girl's head. Instead, I just stood there, fighting back the tears."

Imani raised her eyebrows, because Kenya wasn't violent. She was always the one who helped her avoid conflict. "Don't do anything crazy. The last thing you need is to get suspended from school at this late juncture."

Kenya groaned loudly. "Everybody's going to know. You know how this campus is. This story is going to grow into something else before it's all said and done."

Imani nodded. "You two did have celebrity status. You were like Will and Jada, Denzel and Pauletta, Russell Simmons and Kimora Lee."

Kenya glared at her. "Aren't you supposed to be comforting me?"

"Hey, I'm just being honest. If the rumors about Lauryn are true, this is going to be all over campus before dinner. She has a mouth like a motor, and if she can make herself look good, then she's going to spread the rumor. You can do better than Maurice, though. He walks around like his crap doesn't stink. Forget him."

Kenya turned away from her friend. "I wish it were that easy."

Imani shook her head and returned to her computer. "It's a shame he doesn't feel the same way. Seems like he's already forgotten you."

Hugging her pillow and leaning against the wall, Kenya closed her eyes and cried silently.

Maurice sat on the edge of his bed, his head buried in his hands and his heart feeling as heavy as a lead brick. Though he'd wanted to end things with Kenya, he hadn't wanted to hurt her. Not after all she'd done for him. Before anything had ever happened romantically between them, Kenya had been his friend. Now she hated him; her eyes had told him that when she'd left the room. She had every right to, though.

"Baby," Lauryn said as she wrapped herself around his torso, "you can't be sitting here thinking about *her* when I'm willing and waiting to do anything you want. I do believe we were in the middle of something before we were so rudely interrupted."

He pushed her away. "I didn't want things to turn out this way," Maurice said, rising to his feet and fishing his boxers out of their pile of discarded clothing. "I've got to find her and make things right."

Lauryn frowned, then stood. "I know she was special to you, but what about me?" She ran her hand down the length of her sculpted body. Her years of cheerleading had given her a figure that was usually reserved for exotic dancers and adult entertainers. She had no qualms about using her perky breasts, small waist, and round bottom to get what she wanted. Right now, she wanted to keep Maurice in this room, and not because she desired him or even wanted to have sex with him. She just wanted to make sure she was in control of him.

So what if he and Kenya had grown up together and were high school sweethearts? This was college, and she wanted Maurice for herself. Why wouldn't any woman want him? He was the star of the Johnson C. Smith football team, and he had NFL written all over his awesome body.

Lauryn wouldn't call herself a gold digger, but she knew a golden opportunity when she saw one. Maurice was her ticket to the good life, and chubby Kenya wasn't going to stand in her way. She couldn't have planned the scene that had happened between them any better herself. Knowing Kenya the way she did, Lauryn knew there was no way she'd take Maurice back. Kenya was one of those "moral majority" chicks or a missionary girl, as Lauryn called it. Obviously, Kenya hadn't been taking care of home, and that was why it had been so easy to entice Maurice and make him hers. When the NFL money started rolling in, she was going to be the one on the receiving end of it, not Kenya.

She had to stop him from going to find Kenya.

Leaping into action, Lauryn grabbed Maurice and pushed him down on the bed. Next, she took his manhood into her mouth and tried to suck him until all thoughts of Kenya disappeared from his mind. At first, he tried to push her away, but it didn't take long for Maurice to succumb to the pleasure of her oral sex.

Kenya who? she thought as Maurice moaned in pleasure.

The next morning, Kenya wanted to skip class, but she'd worked too hard to let Maurice and his wayward penis threaten her future.

However, the moment she walked out of her dormitory, she realized that the story of her twisted triangle had not only spread across campus, but it had a life of its own. When she walked by a group of cheerleaders, she heard one of them whisper, "I heard she was in the hospital last night because she slit her wrists."

Ignore them, she thought as she trudged up the hill.

As she passed a group of football players, guys that she knew because of Maurice, she could see laughter in their eyes.

"Damn," one of them called out. "You can cry on my shoulder, boo."

"Fighting the urge to flip him the bird, Kenya continued on and prayed she could make it to the communication arts building without hearing anything else. But as soon as she opened the door to the building, Yvette Mason, the editor of the student paper, cornered her.

"Kenya, my God! I didn't expect to see you today.

Are you all right? Will you be suspended? You're the best writer that we have on staff, and we have deadlines coming up. Have you turned in your articles?"

Kenya held her hand up. "What the hell are you talking about?"

Yvette looked around as if she was making sure there were no eavesdroppers around. "Rumor has it that you pulled a knife on Lauryn Michaels after you caught her and Maurice in bed together."

"Get out of my face with that nonsense," Kenya snapped.

"Kenya, I don't want to get all up in your business, but I have a responsibility to the paper, and so do you. If you're going to be suspended or even arrested, we have to get your articles."

Exhaling loudly, Kenya took two steps closer to Yvette. "I didn't pull a knife on anyone, I didn't try to kill myself, and I don't give a damn about Lauryn or Maurice. Now, I'm going to class. As far as my articles go, you'll have them when they are due."

As Kenya turned on her heels to head down to the basement, she saw Maurice walking into the building. She wanted to slap him, push him down the stairs, or break his neck, anything to make him feel the pain that she was feeling inside.

"Kenya, I-I . . ."

"Save it," she barked. "I have nothing to say to you."

"We need to talk."

"Go to hell," she replied as she descended the stairs.

Maurice ran after her and grabbed her arm as she reached the bottom of the stairs. "I didn't want things to go down like this. Can we still be friends?"

"Sure," she said sarcastically. "As soon as hell freezes over, you and I will be the best of friends.

Maurice, I hope she gives you a disease and your man parts shrivel up and fall off. Don't ever speak to me again. And tell your whore that if she doesn't stop spreading rumors about me, I'm going to turn her fiction into reality."

Kenya pushed through the double doors leading to the journalism classrooms and promised herself that she wouldn't cry, despite the hot tears stinging her eyes.

When she walked into the classroom, all the chatter stopped, and eighteen pairs of eyes focused on her. Kenya ran her hand over her face and stared them all down.

This has got to stop, she thought as some people began whispering.

"Listen up, people," she yelled. "I know you've been discussing my personal life. I just have one thing to say. Get your own damned lives. I didn't cut anybody, I didn't cut myself, and I'm sick of the rumors. My boyfriend and I broke up. That's it."

Kenya didn't give anyone time to respond before she ran out of the classroom. The main reason she'd decided to attend JCSU, because it was such a small school, was going to be the same reason she'd have to leave. She wasn't going to be the next Eboni.

Kenya remembered when Eboni Sanders, a popular cheerleader, passed out at a basketball game, and rumors swirled for a year about what had caused her to faint. She'd been rumored to be on drugs, she'd been rumored to be pregnant, and she'd been rumored to have HIV.

As it turned out, she was diabetic, and her blood sugar had been extremely high that day. But the rumors had dogged her until the day she dropped out of school. Kenya wasn't about to allow that to happen to her. Her last few months of college weren't going to be spent dodging rumors and Maurice.

While heading back to her dorm room, Kenya came face to face with Lauryn and her crew. The smirk on Lauryn's face spoke volumes. She looked as if she'd beaten Kenya. And in a sense, she had. But if Maurice was the prize, Kenya hoped it would rust.

"Hey, Kenya," Lauryn said. "Listen, I'm so sorry about what happened yesterday. But that's life. Men leave women. Don't let it consume you, and please don't try to kill yourself."

"Lauryn, go straight to hell, and take Maurice with you. You guys deserve each other," Kenya replied, then shoved Lauryn as she blew past her. She didn't stick around to watch Lauryn tumble down the hill, but from the laughter that rose from the football players watching them, she knew it was a funny sight. But she didn't take any pleasure in her irrational act. She was acting the way everyone had rumored that she was.

What am I doing? I can't sink to her level, she thought sadly.

When Kenya made it back to her dorm room, she sat down at her computer and logged on to Clark Atlanta University's Web site. She had to laugh as she perused the CAU site. Her mother, Angela, had urged her to go to her alma mater, but Kenya had wanted to attend the same college as her boyfriend.

Mother always knows best, Kenya thought, remembering the conversation she'd had with Angela before applying to Johnson C. Smith.

* * *

"Kenya," her mother had said as they looked over college catalogs, "you've always made good decisions, and I want you to choose the college you attend. But following Maurice isn't a good idea."

"Ma, I don't want to go to a school that has an Angela Taylor Mass Communications scholarship. That's too much pressure to live up to."

Angela had folded her arms across her breasts and had lifted her eyebrows. "No matter where you go, I'm not accepting anything less than a three point zero. I will not hesitate to snatch you out of school and let you work at Wal-Mart if you think you're going to Charlotte to play house with Maurice."

Kenya had frowned and shaken her head. "Ma, I want to get an education. Maurice is going to be playing football, and I'm going to be laying the foundation for my future career as a public-relations executive. I love him, but I'm not a fool. Daddy, please talk to her."

Henry Taylor, who had been reading the newspaper while his wife and daughter argued, had dropped the sports section and had looked at them. "Angela, let the girl make her own decision," he'd said quietly. That was Henry's way, nonconfrontational, until he was pushed. "I just know one thing. This better not be about chasing that knuckleheaded boy."

Kenya had folded her arms across her chest and had shaken her head. "Come on, Daddy. I'm not following Maurice."

"Then explain to me why you want to go to Johns C. Smith," Angela had said.

"Johnson C. Smith," Kenya had corrected. "Well, Charlotte is a growing city, and Smith is a small college, which means less competition for internships and things of that nature. There are a lot of new public-relations companies moving to Charlotte. With all the banks in Charlotte, they are always looking for public-relations folks to tell their stories to the media."

Angela had smiled at her daughter. "Well, I see that you've researched *Johnson* C. Smith and Charlotte. If that's where you want to go to school, then I'll support you."

Kenya had hugged her mother and kissed her on the cheek. "I'm not totally clueless, Ma."

Angela had patted her daughter's shoulder. "I know. Your father and I did a good job."

As Kenya picked up the phone to call her mother, she prayed that Angela had enough clout to get her into CAU without much of a hassle. All she had to do was figure out a good reason for the desire to transfer in her senior year.

"This is Angela," her mother said when she answered the phone.

"Ma, hi," Kenya said.

"Hey, baby. Is everything all right?"

"I can't just call and say hello?"

"Not when you should be in class, and not when I'm at work."

"You're the editor, Ma. You don't get busy until later."

Angela sighed into the phone. "And I know when

my daughter has something she wants to ask but is afraid to do so."

"Uh, well, I kinda got into a little trouble."

"Hold on," Angela said.

Kenya heard her mother close the door to her office. She knew this wasn't going to be pretty.

"Kenya Denise Taylor, are you pregnant?"

"No. Ju-just suspended," Kenya said, formulating the lie in her head.

"What! What happened?"

"Uh, I-I got into a fight."

"Kenya, what in the hell is wrong with you? You're a senior about to graduate. Do I need to come up there and talk to the chancellor? I can't believe you did something so stupid as to get into a fight. Tell me that it didn't have anything to do with Maurice."

"Ma, I'm sorry. Okay, I'm not going to lie to you. Maurice and I broke up, and this campus is too small for me to see his face every day, and it was really nasty, and I just want to get away."

For the first time since she'd caught Maurice and Lauryn, Kenya sobbed uncontrollably. She told her mother the entire story about catching Maurice having sex with Lauryn and the rumors.

"You can't run from them, baby," Angela said.

"Ma, you wanted me to go to Clark Atlanta, and now I want to go there. I don't see the problem."

"The problem is, I don't want you to think that you can cut and run when you face some adversity. I know he was your first love, but you will get over it."

"Easy for you to say. You married your first love. Ma, please, I can't stay here and be subjected to seeing him with her and hearing all the rumors. Please, I'll do anything."

"Let me talk to your father, and we'll get back to you tomorrow. Go to class, and ignore all the talk."

"Yes, ma'am," Kenya said, all the while thinking, *Easier said than done.*

Maurice rushed to the infirmary when he heard that Lauryn was there. He hoped that the reason behind her being there was another rumor. There was no way Kenya would have pushed her down a hill. That wasn't in her nature. Then again, Kenya was mad as hell, and there was no telling what she was capable of.

God, I hope Lauryn isn't hurt and Kenya doesn't get into trouble for this, he thought as he opened the door to the infirmary. Maurice found Lauryn sitting on a bench, with a sling on her arm.

"Mo, Kenya tried to kill me," Lauryn said.

"What happened?" he asked as he sat down beside her.

"That fat sow pushed me down the hill beside the student union."

Maurice pulled her into his arms. "I'll talk to her."

"No, don't. Just ignore her. I'm going to press charges with campus police."

"Don't do that. Kenya is upset about us, and you really can't blame her."

Lauryn pushed away from him. "Hello! I'm your woman now, and my arm was nearly broken."

"You want her to get kicked out of school? Come on, Lauryn. Your arm isn't broken. Just let it go."

"Okay, who do you want? Me or her fat ass?"

"I'm with you, but you don't have to bad-mouth Kenya."

Lauryn pushed her hair back with her unbandaged hand. "Fine, but you'd better keep her away from me."

"Forget about Kenya. Come on. Let me pamper you until I have to go to practice," he said as he scooped her up into his arms.

Maurice couldn't help but wonder if he'd made a mistake letting Kenya go.

Two weeks later, Kenya got the okay from her parents to come home to Atlanta. Though she'd have to start over at Clark Atlanta as a junior, it was well worth it. Watching the romance of Maurice and Lauryn was sickening. And to add insult to injury, Lauryn now had the entire campus believing Kenya was out to get her. She was happy to go home.

The day she packed her things, Maurice showed up at her dorm room. "Kenya?"

"What do you want?" she said, not looking up at him.

"What are you doing?"

"Minding my business."

"Are you leaving school?"

She slammed her clothes into her suitcase, then looked up at him. "Maurice, get away from me. You gave up the right to know what I'm doing when you put that girl on top of you."

"You fought so hard to come to school here, and I don't want you to leave because of me," he said. Maurice timidly stepped inside the room.

"Aren't you just full of yourself," she snapped. "Who cares what you think?"

"I still care about you, Kenya. Are you going back

to Atlanta?" What he wanted to do was reach out to her, but the fiery anger in her eyes pushed that thought out of his head.

"Get out. Don't worry about where I'm going. Just know I won't be around you and your little tramp anymore. You win, Maurice. You and Lauryn drove me away. You broke my heart beyond repair, and I'll never forgive you for that. I hate you as much as I loved you. Now, get out of my way before I do something that I will regret. Enjoy, but regret."

"Kenya—"

"Out!" she said. She knew that she was using anger to mask her pain, and though she wanted to hate him, she couldn't and didn't.

"So, this is how it's going to be? We're not even going to try and be friends?"

She took a deep breath, trying to calm herself down. "Friends? Let me put it like this, if you were on fire, I wouldn't spit on you unless I had gasoline in my mouth. You snuck around behind my back to be with her. Would a *friend* do that? Would a *friend* lie to my face over and over again? Hell no, we're not friends, and we never will be again. Now get out of my face."

A wave of sadness washed across his face. "I still have love for you, Kenya, and if you ever need any-thing . . ."

She picked up a broken shoe and threw it in his direction. Quickly, Maurice ducked out of the way.

"I need you to get out of my room and out of my life!"

Maurice walked away from the door, and Kenya thought that would be the last time she ever saw him.